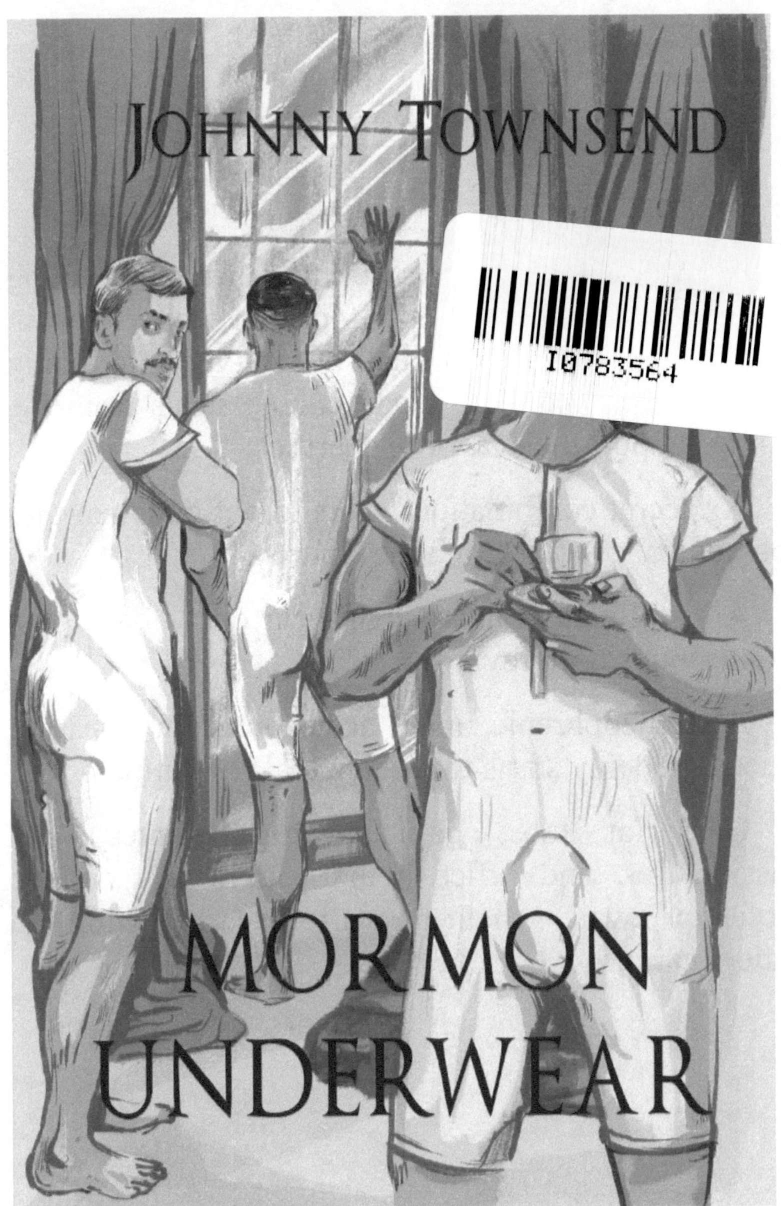
Johnny Townsend
MORMON
UNDERWEAR

Mormon Underwear

In these stories of gay Mormons, we see a young LDS man stripping to his Mormon underwear in public. We watch as a virginal seventy-year-old finally gives in to temptation. A gay couple steals from the rich to support their favorite charities.

A "secret combination" plots to put gay men into positions of power within the Church.

A celibate thirty-eight-year-old dates a promiscuous porn reviewer.

A schizophrenic man accustomed to hearing voices suddenly starts to receive real revelations.

Gay hot tubs, gay bowling leagues, gay missionaries, and office hours with a gay college professor await, whether you're wearing Mormon underwear or not.

Praise for Johnny Townsend

"The thirteen stories in *Mormon Underwear* capture this struggle [between Mormonism and homosexuality] with humor, sadness, insight, and sometimes shocking details….*Mormon Underwear* provides compelling stories, literally from the inside-out."

Niki D'Andrea, *Phoenix New Times*

In *Zombies for Jesus*, "Townsend isn't writing satire, but deeply emotional and revealing portraits of people who are, with a few exceptions, quite lovable."

Kel Munger, *Sacramento News and Review*

Inferno in the French Quarter: The UpStairs Lounge Fire is "a gripping account of all the horrors that transpired that night, as well as a respectful remembrance of the victims."

Terry Firma, Patheos

Gayrabian Nights is "an allegorical tour de force…a hard-core emotional punch."

Gay. Guy. Reading and Friends

In *Sex among the Saints,* "Townsend writes with a deadpan wit and a supple, realistic prose that's full of psychological empathy….he takes his protagonists' moral struggles seriously and invests them with real emotional resonance."

Kirkus Reviews

"Johnny Townsend's 'Partying with St. Roch' [in the anthology *Latter-Gay Saints*] tells a beautiful, haunting tale."

Kent Brintnall, Out in Print: Queer Book Reviews

Selling the City of Enoch is "sharply intelligent…pleasingly complex…The stories are full of…doubters, but there's no vindictiveness in these pages; the characters continuously poke holes in Mormonism's more extravagant absurdities, but they take very little pleasure in doing so….Many of Townsend's stories…have a provocative edge to them, but this [book] displays a great deal of insight as well…a playful, biting and surprisingly warm collection."

Kirkus Reviews

The Washing of Brains has "A lovely writing style, and each story [is] full of unique, engaging characters….immensely entertaining."

Rainbow Awards

Mormon Underwear

Johnny Townsend

Contents

Mormon Underwear

I was never any good at keeping secrets. When I found condoms in my dad's underwear drawer at the age of thirteen, I told my twelve-year-old sister, who promptly told my mother, and I was grounded two weeks for snooping.

The same thing happened when I went on a Boy Scout campout with our church group, and one of the scouts brought along a *Playboy* magazine. It wasn't that I was a tattletale. I just couldn't resist sharing the tantalizing news with my cousin. He, on the other hand, *was* a tattletale, and our whole troop got in trouble over that one.

I could relate dozens more examples of my inability to keep my mouth shut, so it was truly a miracle I'd managed to keep quiet that I'd been going to gay bars on Friday nights ever since I'd turned twenty-five, seven months ago. Somehow, when I realized I was a quarter of a century old, I felt I couldn't waste any more time trying to become straight and started going out regularly. I didn't go out on Saturday nights, of course, because if I stayed out past midnight, that would be Sunday, and I didn't want to be out partying on the Sabbath.

Since I didn't drink alcohol, partying was a relative term. I wasn't sure if my abstinence was me being "smart," or if I was still just hung up on Church teachings. By this point, I absolutely believed the Mormons were wrong about homosexuality, and that obviously threw into question everything else the prophet said, but I didn't want to simply chuck the whole thing all at once. Maybe *some* of the rest was true. Perhaps the Church was just keeping it secret that homosexuality was acceptable, the way they had kept secret for so long the fact that blacks were equal to whites.

This evening, I went to one of the seedier bars in Chicago. I pretty much exuded "white breadness," so I didn't expect anyone to look twice at me there, but I'd only been in the place twenty minutes when a slim yet muscular guy in tight black button-fly jeans and a tight white T-shirt nodded at me.

"Boxers or briefs?" he said.

"Uh, neither," I replied a little uncertainly.

"Really?" The man tried hard not to smile condescendingly. "You don't look the type to walk around without underwear."

"Oh, I'm wearing underwear," I said. "Just not boxers or briefs."

The man's eyes widened. "Don't tell me you have on bikinis. Or a thong. I'll have to leave."

"No." I smiled. "I'm afraid I have on Mormon underwear."

The man frowned. "What's that?"

"Well, it's a one-piece outfit that has a T-shirt for the top portion and knee-length shorts for the bottom. There's a slit in front and a slit in back. And you get into them by crawling through the neck."

The man's mouth fell open, but he didn't say anything.

"And there are little symbols embroidered in them, over the breasts and navel and right knee, that all have special religious meanings."

The man continued to stare. Of course, we weren't supposed to talk about our "garments" to non-members, and we most definitely weren't supposed to mention the symbols, but he'd asked what I was wearing, hadn't he? And I couldn't resist sharing the privileged information.

The man finally shut his mouth and gave me a head-to-toe lookover. "Well," he said finally, "there's a back room in this bar. Can I get inside you through your rear slit?"

I hadn't ever been fucked yet and was anxious to try it, so I nodded and followed the man to the rear of the bar. When we finished, the man kissed the back of my neck. It seemed a little out of place in this high testosterone environment, but it touched me.

"My name's Andy," the man said, zipping back up.

"I'm Bruce."

"Listen, Bruce, you were a lot of fun. Would you mind if I took your phone number?"

"Sure."

There was a message from Andy on my machine Sunday when I got home from church. "I was wondering if you'd like to get together this week. I go to a group called Third Thursday on, obviously, the third Thursday of each month. It's a gay professionals group. I think you'd like it. Anyway, this week is Show and Tell. We're all supposed to bring something interesting. I thought you could show your Mormon underwear. Since you're new, you wouldn't need to participate if you didn't want to. But if you're interested, give me a call."

I'd felt a *little* bad even telling Andy as much as I did the other day. I wasn't sure I wanted to blaspheme to the extent of showing a whole roomful of people these sacred underwear. But I called Andy Sunday night, and he agreed to pick me up on Thursday.

On Tuesday, though, I got a call from the stake president. He was the man in charge of nine Chicago congregations, including the ward I belonged to. Had I been found out, I wondered? Had someone seen me go into the bar the other night?

"Can you come in for an interview tomorrow evening?"

I took a deep breath. I knew it had to come sometime. "Sure," I said. "What time?"

I walked into the stake center the next evening at 6:30 and knocked on the stake president's door. After a little innocuous chit chat, the president said, "I suppose we ought to get down to business."

I braced myself, but I'd vowed to take the order to attend a Church court gracefully. It would be a little awkward since my father was on the stake high council and would be one of the twelve men holding court for me, but before I ever went to my first bar, I'd accepted the consequences.

"We'd like to call you as second counselor in the bishopric."

"What?"

"You're an upstanding young man. We've decided to groom you to be a bishop one day. Of course, that won't happen till after you're married. You really need to make a little more effort on that front. It wouldn't hurt for you to switch over to a Singles ward. But since you insist on coming to one of the regular wards, we decided it was time to push you to the next step in Church leadership."

I blinked. "I don't know what to say."

"You go home and pray about it but let us know by tomorrow. We'll have to call someone else if you don't accept the calling, and if we wait too long, he'll know he was second choice. We don't want that."

"No, of course not."

"What do you think?"

"Well, I'm not that good at keeping confidences…"

"The bishop will handle most of the delicate part."

"Okay. I'll give you a call tomorrow evening."

That night in my apartment, I debated what to do. On the one hand, it was a great honor to be second counselor. On the other, I didn't want to be even more of a hypocrite than I already was. Then again, when the inevitable happened and I was discovered, it would make more of a ripple the higher up I was, and that was good. But I also had to consider that the higher my position, the more embarrassed my parents would be at my fall from grace. And on yet another hand…

I imagined for a moment being groped by that many hands.

I accepted the call and phoned the stake president Thursday evening when I got home from work. Then I called my mom with the news. She said she'd bake my favorite cookies for Sunday. Next, I showered quickly and put on a fresh pair of garments, smiling eagerly when Andy came by a few minutes later to pick me up.

"This is Ivan," Andy said after I'd climbed into the back seat. Ivan sat in the passenger seat up front. I offered my hand. "Ivan's my partner."

"Oh," I said. "Nice to meet you."

Andy chuckled. "Don't worry. He knows everything. We have a very progressive relationship."

"Okay."

Ivan smiled. "I can't wait to see those underwear of yours."

Around forty people showed up for Third Thursday, all dressed on the nicer side, even Andy, who wore Dockers tonight in place of his tight jeans. It was evenly split between gays and lesbians, and between those who could "pass" and those who made no attempt at it.

Andy and Ivan introduced me to several men and a few women, doctors and lawyers and business professionals mostly. It was pleasant to meet people outside of a cruisy bar setting. Everyone seemed a little more real. I'd only made a couple of gay friends over the past several months, not as many as I'd have liked, and always in an environment that limited them to their sexuality.

While the people here were friendly, there was also an element of gossip in the air. "Bob's in AA." "Suzanne was arrested for domestic violence a couple of months ago." "Gerald's into shady dealing." "Bette's a closet Republican." Apparently, I wasn't the only one having trouble keeping personal information private.

Soon the meeting started, and everyone seemed to have a ball with the Show and Tell. One man presented a large ammonite fossil. I wondered if it was named after Ammon in the Book of Mormon. Another man revealed some nice embroidery he'd recently completed. A woman proudly displayed a lovely art deco vase. Another woman showed everyone her favorite mezuzah. A man offered his son's most recent drawing.

And then it was my turn.

"You know," I said, standing in front of the group and slowly unbuttoning my shirt, "you see those Mormon missionaries going around in twos, and they look so innocent."

I pulled off my shirt, which must have puzzled some of the crowd, though so far all it revealed was a fairly ordinary T-shirt.

"But did you know they carry a secret around with them every day?"

There were a few raised eyebrows at this, even more when I started unbuckling my belt. "When they go home at night and get in bed, they don't look like everyone else."

I unhooked my pants and lowered my zipper but held my pants up as I continued. "Mormons are supposed to wear their Mormon underwear at all times except when they're showering or participating in sports that would prevent it. But they have to put them back on as soon as possible, and theoretically they're supposed to wear them even while having sex."

At this point, I dropped my pants to the floor, and there were a couple of gasps mixed with a couple of laughs.

"And he did wear them when we had sex the other night," Andy announced.

"TMI!" someone shouted.

"Anyone wanting to try sex with a Mormon wearing Mormon underwear drop your phone number off here," Andy continued unfazed.

I blushed and pulled up my pants and then put my shirt back on as the next person in line showed off a Wedgwood saucer.

"You were a hit," Andy said later as he and Ivan drove me home. "Sometimes, it's hard to break into an established group. But people there tonight will remember you."

"I did get two phone numbers," I said, laughing.

"And here's my cell." Ivan handed me a slip of paper.

Andy laughed, and I kissed them both when I got out of the car.

On Sunday, I was officially called to be second counselor in the bishopric, and the congregation raised their right hands in Sacrament meeting to sustain me. I was set apart afterward by the stake president and his counselors. My parents belonged to another ward but came to watch. My mom had kept a scrapbook over the years of my rise through the Priesthood and all my various callings.

The most damning thing I ever saw Mom do was drink café au lait at the Café du Monde once on our trip to New Orleans. My dad had only ordered milk, but he did steal a single sip himself. Seeing my parents look so proud now only made me feel like a heel because I knew that feeling was bound to come to an end eventually.

I put it out of my mind, though, and that evening, Ivan came over. He was a French professor at the university and told me Andy was a Spanish professor there. That was how they'd met six years ago when they'd both started teaching the same semester. I'd served my mission in Scotland and so didn't speak a second language.

"I wish I could speak French," I said.

"You can audit my class for free if you like."

"I couldn't get away from work in the day."

"I teach one Monday/Wednesday evening class to make a little extra money. You're welcome to sit in. The semester only started two weeks ago. I can help you catch up."

"Really?"

"Sure. But only if you let me at that front slit."

"I always wanted one of my professors to come on to me."

"You may have one preposition too many in that sentence."

Ivan sucked my dick for a while and then I asked to reciprocate. "On the condition you go in my back slit afterwards."

His back slit, it turned out, was fairly wide, as he was wearing a jock strap. After we finished playing, Ivan gave me directions to his class and added, "Andy and I would like to have you over for Sunday dinner next week. What do you say?"

"Sounds great."

I had to start meeting with the bishop but told the man I wouldn't be available on Monday or Wednesday evenings. Of course, no Church work was done on Monday nights anyway because it was Family Night. I usually met with the Singles for a Single Adult Family Home Evening, but this Monday I went to French class for the first time instead. I sucked Ivan off in his office afterwards, and when I joined the bishop in the bishop's office Tuesday night, I couldn't help but experience a flashback of the previous evening. I put a folder on my lap to hide my erection.

"I'd like you to start going through the inactives list," the bishop said. "Try to visit just one person on the list each week. You know how Home Teaching goes. Most of these people never get visited at all. I've assigned you a new Home

Teacher, too. It's important that at least *we* get visited once a month, and I know Pete will be diligent about scheduling. He's a stalwart member, as you know. He was first counselor for a while before I became bishop."

"Okay."

"Now when you visit these folks, I want you to find out what's keeping them from church, or if they even still want to be members. We can take their names off the rolls if they want."

"Excommunicate them?"

"It's really only excommunication if they're committing some grave sin. Otherwise, it's just cleaning up the records."

"What if they won't tell me why they're inactive?"

"It'll be your job to find out their secrets."

I shrugged. "Okay."

I called my first inactive member when I got home that night and went to see him and his wife Thursday. They stopped coming to church, the man said, because the bishop's wife had made a rude remark about his wife's dress one Sunday. It turned out that this was the previous bishop, who'd since moved out of the ward.

"Do you think you might like to come back?" I asked. "Or did that incident shake your faith?"

The man blushed. "No, I guess that was a silly reason to begin with. We'll be at church on Sunday." I noticed the woman had said very little the entire visit, so I really had no way of knowing if the man's version of events was accurate or not, or if she was willing to forgive, forget, and move on as he was.

I wondered why I still cared about the Church at all, when I certainly had more reason to be upset than these people ever had. Was I just a mindless sheep? Perhaps I should see a psychiatrist to dig up my deep, hidden motivations. There was one I'd met at Third Thursday who seemed nice.

Well, at least his box looked nice.

But truth be told, I was enjoying my little position of power and wanted to keep it a little longer. Despite all the negative energy I got from the Church, I did get some positive things out of it, too. Nothing was all bad or it would cease to exist.

Friday, I went out to the bars as usual, but no one was interested. I wondered if I'd ever find a man of my own. If I did, that would pretty much force the issue at church, I supposed. Maybe I was sending out conflicting vibes. Perhaps people could tell I wasn't completely sure I wanted to meet them.

Of course, I was sure I at least wanted sex. I could worry about dating if that opportunity ever presented itself. Just as fun as the sex, though, was hearing people's life stories. One man a few weeks ago had told me he'd learned how to braid hair while in jail. Another told me he escorted to bring in a few extra dollars. And yet another guy told me he was a cantor and having an affair with a Catholic priest. He said his wife was upset he wasn't having an affair with the rabbi if he had to have an affair at all.

People would tell complete strangers absolutely anything, I decided, and these friendly revelations would probably keep me going out even if I did meet someone special somewhere down the line.

Sunday after church, I went to Andy and Ivan's house for dinner. "I see Ivan recruited you to French before I could get you interested in Spanish."

"Well, I'd eventually like to learn Spanish and Italian, too. I've always been intrigued by Romance languages."

"I know Portuguese and Ivan knows a little Romanian."

"But we don't know any languages in common except English. Makes it hard to talk about people behind their backs. You can't gossip in public."

"Must be very frustrating."

"We're studying sign language together, though. But so far all I can say is, 'You're beautiful' and 'Let's fuck.'"

"As long as you have the essentials down."

After dinner, we watched *A Love to Hide*, about gays and Jews trying to keep their identities hidden during World War II.

Then we all went to the bedroom, where I was able to use my front and back slits at the same time.

On Tuesday, I visited another inactive member. His reason was learning of the Mountain Meadows massacre. "It wouldn't be all that bad just to know it happened," the man said, "but the Church keeps so mum about it. It's like they're trying to hide something."

I couldn't help him with that one, but when I asked if he wanted his name removed from Church records, he was quick to say no. He looked shaken by the very idea.

Friday night, I went home with a guy who picked me up at a bar. But as we were making out on his sofa and he started unbuckling my belt, I said, "You're in for a surprise." I of course was referring to my underwear, but the guy stopped working on my belt immediately and looked shocked, as if I'd just announced I had two dicks. He sat up and asked me to leave.

As I drove home, I wondered if I should stop wearing my garments altogether if they were going to keep me from having sex. Even those who tolerated the strange underwear certainly didn't find them very sexy.

And there was also the possibility that wearing them while out cruising just added points to my sin tally.

But I *liked* the garments, as odd as they were. Lots of members had moved to the relatively new two-piece garments, but the one-piece was so different that it made me feel special, and I liked feeling special.

So I wore them again Saturday night when I went back to Andy and Ivan's place for a sleepover. We had an early dinner and then played cards, which of course was forbidden by the Church as well. Then we watched a movie. While it wasn't a gay film, it was rated R, and that was forbidden by the Church, too. Somehow, though, I suspected the movie and the cards would be the least of my worries if tonight's activities were discovered.

We played a version of Truth or Dare, where at one point Ivan had to reveal his first sexual experience. "The first time I had a cock up my ass," he said, "was when I was twelve."

"Twelve!" exclaimed Andy. "You said you were eighteen the first time you were with a man."

"Now that's true," Ivan agreed.

"So?"

"The first time I had a cock inside me was when I was visiting my grandparents one summer and found my grandmother's dildo."

"Oh, no," said Andy.

"Are you sure it was your grandmother's?"

"It was in her lacy underwear drawer."

"You sure those were *her* underwear?"

"Why didn't you ever tell me about this?" asked Andy.

"It's embarrassing."

"You know you can tell me anything."

"Even gay people can be judgmental."

I slept between Andy and Ivan that night. They were both nude, but I liked sleeping in my garments. We were too tired for sex by the time we went to bed, but at some point in the middle of the night, I felt my back slit being opened, and

Andy pushed himself inside me. I only half woke up, and even Andy seemed to fall asleep before he finished, lying quietly next to me, still inside me for several minutes before he slipped out.

Sunday was a long day at church, including an extra meeting with the bishop and his first counselor. Despite what the stake president had said, the bishop decided to confide in us what one of the members had told him the previous week. One of the elders in the Elders' quorum had confessed he was attracted to his twelve-year-old daughter. He hadn't acted on it but was afraid to get counseling, afraid the police would find out his hidden desires. I didn't much like learning about them either.

Weeks went by in much the same manner. I was learning French, and seeing Andy and Ivan usually once a week, and meeting with a new inactive member every week, and still going to the bars on Fridays where I occasionally hooked up with other guys, none of whom ended up being date-worthy. I saw my home teacher Pete and his companion once a month and my parents every few weeks. My mother gave me Jello on each visit to take home.

As Andy had predicted, people did remember me at Third Thursday, and I made a couple of decent friends. I spent an occasional Friday evening with one friend, a Sunday evening with another, and enjoyed a fairly satisfying social life. Eventually, though, I was spending almost every Saturday night on sleepovers with Andy and Ivan. It was at their place one Saturday night when Ivan told me I'd made an A on my final exam.

"Whoo hoo!" I clapped. "Does anyone teach the second semester at night?"

"It'll be offered as an evening class in the Spring, but after that, you may have to study on your own."

"Yikes."

"You seem like a self-motivated type."

"Well, it *is* easier to study when I get a blow job after each class."

We played naked charades for a while. It was amusing trying to find hidden meanings from someone who had nothing at all hidden.

This seemed to evolve naturally into a discussion of more sexual secrets. "The son of our department chair took my class one semester," Andy said. "He came to my office one day and bent over my desk. I took a chance and went for it. I don't know if there's any connection, but I ended up with a raise a month later."

"I wondered why you got a raise that year and I didn't!"

"The chair's daughter will be a freshman next year."

"No, thanks."

But Ivan had a secret of his own to share.

"The first week of this semester, one of my student athletes left a gym bag in class," he said. "I brought it to my office and gave him a call to let him know I had it. But I couldn't resist looking through it, though I don't know what I expected to find.

"What I found, though, was a jock strap," Ivan went on. "I took it, and the student never said anything. Anyway, he left his bag in class another time a few weeks later, and I brought it to my office and called him again. And I couldn't resist looking in the bag again."

"And?"

"And I took another jock strap for my personal collection. I knew he couldn't help but notice it the second time, but I really wanted it."

"You look so professional and reserved on the surface."

"But underneath, I'm a pervert."

"You say that with just the right amount of self-confidence."

"Anyway, the other day when he turned in his final exam, he gave me a little Christmas gift."

"A pair of your own jock straps?"

"No. Another of his." Ivan paused. "But this one had dried cum in the cup."

"Oh, no."

"I still don't know if he was gay or just flattered. But I bet he keeps that little gift a secret for a while."

"How about you, Bruce?" said Andy. "Tell us one of your dirty little secrets."

I tried to think of something I could reveal without embarrassing myself too much. But I finally decided to just let go. "When I was a teenager," I said, "I used to beat off while looking at a picture of Joseph Smith."

"No way."

"And after my mission, one night I wanted to feel the weight of a man on top of me. So I stuffed some clothes with my bedspread. I put some of my free weights in the dummy, too, to make it heavy, and..."

"And? Let's hear it."

"And I made a head and posted a full-page picture of Joseph Smith on it, so while the dummy was on top of me, I masturbated pretending Joseph Smith was in bed with me."

Andy and Ivan howled.

"Now, if you'd just put a cum-stained jock strap on Joseph Smith, I might try that myself."

"Are all people as weird as we are?"

"I'm ignorant about women's fantasies," said Andy, "but I would be very surprised if almost every man, both gay and straight, didn't have some kinky fantasy or experience he'd like to keep hidden."

"So I'm not going to hell?"

"Well, I can't guarantee that. But it won't be for having sex with Joseph Smith."

The next day in church, I looked at the other congregants, mostly the men, and wondered what secrets they were carrying. They seemed good and decent. Surely, Andy was wrong in his judgment. But then I looked at the member I knew was lusting after his daughter, and he looked perfectly normal. And undoubtedly, most people still thought I was an innocent virgin. So how reliable were appearances?

"Hey, Bruce," said Pete, coming up to me after Priesthood meeting. "I still haven't seen you for December yet, and it's getting close to the middle of the month. Things'll get too crazy if I don't get my home teaching done this week. Then you'll be busy with everyone's tithing settlement before the end of the year. Can I come by your place tonight?"

"Sure."

"My home teaching companion is sick. I know it's a little unorthodox, but do you mind if I come by myself?"

"No problem."

Pete did come over that evening. He was in his late thirties, with two teenage boys, twelve and thirteen, both deacons. He gave a brief lesson about the Christmas spirit and then asked how things were going for me personally.

"Oh, just fine."

"Are you seeing anyone? I hear you're not going to the Singles dances anymore."

"Just hanging out with friends. I'm not really in the market right now for a wife."

Pete nodded. "Sometimes, I wish I'd waited longer. Maybe…"

I wasn't sure I was up to hearing any more confessions, but at the same time, I wasn't able to resist the hook.

"Maybe what?"

"Do you ever wonder what life would have been like if you'd taken the path less traveled?"

"How much less traveled?"

Pete looked at me. "Traveled by about one tenth of the population." His eyes locked onto mine.

Pete then told me when he was about twelve, he'd gone camping with his father, his father's best friend, and the best friend's son, about Pete's age. The two men shared a tent and the two boys shared another. Not long after they'd gone to bed, the other boy propositioned Pete, who was horrified and ran to his father's tent. When he opened the flap, though, he saw his father making love to the other man. He closed the flap and walked slowly back to his tent, where he and the other boy had sex as well.

Pete and his father never talked about what happened, and though the two men continued to go camping once in a while, Pete never returned to the woods with them. But he remembered that night over the years, and the older he became, the more he wished over and over he'd gone camping again.

"I have a sleeping bag," I said. "Would you like to go camping with me sometime?" I knew I was taking a chance saying such a thing to another Mormon, but I liked Pete.

"It's a nice night out," said Pete. "Not too cold, just cold enough to cuddle." He looked at me again.

Pete called his wife a little later to tell her the car wouldn't start and he was going to spend the night with me and call a garage in the morning. Then we carried the sleeping bag outside. Pete crawled in first, still fully clothed, and I crawled in after him.

It started out as a back rub, but the foreplay went on non-stop for six more hours. Finally, still fully clothed, Pete pulled himself on top of me and pumped away for about ten seconds. He groaned and collapsed at the same time I came.

Tuesday night, I got a call from the bishop. "Uh, Bruce, we need to talk."

I'd finally made a mistake, and events now began to unfold rapidly. After I told the bishop everything that night, I had to speak with the stake president on Wednesday, and my court was held Thursday.

My father was present and heard all the accusations against me. I denied nothing, and after half an hour of prosecution and "defense," I was asked to wait in an adjoining room while the High Council made their decision.

It was a foregone conclusion, of course, so when the stake president came in my room a few minutes later, I was prepared for the verdict.

Or so I thought.

"You're being excommunicated, Bruce," the stake president said sadly. "You need to take off your garments now."

"What?"

"You're no longer a member. You can't wear them anymore."

I started unzipping right there, and the president almost tripped while running away. I zipped back up and walked out of the building. I went back home, and not half an hour later, there was a knock at the door.

"Mom. Dad."

"Hi, son."

I ushered them in, and they both hugged me. I expected Mom to be a little weepy, but she wasn't.

"Thank God it's finally all out in the open," she said. "We've known you were gay since you were seven years old. It's been no secret to us. All these years, it's been like the elephant in the living room no one can talk about, but now we can finally have an adult relationship."

"You knew?"

"We can't even put our finger on just what it was. Maybe it was the way you insisted on having two G.I. Joe's so just the one wouldn't be lonely. Or the way you never took to sports. Whatever. It was just a sense, but we knew we weren't wrong. We just wanted you to have a few nice experiences in the Church before it all came out."

"You're not upset?"

"Well," Mom said slowly. "I always knew something awkward had to come out of my pregnancy with you." She paused. "Your father and I weren't married when you were conceived."

"You're kidding."

"I was still on my mission," my mother went on. "I was having my final interview with the mission president. Then he said he'd tell everyone I had come on to him and he'd send me home dishonorably if I didn't… well, a month later, your father and I were married."

"I'd waited for her just like she'd waited for me on my mission. When she told me what happened, we got married in the temple as soon as she missed her period."

"Oh my god."

"But you're sealed to me, so you'll always be my son," my father said quickly. Since I was ex'ed, of course, the sealing was no longer in effect, but I knew what he meant, and I smiled.

"What a relief to finally get the cards on the table." My mother sighed heavily.

We talked a while more, and when my parents stood to leave, my mother said, "Now when you meet a nice young man and get married, we want him to be part of our lives, too."

We hugged and then they left. I sat back on my sofa and stared at the floor for a while.

I didn't go out Friday night.

But Saturday, I headed back to Andy and Ivan's place. After dinner, we played Trivial Pursuit and then watched a couple of episodes of *Bewitched*, the ones with the gay Darrin. Then we got ready for bed.

"Boxer briefs?" asked Andy in surprise.

"What happened to your Mormon underwear?"

"I'm moving on to a new stage in life." I told them briefly what had happened. They both hugged me at the same time, a long, sweet, comforting hug.

"Can I tell you guys a secret?" I asked as we climbed into bed.

"You know you can."

"I love you both."

There was silence for a moment, and my heart started beating faster.

Then Andy said slowly, "Even though you're not a Mormon anymore…" He hesitated. "Do you think you could consider polygamy?"

"No," I replied firmly. Then I smiled nervously. "But I've been thinking a lot about polyandry, and basically I'm all for it."

"We'd love to marry you," said Ivan. "We were just wondering when to bring it up."

"You really like us?"

"You're the most normal guys I know."

"I'll try not to take offense at that."

"We have a spare bedroom where you can put your books and things. And we'll fit anything else you need throughout the rest of the house."

We got down to sharing our bodies and had the most passionate sex we'd had to date. As I lay on top of Ivan with cum on my back, I wondered briefly if my parents were prepared for me to bring two husbands home for Christmas dinner.

We'd work that one out as we came to it, I decided.

Feeling Andy softly kissing my back, I wondered if the secret to life was to truly love someone no matter what anyone else thought, no matter what the consequences, just to love as long as you were able, the best you could.

It was too obvious to be a secret.

So why didn't more people know about it?

A few years ago, I'd been begging God to make me straight. I'd had no idea of the secret he held in store for me. I wondered now what other secrets lay ahead.

I lay down next to Ivan, and Andy lay down next to me. We didn't clean up but just lay there all sticky and covered in sex and love. Then we turned out the light and, one arm on top of another on top of another, we unhurriedly drifted off to sleep.

Splitting with Elder Tanner

"Flip! It sure is hot." Elder Tanner stopped for a moment and wiped his brow. Jason stood off to the side and looked at him appraisingly. The 95-degree Georgia heat with its 90% humidity was unbearable even for natives like himself, but it did offer one perk. Elder Tanner had sweated so much that his wet shirt clung tightly to his body. Even with his garments on underneath, Jason could see the outline of Tanner's pecs, even see his nipples. He smiled.

"It'll just make Vancouver seem that much better when you get home to Canada," Jason said.

"I *already* liked Vancouver," Elder Tanner complained.

"Maybe you can take a cold shower when we get home."

"I'll have to anyway, after that last door."

Jason was going on "splits" today with the missionaries, and Elder Tanner always chose working with him over Kirk, the other stake missionary. Jason hadn't particularly enjoyed his own two-year mission to North Dakota and hadn't been all that excited when the bishop called him as a stake missionary just six months after his return to Atlanta. But four months later, Elder Tanner had been transferred to the ward, and missionary work seemed fun again.

"You thought she was pretty?" Jason asked.

"Are you kidding? You must be taking salt peter if you didn't get a hard on."

Jason laughed, enjoying the sexual talk. He and Elder Tanner went tracting door to door three hours almost every Saturday and went on teaching assignments usually one weeknight each week. This gave them lots of time to talk, and Elder Tanner had told Jason about discovering masturbation at eleven, how disappointed he'd been to learn two years later it was a sin, and how even now as a missionary he sometimes succumbed. He told Jason about the first girl he kissed, and about dry humping his college girlfriend, only to find out in his missionary interview that this wasn't allowed, either.

"I have all this sexual energy," he complained. "My companion doesn't like talking about these things. I'm glad I can talk to you, Jason. You're a good friend."

Jason punched Tanner lightly in the shoulder, and Tanner smiled sheepishly. "I'm sorry," the young missionary said. "I'm always talking about me. How's *your* girlfriend?"

"Amy's fine," Jason said.

"Is she soft?"

"Yes." Jason looked again at Tanner's wonderful, hard body. He watched him lift weights sometimes at the apartment. There was one little muscle in Tanner's forearm near his wrist that was particularly attractive.

"Does she smell good?"

"I don't really like perfume."

Though the combination of Tanner's sweat, body oils, and deodorant could be rather intoxicating.

"You going to see her tonight? You going to kiss her? French kiss?"

Jason shook his head. "We're going to wait till we get married before we kiss."

Elder Tanner stopped halfway up the walk to the next door. "You're kidding, right?"

"We read somewhere that it's safest this way. If you don't take the first step toward sex, you won't take the last."

"You're a stronger man than I am." Elder Tanner put his arm across Jason's shoulder and pulled him close. "I guess that's why you're so gung ho on missionary work. Keeps you pure."

Jason looked at Elder Tanner's smile and felt a warm sensation spreading through his chest. "Yes," he said, "we want to be good Mormons."

They tracted for another hour. Elder Tanner talked about his dog, Scruffy, and about his plans to become a CPA. Jason talked about his sister's marriage to a returned missionary and their seven-month-old baby. He told Elder Tanner about how his mother loved being organist for the ward and how his father enjoyed working as physical facilities rep for the stake. Elder Tanner spoke about how his girlfriend at BYU-Idaho kept sending him photos of herself in tight T-shirts. Jason talked about the latest email from his brother serving a mission in New Zealand.

His brother had gotten New Zealand while all Jason got was North Dakota. His brother had all the cheerleaders in high school. All Jason had was chess club.

"He's already a district leader," Jason said, "and he still has nine months left. He'll surely be ZL. I was only senior companion."

"Zone leaders are assholes. I'd have been happy to have you as my senior companion."

Finally, it was time to head back to the apartment and meet up with the others. "Thanks for your help today, Jason," said Tanner. "The others'll be back soon. You don't have to wait."

They were inside, Tanner in front of the fan, with his white shirt still clinging to his body.

"No, I know you. You just want some alone time so you can masturbate in peace."

Elder Tanner laughed. "Aw, now why did you have to go and say that? Now I *do* want to masturbate."

"Just keep looking at me and the feeling will go away." Jason laughed, too.

Elder Tanner looked at him intensely and rubbed his crotch. Jason felt a twitch in his own penis. "Yep, you're right," said Tanner with a smile. "Thanks again for keeping me on the strait and narrow."

Jason felt a little disappointed, but really, he did want Elder Tanner to stay righteous. He wished he could be righteous himself. The Church was the most important thing in his life. He'd cut his own masturbation down to once a week, yet it was only a modest victory. He found himself jacking off to his photo of Elder Tanner every Saturday evening before going to pick up Amy.

He did the same this evening, feeling calm as he walked up to her door. Amy's father answered. Jason's girlfriend was only twenty and still living at home as she studied for her junior year at the university. Jason lived at home as well. At twenty-two, he was just finishing up his sophomore year. Two years in North Dakota put him way behind other kids his age.

Amy pushed past her father and walked with Jason back to the car. "You look lovely tonight," he said. Amy lowered her eyes. "Did you have a good day?"

"Worked on a paper for class. You?"

"Me, too. I like psychology." Jason planned on earning his Masters' in Social Work after finishing his psychology degree, but that meant at least four additional years of intense studies. He wasn't sure Amy was willing to wait that long to marry. The bishop was already pressuring her.

They drove to Burger King for dinner, and then Jason drove back to his parents' house. "Hello, Amy," his mother said as they walked through the kitchen. Jason led Amy to his bedroom, where they closed the door behind them. There was a bookcase against one wall filled with science fiction novels. Jason's desk was only neat when Amy came over. The rest of the time it was deep in clutter. He had posters on the walls, one of Gandhi, one of his favorite movie *The Day After Tomorrow*, and a vintage one of Donny and Marie.

"What did you pick for tonight?" asked Amy.

"The new *Star Trek* just came out on DVD."

"Another science fiction movie." Amy sighed.

"It gives me hope for the future."

"All right."

Jason and Amy sat in two chairs separated by a couple of feet. Jason felt particularly pulled by the new Spock's dual nature, and the new Spock's magnetism. He wanted to be Uhura and comfort him, too. He and Amy talked for a few minutes after the movie ended, and then Jason drove her home. He shook her hand at the door, and she smiled wistfully. "Another cold shower tonight for my poor Jason."

"Yes," he lied, smiling. "You Jezebel."

The next day was church. Amy was nursery teacher in her own ward, so she didn't come to Jason's. He was the Sunday School instructor for the twelve- and thirteen-year-olds. He enjoyed it well enough, but the best part of the day was sitting next to Elder Tanner during Sacrament meeting. When they shared the hymnal, Elder Tanner's arm would brush against Jason's ever so slightly. Jason looked at the hair pattern on Tanner's arm, and at that attractive little muscle near the wrist. Elder Tanner always grinned impishly at him. Heaven couldn't be any better than this.

The bishop made an announcement at the end of the meeting, reminding everyone that civil unions for same-sex couples was going to the state legislature in a couple of weeks. All Church members were to send letters to every politician from their district and make phone calls, too.

"Several states have already legalized gay marriage. The liberal media has made homosexuality seem normal. We must fight to the death to defend the sacred institution of marriage."

Jason accepted without question that homosexuality was a sin. He'd read the scriptures. He'd heard all the talks from General Authorities over the years. Still, he wasn't quite sure why it was wrong to allow secular gay marriages. The law allowed smoking and drinking and gambling. It allowed coffee and tea. It allowed premarital heterosexual sex. And shopping on Sunday. It allowed lots of things that were technically wrong. Jason wondered why the Church couldn't just insist that its own members remain pure without trying to force everyone else, too.

But Jason idolized Orson Scott Card, the most prominent Mormon writer. And Card had insisted that if the country allowed gay marriage to take effect, it would become his primary duty to "overthrow the government," which would at that point become his "mortal enemy."

Jason realized his own mind was tainted simply by being gay, despite still being a virgin. Even though he never intended to act on his gay feelings, it was depressing to hear the Church repeat over and over how despicable gays were. He *tried* to be good, didn't he? Jason wondered if things would always be this way. In the past, polygamy was a commandment. In the past, interracial marriage was against Church teachings, and Blacks couldn't hold the priesthood or go through the temple.

It was *possible* that at some future date, the prophet would have a revelation accepting homosexuality. At every

General Conference, Jason waited to hear the announcement. But the words never came.

Just a list of new temples to be built.

He would have to marry Amy and hope for the best.

"Hey, we're going skating this P-day," Elder Tanner told him after the closing prayer. "You want to come?"

"Sure." Jason smiled. Elder Tanner had invited him to join the missionaries on other Preparation Days, to go to the zoo, play Frisbee in the park, and play basketball in the church gym. Being stake missionary was the best calling he'd ever had.

Classes the next couple of days went well. And Jason saw Amy again Monday night at Single Adult Family Home Evening. They played Truth or Dare. Amy had to tell everyone about her first crush. That was why Jason always chose Dare. Tonight, he had to take a frozen burrito and go to a neighbor's door and ask if they'd ordered it.

On Wednesday after class, Jason went to the elders' apartment, and they all headed over to the skating rink. Jason enjoyed watching Elder Tanner skate backwards and dance on his skates. When they played Snap the Whip, Jason got to be the tail, only fun because it meant holding Elder Tanner's hand. As the elders skated faster, it became harder to hold on, and finally Elder Tanner's hand was torn from Jason's grasp.

But he'd gotten to hold his hand for a little while anyway. Jason understood what fans must feel when they got to touch their favorite celebrity. He could imagine some kind of mystical residue on his hand even after they all left the skating rink.

Jason drove everyone to Baskin-Robbins and offered to treat them to banana splits. The elders eagerly accepted, which gave Jason an excuse to hang out a bit longer. Jason chatted and joked with all four, but it didn't keep him from noticing things like Elder Tanner licking ice cream off his upper lip, noticing how Tanner accidentally brushed against Jason's leg while changing positions.

"Hey, this banana is the same shape as my dick," said Elder Tanner's companion, Elder Holmes, eyeing it approvingly.

"Aw, why did you have to say a thing like that?" asked Elder Tanner. "How can I eat this now?"

"Your dick is split?" another elder asked.

"You know what I mean."

"You're gonna make me waste this."

Jason picked up his banana and took a big bite. The others all laughed and groaned, and everyone finished their treats.

Jason and Elder Tanner went out teaching the next night. They were at the apartment of a single mother with a young child. The woman must have been at least twenty-six, but Jason could still see she was flirting with Elder Tanner, who seemed oblivious. Jason realized all along he'd have to share Elder Tanner. One day, Tanner would get married. But he was still glad he didn't have to share tonight.

"Can you see her as a member?" Elder Tanner asked him afterward, apparently trying to get a feel if further teaching appointments were necessary.

Jason shrugged. "Yes," he said slowly. "Maybe not as an active member, but…"

"Is it worth baptizing her if she doesn't become a good member?"

"That's her path to decide."

"Aren't we just cursing her if we give someone the gospel and they aren't strong enough to live it? Better to be ignorant than torn in two directions." He looked at the ground a little morosely.

"Are you torn in two directions?"

Elder Tanner looked at him. "Sometimes, I want to be a good missionary, and other times I want to go to an R-rated movie."

There were times Jason felt he had a split personality. One half of him wanted to be a good Mormon boy, and the other half longed to be a decadent pervert. But it *was* better to be torn than just be the pervert outright.

"It's okay to want the wrong things." Jason put his arm around Elder Tanner. "As long as we *choose* the right ones."

They'd finished early but had nowhere else to go, so they headed back to the apartment. "You don't have to stay if you don't want to. The others will be back soon."

"You're always trying to get rid of me," Jason joked. "But I know the rules." Missionaries were never to be left alone.

"It's been a long day. You mind if I go take a shower?"

"Oh, go ahead. I'll just browse through your Church magazines."

"You don't know how big a help you are to us," Tanner said, taking off his tie and unbuttoning his shirt. "To me, anyway," he said. "Elder Holmes is okay, but he's hard to live with twenty-four hours a day." Elder Tanner kicked off his shoes and pulled off his pants. He stood now in just his garments. "You make me realize there are good people out there, righteous people who are actually fun to be with." He slipped off his T-shirt. "It makes a difference, I can tell you."

Jason looked at Elder Tanner, nodding in what he hoped was an empathetic manner. The missionary was now standing in only his knee-length underwear and socks. The man had the exact body type Jason preferred. Lifting weights gave him definition without bulking him up too much. And his nipples were so pointy. Jason's own were wide and soft, even though he wasn't overweight. Elder Tanner's nipples were hard. It was a good look.

Tanner turned his back to Jason. "You don't want to see my dick. I'll turn around so you won't be grossed out." He leaned over and tugged off the bottom half of his garments. Jason saw the beautiful split of his butt crack and had to force himself to close his eyes.

When he looked up a moment later, Elder Tanner was still leaning over, taking off his socks. The physical pain

Jason felt as he turned away was almost unbearable. His chest hurt.

"I'll be out in a few minutes."

Elder Tanner went in the bathroom and pulled the shower curtain shut, but he left the door open. In his own mission, Jason had only been allowed to shut the bathroom door when defecating. At all other times, the missionaries were ordered to keep it open, to reduce the risk of masturbation.

Jason could hear the water running and moved to the bathroom door. The shower curtain wasn't completely transparent, but Jason could see the color of flesh as Tanner showered. He wondered if he should talk to Tanner, to give himself a reason for standing in the doorway, but he didn't want to talk.

He looked at his watch. The others weren't due back for twenty more minutes. Of course, he and Elder Tanner hadn't been due back, either. Jason quietly unzipped and pulled out his penis. He began softly stroking himself as he watched Elder Tanner washing his short hair.

It was wrong to look at a platonic friend in a sexual manner. It was a sin to make a stalwart missionary into a sexual object.

Jason watched as Elder Tanner rubbed soap over his body, as he leaned over and let the shower rinse his ass cheeks when he pulled them apart. Jason watched as Elder Tanner lathered his pubic hair and even stroked himself a time or two, obviously unaware he was being observed.

Jason shot off into his hand just as he heard a key in the front door lock. He quickly licked his hand clean and shoved his dick back in his pants.

"You guys have a good lesson?" Jason asked, smiling.

"We got a commitment to baptism."

"Good deal. Our contact is still on the fence."

Elder Holmes shrugged. "Some people don't know which fork in the road to take."

"All you can do is encourage them to fork correctly."

Just then, the other two missionaries showed up, and Kirk, who'd been working with Elder Holmes, shook everyone's hand and took off. A moment later, Elder Tanner came out of the bathroom with a towel around his waist.

"Leaving your clothes all over the floor again?" asked Holmes. "Didn't we talk about this in Companion Inventory?"

"Sorry."

"Well, I guess I'll head on, too," said Jason. "See you guys on Saturday."

Jason shook hands with everyone, but as Elder Tanner shook his hand, he looked intently at Jason and said softly, "Thanks for this evening."

Jason felt uncomfortable and smiled uncertainly, but out in the car, he put both his hands to his face. The one hand smelled like cum, and the other smelled like a clean Elder

Tanner. Jason sat behind the wheel and breathed in deeply for a few minutes before turning on the motor.

Classes on Friday were rough, concentrating difficult. Jason wondered if he should ask the bishop to release him from being stake missionary. There was no point putting himself in the grip of temptation. He wanted to live a Celestial life, and that meant no more masturbation or fantasies about Elder Tanner or Jake Gyllenhaal or anyone else.

But was facing temptation too heavy a price to pay for good deeds? When Jason worked with Elder Tanner, he was teaching the gospel, he was reaching out to Gentiles. He was offering emotional support to a struggling missionary. Those were good things. If his spiritual credit score was dinged a few points in the process, wasn't it more important to do the job God had called him to do?

There was a stake Single Adult dance that evening, and Jason and Amy danced for hours. She told him how her younger sister had just gotten braces and was devastated, and how her brother had gotten suspended from high school for getting in a fistfight with another boy over who the sexiest female pop artist was. Jason knew he should be interested in what was going on in Amy's family. He liked Amy, after all. So why didn't he care? What kind of person was he if he couldn't generate a little sympathy?

After Jason dropped Amy off when the dance ended, he walked around the side of her house to her bedroom window and started singing her current favorite love song. She opened her window, laughing, and threw a box of Kleenex at him.

On Saturday, there was a work project at church in the morning, trimming the bushes and bagging the clippings. A few men from the Elders' quorum came, and Jason enjoyed the physical labor in the early morning heat. He appreciated being able to do a tangible good, when so many other good acts were intangible. Getting people to the right agencies and signed up for financial and emotional assistance were only occasionally tangible goods, and he couldn't even do that unless he made it all the way to becoming a social worker. Jason went home and studied intensely for an hour before meeting the missionaries later for splits.

Jason's mom had baked some cookies for him to take over, and the elders swarmed on the Tupperware container when Jason opened it. "This is great," Elder Holmes said. "Our dessert budget is kaput for the week."

"The dishwasher is kaput, too," said Elder Tanner dryly, pointing to his companion.

"I'm not in the mood."

Jason went to the kitchen and turned on the hot water. Within five minutes, he had all the dishes cleanly stacked in the drain board.

"That's very subservient of you," said Elder Holmes with a knowing smile. Jason frowned. Had he just given himself away?

"That's *thank you*," said Elder Tanner. "Come on, Jason. You're my comp now. Let's get going."

They were soon tracting, and it was not going well. Two people cursed them out, one threatened to call the police, another laughed at them, and one coldly promised to shoot them if they ever came back. Worse, though, was the complete indifference that 95% of people showed. They simply couldn't have cared less. Understanding the purpose of life was absolutely unimportant to them.

"You ever feel you're playing for the wrong team?" Elder Tanner asked once between houses.

"Just because lots of people are addicted to heroin doesn't make me want to stick a needle in my arm."

"These people don't seem any less happy than we are, though, do they?" He paused. "That's not a very high standard, I guess. I'm usually not very happy. Isn't the Church supposed to make us happy?"

Jason waited a moment before answering. He'd been terribly unhappy for most of his own mission as well. He only had one companion he liked, and that lasted only three months. The other twenty-one months had been unbearable. Jason had almost bought a ticket and come home early more times than he could remember. The zone leaders were always criticizing him, always pressuring, always intimidating. His companions were either loafers who dragged him down or zealots who critiqued every word that came out of his mouth.

Jason didn't know what Tanner was facing here, but it had to be a less than perfect existence.

"We don't do the right thing for social rewards," Jason said. "We do them to please God."

"Why do I always have to adapt to what God wants? Why can't He be big and adapt to something I like once in a while?"

"Is what you want so unacceptable?"

Tanner looked at the sidewalk and kicked at a twig. "I don't want to tell people what to do all the time. I don't want to tell them they're wrong. I don't want to set myself up as the single Truth Bearer in the neighborhood, as the only person who has a monopoly on Righteousness."

"But we *do* have the truth," Jason said quietly. "And that gives us an obligation."

"I don't want an obligation. I want to live my life and let other people live theirs." He looked up at Jason. "Is the same thing right for everyone? We all have different jobs, read different books, play different sports. Why can't there be more than one way to live a righteous life?"

Jason's chest hurt again. It was painful to listen to another person's suffering. "I don't know," he said slowly. "I don't know." He wanted to hug Elder Tanner, hold him and kiss him and tell him everything would be all right.

Instead, they knocked at the next door.

Before much longer, though, it was time to drive Elder Tanner home. "Thanks for helping today. Sorry I was so negative."

"You're always a pleasure to work with."

Jason went home and studied, and when it was time to go to Amy's house, he almost called and told her he was sick.

They watched *The X-Men* in his bedroom, and then Jason drove Amy home. To be human and a mutant at the same time, Jason mused, thinking of Hugh Jackman. It must be a terrible thing. But he still wished Wolverine were there.

Elder Tanner was in a better mood at church the following day, and Jason sat next to him again. He caught the bishop's eye at one point and thought he saw suspicion cross his face. It was so hard to be on guard all the time.

The next couple of days went well. Jason made a 98 on a test and an A on a paper. He was making A's in four of his classes and a B in the other. He studied a little harder for the B class this week. He had to save his senior year for B classes. His GPA couldn't handle B's now if he was going to have difficult classes his last semester or two. He had to be prepared with a strong GPA going in. His years as a Boy Scout had taught him about preparation. You always had to push now in case you were weak later. Store up bonus points. That was probably one of the reasons the Church had people serve missions while they were young.

Tuesday night, he got a call from Elder Tanner and smiled. Maybe they'd go to a museum together on P-day. "Hey, pal," said Tanner, "I've got bad news."

"What is it?" Jason's throat felt tight. Had Tanner told the mission president how he felt? Had he been caught masturbating? Was he found with a porn magazine like one of Jason's companions? Was he being sent home? What could it be?

"I'm being transferred tomorrow to Macon. I'll miss you, buddy."

Jason sat down. He felt dizzy and a little nauseated. Elder Tanner had only been in the ward two months. Transfers were unpredictable, but this seemed so unfair.

"Do you…do you need a ride?" asked Jason. "I can skip class for a day."

"Oh, no, but thanks. I already have my bus ticket."

Jason felt he was in a trance. "Well, send me your address when you get there."

"We're not allowed to write anyone within mission boundaries. And we can only email our direct family. But you know that."

"Yeah."

"I've gotta go. Just didn't want to leave without saying goodbye." He laughed. "Till transfers do us part, hey, bud? So long, comp."

"I'll be praying for you."

They hung up, and Jason looked at the class notebooks sprawled across his bed. He pushed them onto the floor in disgust. Why was God doing this to him?

He stared at the pile of notes.

Perhaps it was a blessing, he decided, nodding slowly. If Elder Tanner stayed longer, the inevitable separation would be even harder. Or maybe it was a punishment for the masturbation. If he stopped sinning, though, could he have Elder Tanner back? He'd do whatever it took. He got down on his knees and prayed.

And just like in the scriptures, he had a revelation. There was no clap of thunder or bright light, but Jason heard a whisper, and he knew it was the voice of God.

The voice in his head told him to submit his papers again to go on a second full-time mission. It might be as miserable as the first time, but it was the only way he could morally be with another man. Same-sex marriage was a sin, but being with a missionary companion twenty-four hours a day would be the next best thing.

If Jason was serving God to get that, it couldn't be a sin. If it was hard and he suffered, that would only be appropriate for a sinner like him. But even if he only had one decent companion in two years, for just two months, it was better than nothing. To be one with another man legally. He had to do it.

And it wouldn't hurt to show up his brother in New Zealand, always the good one, always the strong one. A second mission would really set Jason apart. It was practically unheard of in modern times. He'd be at the mercy of the mission president and zone leaders, but maybe, *maybe* he'd have a few weeks of happiness.

Jason had a small inheritance from his grandmother that he'd been planning to save for graduate school. His parents let him live at home rent-free, and Jason worked summers to pay his tuition the rest of the year. His father had paid for his first mission, but if he wouldn't pay for this one, Jason could use his inheritance. He could always take out a student loan for graduate school. This was the opportunity of a lifetime, and he couldn't let it slip away. Perhaps this was the sole reason God had called him as a stake missionary, to make him see he needed to serve a second full-time mission.

Jason wished he could get on the bus with Elder Tanner and run away with him somewhere.

He pulled out his picture of Elder Tanner and caressed it. He'd probably never see the man again. It wasn't as if he could run right over to the elders' apartment and kiss him goodbye. He'd end up with a split lip. At least he had this photograph, though. He lifted it to his face and smelled it.

It smelled like paper.

Maybe he could just show up tomorrow and drive Elder Tanner to the bus station without being asked.

Jason picked up the phone and dialed the bishop. "Yes, Jason?"

"I want to serve a second full-time mission. These are the Last Days, and they require sacrifice. We need everyone to do their part and go the extra mile. I have the money and the desire. I want to go."

The bishop was silent for a moment. "What does Amy have to say about this? Are you two splitting up?"

Jason had forgotten about Amy. But if she was the right girl for him, he thought now, she'd wait. Besides, maybe a second mission is what it would take to finally make Jason straight. It would be in her best interest to let him go.

And maybe she'd find someone better while he was away.

"No, she wants to finish school first anyway. This will give her the chance."

"You shouldn't put off marriage till you graduate. Marriage is too important to postpone. It's one of the main reasons we come to Earth. It's a prerequisite for the Celestial Kingdom."

"Marriage *is* important to me," Jason said. "I just feel I need to do it my way."

"It isn't good for man to be alone. It leads to sin. And I can absolutely predict that Amy won't be waiting when you get back. It's a mistake."

"There are other righteous girls I can marry, Bishop. It's important for me to serve God."

"You serve God by getting married and having children."

"Going on a mission and having children aren't mutually exclusive. I can do both."

"Obviously, we're divided on this. I can tell you, though, as your spiritual leader, you need to marry Amy."

"Bishop, I'm going on another mission. If you won't submit my papers, I'll move to another ward where I can find a bishop who will."

"Jason, you sound desperate. What's really going on?"

Jason tried to answer but found he couldn't formulate a response. No words would come. He just wanted to scream, to curse, to hit someone.

"Are you in love with him, Jason?" the bishop asked quietly.

Jason started sobbing.

"You can never be with another man, you know. Homosexuality is a sin. Same-sex marriage is unacceptable. There's never a right to do something that is morally wrong."

"But there is!" Jason spluttered. "People have the right to play football on Sunday. They have the right to see R-rated movies. Hell, they even have the right to see X-rated movies! People have the right to be atheists. People have the right to have abortions. Those are all legal rights. Why can't I just love someone?"

"It isn't real love and you know it," the bishop said. "It's lust. You have to admit it to yourself if you expect to escape. By definition, it's all about sex. It's the devil trying to enslave you."

Jason sobbed some more. He *did* want to have sex with Elder Tanner. Maybe the bishop was right. It wasn't the same as the bishop wanting to have sex with his wife. *This* was a sin. It was making him deny Amy. It was making him delay school. It was making him waste money. It was making him stagnate in the past rather than move forward.

"Bishop, I *need* to go on another mission. I absolutely need the spiritual experiences of a mission. I didn't have any on my last one."

"I can't let you go for the wrong reasons."

"But my first companion went so his father would buy him a car. My second companion went so his father would pay for college. My third companion went so he could marry his girlfriend who was a General Authority's granddaughter."

"Your third companion went for the right reason."

"I'm submitting my papers, Bishop."

"If you do, I'll hold a Church court."

Jason wanted to scream again. He wanted to throw something. But how could his feelings be right if what he wanted to do was curse the bishop? He hung up the phone and cried.

He would have to quit school and move to another ward, after all, another stake, and submit his papers there.

Then he had another idea.

Perhaps he should simply look for a man here, a man outside of a sanctioned missionary companionship. Someone like that nice guy one row over in his Adolescent Psychology class.

Yet he wanted Elder Tanner. He wanted the Church.

The phone rang and Jason leaped for it. Maybe it was Tanner calling to give him his new address, despite the rules, or his email address. Maybe he was going to ask for a ride and sell his ticket back.

"Jason?" It *was* Elder Tanner!

"Hey there!"

"The bishop just called and told me everything."

Jason's heart began beating furiously.

"You queers have to ruin everything."

"But—but—"

Elder Tanner laughed. "Just kidding, buddy. Doesn't bother me in the least. I just wanted to tell you I still love you."

"Still?"

"You're the best companion I've ever had, even if it was only for a few hours at a time. But I do have my girlfriend back home."

"Right."

"Stay good so I can at least see you again in the Celestial Kingdom."

"Okay."

"I gotta go. You take care."

"You, too."

There was a pause during which neither of them seemed to want to hang up, and Jason's heart began beating faster again.

But then there was a click, and Jason felt all the air rush out of him. He leaned over slowly and gathered his notebooks off the floor. He stared at them a long time and then opened one and tried to study. "It is in adolescence that one first feels the longing for love."

Jason closed his notebook and pulled his pillow to his chest. He sat on his bed and rocked gently back and forth, looking about the room in a daze.

He was still rocking when the sun came up in the morning. He should have felt too tired to drive to the university but was determined to go anyway.

First, though, he took off his garments. He didn't own any secular underwear, though, and so pulled his pants back on without.

He tossed his scriptures in the trash, drank some orange juice, and headed off to class.

The Pool Room

Glennon pushed hard against the iron gate and then walked up the steps to The Pool Room. Mike had died yesterday, and though Glennon never used to read the obituaries, over the past few months, reading them had become a near-daily habit. Glennon didn't really know Mike well. Just that he was the guy who'd composed the AIDS requiem for the Gay Men's chorus to sing last season, the requiem they'd sung in the St. Louis cathedral on Jackson Square. At least Mike had lived long enough to hear it performed. 1990 was supposed to be the start of the Gay Nineties, but so far, things didn't seem very gay.

Glennon walked down the long hallway, its floor covered in decaying carpet. He passed a couple of empty rooms, then the kitchen, and the pool table and jukebox, before coming to the bar. Jim, the cook, was already seated there, his white apron tied tightly around his waist. Annie was bartending, having started back to work the week before after spending most of the summer in the hospital.

Glennon sat on a corner stool so he could see everyone at the bar but could still look back down the hallway toward the front gate. The Eurythmics were telling everyone, "It's All Right," and Glennon could hear someone diving into the swimming pool out back. The motor of the hot tub was humming away, so someone was enjoying that as well. Probably two someones.

"Can I get you anything?" Annie asked. She brushed back her blond hair, her roots freshly bleached. But no make up allowed yet.

Glennon ordered his usual rum and Coke and left a generous tip. He liked the bartenders here and had gotten to know all of them since he only lived five doors down in this same Bywater neighborhood. He tried now to come mostly during Annie's shift. She set Glennon's drink in front of him and playfully stabbed a straw into it. As Glennon began stirring slowly, he looked at his right hand.

He remembered the time he'd burned himself when he was eight, trying to cook a Mother's Day breakfast. His brother, George, only ten, had volunteered to do all Glennon's chores for the rest of the week. Glennon remembered feeling jealous seeing how good George was.

But his brother was always like that. George had been the one to start the family "pixie" program a few years later, where the family would get together and choose two other families in the neighborhood each Christmas, leaving goodies on their doorsteps at least once a week for the three weeks before Christmas.

And George was the one who'd gone through the neighborhood looking for elderly people and then volunteering his own time as well as Glennon's mowing lawns or washing cars or whatever else George could think of. George always studied his scriptures. He became a zone leader on his mission to Japan. Glennon had resented helping the neighbors or serving as a missionary later himself, but George always seemed so happy to find opportunities to serve that Glennon often pretended he was enjoying himself, too.

He wanted to watch a movie or go swimming or sing a song.

Of course, everyone always praised Glennon for being so good and helpful, but he always felt scared, knowing one day they'd find out he was a fake.

Annie picked up her tip from the bar and patted his hand. God knows Glennon didn't have much money to spare these days, not since rushing off to Pensacola when he learned George was dying in the hospital with AIDS. The family hadn't even known he was positive. His brother had been in a monogamous relationship for five years. But it was only a matter of weeks now. George's liver and heart were almost destroyed.

While cooking a hamburger for Glennon one day, Jim had told him of his I.V. drug using sister who'd contracted AIDS. After three weeks in the hospital, she'd said good-bye to everyone and unplugged everything stuck into her. She'd died the next day. Glennon didn't believe in miracles and so wished George would hurry up and die, too, but George didn't want to go. "There's so much more I need to do first," he kept saying. "Things'll change for us. You'll see. We're making the world a better place."

"Annie!" Glennon said suddenly. "Where are your gloves?"

"I've only got the one body suit," she said. "I have to wash it sometime." She laughed. "Or you guys would stop coming in."

Annie was straight and had begun working at The Pool Room in May. Then one Wednesday night after the Bring-Your-Own-Meat barbecue, she'd gone home from her shift and started to feed her two kittens. She stood up, thinking she smelled something, and opened her bedroom door. That was when the neighbors heard her scream.

She had collapsed right there in the hallway, overcome by the heat and fumes, and before her gay neighbors could break in and pull her out, she'd suffered third degree burns on her chest, arms, and face, and second degree burns on her legs. Her kittens had died, and all the water had boiled out of her fish tank. Glennon had only visited Annie three times the two months she was in the hospital. He remembered that the tips of her ears had been black for the longest time.

Glennon had never thought he'd know anyone in her condition. He'd always just thought, "Oh, that poor person," when he saw a burn patient in the news, but he'd never really had to deal with it. Just feel a moment of sympathy and then move on to something else. But now there was no way to deny the suffering. Hearing Annie cry after having her scabs scraped off was awful. It hurt too much to watch her suffer, and yet Glennon knew that even if he and Annie weren't close friends, he owed her something simply because he was capable of giving and she needed whatever he could offer.

She'd asked him to read to her since she could no longer hold a book, so he'd read Erma Bombeck and Florence King and Jean Kerr. The only halfway humorous comment Annie had made her first six weeks in the hospital was, "I think I'll quit smoking. It doesn't do much for me anymore."

Annie's face had red splotches now but was not otherwise disfigured. Her right arm, on which she'd been wearing ten bracelets, was badly scarred where the metal seared the skin. Annie would need to wear a tight body suit for the next eighteen months to prevent further scarring. She even had a face mask she wore when not at work.

"And I'll tell you what," she added. "When I get enough money for the next suit, after the elastic wears out in this one, I'm going to see if I can dye it. This tan is getting old."

George Michael was singing, "I gotta have faith, faith, faith," a song which usually set Glennon to dancing no matter where he was. Today, though, he couldn't even manage to tap his foot. He turned, though, when a man glistening with pool water stuck his head in the door and ordered a cheeseburger.

Daisy followed him inside and stayed even after the man returned to the pool. "N-n-nice legs," he whispered, sitting beside Glennon and motioning back toward the door.

"Nice everything," Jim said, closing the book he'd been reading and heading for the kitchen.

Glennon put his hand on Daisy's leg and squeezed. Daisy's real name was Richard, and Glennon never did hear how he got the nickname, but Daisy seemed happy with it. He was nearing fifty and almost continually drunk, with a permanent three-day beard. He also flopped out of the baggy shorts he wore while trimming the weeds at The Pool Room and picking up trash.

Daisy had been quite depressed when Annie was burned. He hadn't liked her working so late in this neighborhood and often said he was afraid for her. At first, Annie just assumed he was paranoid because of the time five years earlier when a gay basher had beaten him in the head with a hammer, but after a while, she'd become spooked and told him to stop talking about it or he'd will something bad to happen. The next week, Annie was burned, and Daisy cried for three days about how he had willed it on her.

Glennon squeezed Daisy's leg again and rubbed his back as he finished his rum and Coke.

"H-how are y-you?"

"I'm okay. Thanks."

"Do you want a b-bwow job?" Daisy laughed. Having heard someone say that to Glennon one day and thinking it a great line, he repeated it almost every time he saw Glennon.

"Oh, not today." Glennon smiled and pulled Daisy closer for a moment in a half hug.

"Why don't you go after the guy in the cute little bathing suit?" suggested Annie, smiling mischievously.

"I d-don't think so," Daisy answered but went out back anyway.

Diana Ross shouted about a "Chain Reaction," and Glennon ordered just a Coke this time.

The gate squeaked open, and Glennon peered down the hallway. Brad was coming up the steps. He was overweight, and his ears stuck out too far, but he was pleasant enough, a former Metropolitan Community Church minister who was now a house painter.

Since Glennon had been excommunicated from the Mormon Church, he had little interest in religion and at first resented Brad trying to interest him in the MCC, but they'd finally both made their points clear and didn't bring up church again. They usually just talked about Brad's work with the "buddy" program.

Glennon enjoyed hearing Brad discuss working with people with AIDS, though it reminded him he wasn't a good enough person himself. He'd helped a blind man past some road construction last week, and the other day, he'd let an old woman cut in front of him in line at the grocery even though he knew she'd be slow.

And there was the time he'd seen a kid knocked off his bike by a speeding car. Glennon had knelt beside him and sung Primary songs to keep the boy calm while waiting for the ambulance to arrive. But those were all one-time, easy things to do, certainly nothing that required much effort.

It wasn't as if he gave three nights, or two, or even one every week helping the people who needed him so badly. Glennon was afraid that once he was caught up in dealing directly with AIDS, he'd never be free of it the rest of his life. Couldn't he have just a few good years before having to deal with misery the entire remainder of his life?

He'd only just come out two years earlier. Was it so horrible to want to have a little freedom now? A few happy months? Did he have to look at sores and boils and lesions right now? This very minute? Couldn't he have a tiny bit of fun first?

Or was it already too late for that?

Glennon watched as Brad approached, wondering briefly what Brad's HIV status was. They'd never discussed it, and Glennon pushed the thought away.

"Hey, Glennon." Brad sat where Daisy had a moment earlier and shook Glennon's hand. "How's chorus?"

"Well, we're killing ourselves. *Aida* is only a few weeks away. We're working our tails off to memorize all that music, and we haven't even started on our Christmas program yet. After the opera, we'll only have two months before our holiday concert. We'll still have to keep killing ourselves. It almost isn't even fun anymore."

"You could always join our chorus. We're pretty laid back."

"No, but thanks." MCC members did hospice volunteer work and some direct care for PWA's. If Glennon joined the MCC, he might not be able to avoid it. But as he took another sip of his drink, he remembered that it was many of these people in Pensacola who were taking care of his brother now.

Just because *they* were saints, though, didn't mean *he* was. He could appreciate their sacrifices without making those same sacrifices himself. Was he so terrible because he liked to watch *Nova* and the Discovery channel every day? Did it make him a bad person because he read at least one science book a week? He *liked* to learn about the world. It was fun. Interesting. Intriguing. Wasn't being knowledgeable a good thing?

So why did he feel so defensive? Not *everyone* had to do the exact same good things, did they? Glennon worked hard for the Gay Men's chorus. That gave the world a better impression of gays, didn't it? It helped promote gay rights.

And the science programs and science books were important, too. Glennon taught science to high school students. He needed to keep abreast of things and read and study daily. It made him a good teacher. Being a good teacher was a good and useful thing.

Brad pushed a button on the jukebox, and a country voice twanged out, "There's a Tear in My Beer," making Glennon smile as he remembered the country/western dance at the Corral a couple of weekends ago. That at least had been a nice opportunity to relax and forget everything else. Almost every guy there had a beard and a pot belly and wore a cowboy hat and boots. They looked like most of his neighbors back in Amite where he'd grown up.

Watching gay rednecks doing the two-step together had made Glennon laugh with delight. One relatively cute guy with a nice smile asked Glennon to dance, and though Glennon was a poor dancer, he'd tried his best. After several more songs, they'd gone over to Glennon's place.

Another wet man came into the bar from out by the pool. "Hey, Fred." Glennon waved.

"Hey there."

Fred ordered a beer and headed for the bathroom. He was a doctor working in the AIDS ward of Charity Hospital and the husband of another chorus member. His husband Kurt did volunteer work for the NO/AIDS Task Force. He was the one who'd counseled Glennon when Glennon had gone recently for a blood test, which had come out negative, thank God. He was also the one who'd organized the benefit concert, auction, and dinner to raise money for Annie.

Glennon was always grateful to see people so organized and helpful. The necessary work was being done, and by someone who was good at it, as Glennon surely wouldn't be. He could never seem to concentrate on more than a couple of activities at a time. As a missionary in Brazil, he could either study his Portuguese or the missionary lessons. When he tried to do both, one suffered. George, of course, had not only become proficient in Japanese on his mission, but he'd also baptized almost twice the average number of converts.

In college, Glennon could either get good grades or be a competent membership clerk for the congregation. He usually chose good grades for a month, then spent a month with his church work, went back to studying for school, and then tried to catch up at church again. He'd look at his bishop, a CPA with five kids who also managed what had to be almost a full-time volunteer job at church, and pray never to have a calling any more demanding than what he already had.

Being excommunicated, while upsetting, had almost come as a relief. No more church work to juggle with everything else. It seemed the only way he could be good at service was if that was all he did.

Other people managed to balance things. It wasn't as if Kurt led a life of pure service. He'd slept with almost every good-looking guy in town and still had time for his gardening, chorus rehearsals, and poetry writing. He also seemed to have achieved a successful eight-year relationship with Fred.

Glennon wondered again how one person could do so much, could have a personal life and yet still give to the community. He wondered what would happen if Kurt or Fred were suddenly to die. Who would take their place?

Glennon frowned and sucked hard on his straw.

Fred came out of the bathroom and gave Glennon a peck on the lips. Madonna began urging everyone to "Express Yourself," so Glennon gave Fred a big hug, getting dampened in the process.

Fred said hi to Brad and then turned back to Glennon. "I can't wait for you guys to finish *Aida*. We listen to that damn practice tape every night. If I hear people shouting, 'A morte! A morte!' much longer, I'm going to look for another place to sleep until after the performance." He gave Glennon an appraising look. "You got room in your bed?"

"Yeah, but I have the same tape."

He shrugged. "Maybe I can pick someone up tonight." He winked as he grabbed his beer and walked back outside.

"I think I'll go out back, too, and read for a while." Brad showed Glennon a copy of the book *Beyond Survival* by Theresa Saldana and walked out the door.

"Daisy ought to read that," Glennon murmured.

"If he could read anymore," Annie said. "At least Brad only got a broken rib."

"What are you talking about?"

"He was mugged two nights ago."

"God," said Glennon, shaking his head. "I hope the book helps." He frowned, realizing how lame that sounded. Surely, there was something *he* could do to help Brad feel better.

Twirling his straw, he began thinking where he might go to buy another wallet for Brad. But somehow that wasn't quite enough. He began thinking of which Bible verse he might have embossed on it, though maybe even this was just an attempt at a quick fix to help ease Glennon's conscience.

Not that his conscience needed easing, of course. Glennon had given up guilt two years ago when he left the Church. Besides, what was there to feel guilty about? He didn't owe Brad anything.

Glennon watched as Annie disappeared into a back room, wishing he knew what to say. He hadn't visited her once since she'd been released. Maybe he could go over for just a little while every few weeks, maybe clean her bathroom or kitchen while she was getting back the full use of her hands. He jotted a note down on a Task Force newsletter to remind himself and then began browsing through the newsletter.

Looking toward the end of the bar, Glennon saw that the food basket was full. Tomorrow he'd have to make his rounds to pick up food for the hospice. That was easy participation. He never told anyone he worked for the Task Force, but he knew if they asked, he'd be able to answer without too much shame.

Annie returned then and carefully poured half a bucket of ice into a bin as two men, dressed, came in from out back and racked the balls to play pool. "I can't wait till I can really hold a pool cue again," Annie said. "I even lost to Daisy yesterday."

Yet again, Glennon didn't quite know what to say. He waited a moment and then shrugged. "I guess you can at least appreciate things more than a lot of us," he offered.

Annie had been slowly wiping off the bar but now put her rag down. "That's a bunch of crap," she replied, a steely note in her voice. "Any 'insight' I may have gained from this I'd give up in a second if I could make this never to have happened."

Glennon nodded and began thinking again of his brother. George was two years older than he but had come out four years earlier than Glennon, before there was much talk of AIDS. If only George had been a little more dedicated to the Church and hung in there a few years longer, the one thing Glennon had managed over George, he'd be healthy now. Then again, if the Church had accepted gays in the first place, George could have remained celibate until marrying another guy, and he'd still be well. But there were different norms in different communities, and now at the age of thirty, George was dying.

Glennon remembered a Church song he used to sing, "My Turn on Earth." The lyrics that kept going through his head were those comparing life to carnival rides, like a Ferris wheel going around, up and down, and like a carousel. "Some horses are high, and some horses are low. Some turns are short, and some turns are long."

Glennon remembered that the husband of Carol Lynn Pearson, the woman who'd written those lyrics, had also been excommunicated for being gay. When the Quilt had come to New Orleans, he'd seen the name of Gerald Pearson on one of the quilt panels.

"Hey, how you doing?"

Glennon turned to see Tory standing beside him. He smiled, and Tory gave him a peck on the lips before ordering a 7-Up.

Glennon had seen Tory at The Pool Room all summer and had wanted to talk to him but never had the nerve to approach because Tory was so good looking. Then for a week Tory never showed up at all, and when he came back, he was limping. It turned out he'd been insulating his attic and had fallen through the ceiling and been badly bruised.

It had at least given them a topic to open a conversation with, and they'd started talking more when they ran into each other at the bar. They'd even gone to see a movie together twice, and Glennon had been meaning to invite Tory for dinner, when the sudden phone call had come from Pensacola.

"Haven't seen you in a couple of weeks," Tory said. "You been okay? Don't tell me you fell through a ceiling."

"No, I went through the roof." He smiled.

"Oh?"

"Well, maybe it was more just bouncing off the walls."

Tory groaned. "Please, you know I have to watch the poisons I take into my body." He smiled, and Glennon's throat started to hurt. Tory had told him about learning a couple of years earlier he had muscular dystrophy. It affected his arms and legs to some extent but seemed mostly centered on his facial muscles. It would someday make it impossible for him to smile. "So I'm going to smile all I can for now," he'd said.

"I've been busy," Glennon told him. "Thought I'd come relax."

"You going to swim?" Tory asked.

"I'm not sure."

"Well, I am. Come on."

Glennon followed Tory outside to the dressing room. Two guys were in the showers, one of them kneeling in front of the other.

"Don't mind us," Tory said, not even looking at them. "We'll be out in a second."

Tory stripped and put on a pair of trunks. Glennon hadn't brought a suit and so just stripped to his underwear. They left quickly, both to give the other men some privacy and to avoid the mosquitoes that always seemed to be everywhere in the dressing room. Every time he was back there, Glennon remembered the joke, "Can you catch AIDS from a mosquito?" "Only if it's a gay mosquito."

The pool was a little too cool today, but after several laps, Glennon began to feel warmer. He stopped to rest while Tory continued swimming, and he saw Tom and Tom walk out. Glennon waved and mouthed a wide, "Tom!" and then signed, "Hi, beautiful!"

Tom waved back and mouthed, "How are you?" while pointing to him. The other Tom just smiled and waved.

Tom #1 was fifty-two, deaf, and an elementary school teacher. He'd been married for twenty-three years, and after his wife died, he'd decided to explore the part of his personality he'd kept hidden so long. After a year, he met Tom #2, whom Glennon knew from the Corral, where Tom #2 tended bar on weekends. Tom #2 was forty-six, a hairdresser, and had given Glennon a terrific blow job one very quiet night at the Corral when they were alone, before Tom met Tom, about six months ago. The Toms had been quite monogamous since their first date.

Donna Summer began claiming, "This Time I Know Is for Real" as Tom #2 leaned down to kiss Tory. Then Tom kissed Tom, and they went to sit at a patio table to sip their drinks. Tory came up beside Glennon and wrapped his legs around Glennon's waist.

"You want to come to the kiss-in with me next week?" Tory asked. "ACT UP is staging a demonstration."

"Lots of media?"

"I hope so."

"Sure. I guess kissing you in public is the least I can do to ask for my rights."

"Fuck asking. We're demanding. Besides, you belong to the Gay Political Action Caucus, don't you?"

"We never really do very much."

"Why don't you join ACT UP? We don't do as much as we need to, but we do believe in more direct action. LAGPAC has its place, but so does ACT UP. I'm also marching for women's reproductive rights in a few weeks. Can you come to that, too?"

Glennon shrugged. "Let me think about it." He'd already heard of the march, but it was taking place the same day several of his friends had set aside to go canoeing, and Glennon only got to go canoeing once a year. But it wouldn't hurt to join the protest. Maybe he'd go to ACT UP's next activity after the kiss-in.

No, not maybe, he *would*. It was time to start *doing* something. He'd go to their next activity. Glennon would have to remember to ask Tory to keep him posted.

"I rented a couple of movies for this evening," Tory went on. "Would you like to watch with me?"

"Sounds fun." Glennon pretended to struggle to get out of Tory's grasp but then held Tory's legs firmly to keep him from removing them from about his waist. "I guess I should ask what they are first, though, shouldn't I?"

"*The Accused* and *Overboard*. Still interested?"

"Sure." Glennon kissed Tory before slipping out of his legs and swimming away. They both swam for several more minutes and then climbed into the hot tub.

Listening to Aaron Neville and Linda Ronstadt sing, "All I Need to Know," Glennon rubbed the tops of Tory's feet with the bottom of his own but didn't get any more physical than that. After a while, Tory climbed up to sit on the deck behind the hot tub, letting just his legs stay in the hot water.

He sighed loudly, as if finally letting the tension flow out of his body. "What a week. The same tire went flat on my car twice, I was passed over for a promotion at work, and I just found out a friend of mine tested positive."

Glennon closed his eyes.

"Jeremy only went out maybe once a year he was so paranoid about catching something. It wasn't supposed to happen to him."

"It shouldn't happen to anyone, should it?"

"We put people in categories, though, don't we? This friend probably won't get it, that one will, this other almost surely is already infected, this other will almost surely never get it, and so on. Jeremy was in my 'almost surely never' category. But his lymph nodes had been swollen for two months, so…"

God. Glennon felt his jaw tightening. Was the whole world going to die? How many more people did Glennon know who were going to get sick? His brother, his brother-in-law, seven members of the chorus, several bar buddies, countless acquaintances, and…who else? Who was next?

He remembered a year ago walking through the Quarter with his mother, and Glennon had stopped for just a moment to talk to a casual acquaintance with Kaposi's lesions on his arms. After they moved on, Glennon's mother had said, "You shouldn't be friends with people like that."

Glennon had turned to her. "You have two sons who may become people 'like that' one day." But God, he didn't mean it.

When Glennon had arrived in Pensacola two weeks ago, his mother had hugged him in the hall outside George's room. "I didn't understand," she said. "I'm so sorry."

Just before George became ill, Glennon's mother had been discussing what it was like to move to a retirement community in Florida. "Everyone you know is old," she said. "Every day, I hear of people back home or people here who are dying. You just don't know what it's like."

"Sure, I do," Glennon had replied. His mother had stared for a moment and then changed the subject, the same way Glennon often tried to change the subject now when he felt any of his friends were about to suggest he become more involved in AIDS work.

But now Glennon felt more and more every day like the last bunny in a carnival shooting gallery, watching the others being shot down right and left. So far, he was untouched, but how many more trips across could he make before he went down, too? And what choice was there but to keep roving back and forth in front of the guns?

"There's so much more I want to do." That's what George kept saying, and it was what he meant, too. George legitimately enjoyed helping. Glennon did it, the few times he did do it, because it was the right thing to do. There was a difference. But it wasn't as if Glennon didn't care about people. He cared.

Just not enough, though that hardly mattered any more. He wouldn't have to "serve" so he could feel good about himself. He was going to have to do it out of necessity. He didn't even want to think about what the coming years might bring.

Glennon glanced up at Tory. He wasn't sure he was in the mood to listen to anyone else's troubles, but maybe Tory needed to talk tonight. "You sure you're up to a movie?" Glennon asked, reaching over to rub Tory's calf.

"Are you kidding? I need *Overboard*. I've only got so many smiling days left." He shrugged. "I need *The Accused*, too. I was raped once about a year ago, by two muggers." He closed his eyes, shuddering. "There are a lot of things I still need to process."

Glennon looked up at Tory for a moment, but Tory looked away. Glennon saw he was watching one woman rub another woman's back. Glennon began to sigh but stopped.

Sighing wasn't a solution.

"What time does that march start?" he asked. "I need to put it on my calendar. I'll be there."

Tory smiled and gave him the information.

Glennon stood in front of Tory and pushed his legs apart, pressing against him. They looked at each other a moment, and then Glennon pulled Tory's head down toward him and kissed him softly on the lips. When he stood back, they looked at each other intently for another moment.

Then the first notes of Louis Armstrong's "Wonderful World" drifted out over the pool, and Tory smiled again.

"Come on," he said, standing up and taking Glennon's hand. "Let's dance."

Tory climbed back down into the hot tub, and with water bubbling up around their waists, Tory and Glennon pulled together in a gentle hug. They slowly swayed to the music, continuing to dance even after the song was over and there was no more music to hear.

Revolt of the Morlocks

I'm afraid I've always found myself rooting for the wrong team. Here in Salt Lake, my favorite basketball team was never the Jazz. When BYU played Notre Dame, I liked Notre Dame. Even when I read such books as *The Time Machine* by H.G. Wells, I couldn't help but feel it was the Morlocks who were getting the raw end of the deal.

So perhaps it was no surprise that even though I knew homosexuality was wrong, part of me sympathized with the gays.

"All this legalizing of homosexuality is a sin," Daniel, the Elders' quorum president, said in class one Sunday. "If we made it against the law in this country, we could put all the gays in prison."

"And what do you think they'd do there?" I asked. "Even straight guys have sex with each other in prison."

This comment, of course, did not go unnoticed. The following week, I was called into the bishop's office. "James," Bishop Olsen said, looking at me intently, "are you gay?"

"What?" I spluttered. "I'm a twenty-five-year-old virgin."

"You didn't answer my question."

I shook my head, swallowing. I'd been asexual longer than most boys, not even discovering masturbation till I was a junior in high school. Even then, it happened by accident. I was out camping with my dad, and I got some kind of bug bite on my penis. A few days later while I was scratching the bite, I realized that satisfying the itch was indeed very satisfying.

When I discovered that what I liked to think about while satisfying the itch on later occasions was my high school gym teacher, I knew I was in trouble. But as a good little Mormon boy, I vowed never to act on my feelings.

While I knew it was wrong for *me* to be gay, however, I certainly didn't feel like oppressing others who were in my situation. I didn't particularly want to be suspected, though, so I always hocked a loogie onto the sidewalk as I walked up to the church. I stuck my finger in my ear during Sacrament meetings to clean out the wax. I wore ugly ties.

Now it looked like the charade was over.

"No, Bishop, I'm not gay." I could feel my face burning.

"Would you have trouble associating with gays?"

What in the world was he getting at? "I suppose not. Live and let live."

"Oh, absolutely not," the bishop said. "There's a group of gay Mormons called Affirmation. They tell each other it's okay to be gay. They undermine the gospel. There are active Mormons who participate. We need to find out who these people are and excommunicate them."

I nodded nervously.

"We're really doing them a favor," the bishop continued. "If you sin as a Mormon, it counts against you far more than if you sin as a non-Mormon."

"That's very thoughtful of you."

Bishop Olsen handed me a piece of paper. "I'm calling you to be a spy in Zion. We want you to go to Affirmation meetings. And PFLAG meetings."

"PFLAG?"

"Parents and Friends of Lesbians and Gays. Get on the mailing lists. Participate in their activities. Infiltrate the gay community here in Salt Lake. Write down names and report back to me."

I accepted the calling with rather mixed feelings. It would be great to have a legitimate reason to meet other gays. At the same time, that might make it too tempting to remain celibate. While I was intrigued to discover how the gay community functioned, I certainly didn't feel like ratting on anyone. So I didn't know exactly how I was going to handle this. Perhaps I could trick people like Daniel from the Elders' quorum into coming to a PFLAG meeting, take a picture of them there, and get homophobes excommunicated for being gay. It was worth thinking about.

I went home and logged onto my computer. I put myself on the Affirmation email list and then looked up the next PFLAG meeting. I signed up for gay bowling and gay softball. There was even a gay country/western line dancing class, and a gay men's chorus. I'd had no idea. This calling looked like it might be more fun than being the Single Adult rep for my ward.

My mom called me Thursday at work to invite me for dinner, but it was PFLAG night, so I told her I had to meet with the Single Adult planning committee. "Well, at least let me stop by and drop off some homemade cookies for you guys. I'll get to see you for a minute anyway."

Feeling like an idiot, I brought a Tupperware container of chocolate chip cookies to my first PFLAG meeting. "We got another Mormon," someone called out when they saw me set the container on a table.

"I couldn't help it," I said a little sheepishly. "My mother is Relief Society president."

"Oh, good. Cookies every month."

I was surprised to see one of my former professors at the meeting with his partner, plus a woman who worked in the bakery section at the grocery, a lot of college kids just a few years younger than me, and several teens still in high school. Some were there with relatives and some weren't. One of the priests who blessed the sacrament every week in my ward was there with his father. This was exactly the kind of thing I was supposed to be writing down, but I was listening, not writing.

"We've known since Adam was five he was gay," the priest's father said when it was his turn to speak. "He asked us when we were going to visit 'the pretty grandpa.' We've spent the last ten years trying to figure a way to keep the Church from finding out."

"Fuck those homophobes," someone else hissed. "You're better off without them. Feel free to evolve."

"My Patriarchal Blessing says I'm going to become a general authority one day," the boy said. "I *want* to stay in the Church." Several people rolled their eyes.

After the meeting, I saw three men approach the priest and his father. I heard one of them say something about a 'special' Affirmation chapter, and I asked what was special about it.

"You didn't say much during the meeting. Are you out at church?"

"Oh, no. I have an uncle who's a regional rep. And a cousin who's a bishop. I—I like the Church. I don't want to be ex'ed."

The three men consulted each other silently, as if by telepathy, conveying whatever they could with their glances. A stray thought passed through my mind that they might be the Three Nephites.

"Then maybe you should come to our meeting, too," one of them finally said. "Are you free tomorrow night?"

At 7:00 Friday, I showed up at the address given to me after the meeting. The priest, Adam, and his father were there, two of the men from PFLAG, and one other man I didn't recognize. I was a little disappointed. I'd been especially interested in pursuing Affirmation, as I truly did want to stay in the Church, but this group looked rather unimpressive.

"Not many gay Mormons, I take it."

"This is a cell," one of the men said, introducing himself as Robert.

"A cell?"

"We aren't typical Affirmation. We work to infiltrate the Church."

"What?"

"We specifically aim to get gays and lesbians who can 'pass' into leadership positions in the Church. It isn't for everybody. To be eligible for the highest positions, 'passing' means being heterosexually married."

"I want kids," Adam said.

"For you, our goal is just to get you on your mission. We'll go from there once you get back. But we'll try to get you into a position of district leader or zone leader. We want to groom you for success."

"And you," said a man the others called Mark, turning to me, "you're already in low level leadership positions. We have some girls for you to meet, either lesbians or young women who are willing to marry gay men. We'll get you married and see if you can't be called as a counselor in the bishopric."

"How can you possibly arrange for callings like that?" I asked.

"We have a couple of stake presidents and high councilors in the area on our team. One seventy. We can't tell you the names. And we may have to ask you to move to a different ward eventually. We realize we have no power once we're excommunicated, so we try to effect change from within. There's a big debate over whether that will ever be possible unless we get a gay prophet and several gay apostles, and even we aren't *that* ambitious."

"Yet," someone said.

"It may take a while, but we'll get someone in a real position of power one of these days. In the meantime, we'll help with bishop roulette."

I was at once shocked by their audacity yet intrigued with the possibilities. Why they'd let me hear about all this without deeper screening, I didn't know, and I hoped no one else who learned of the group would blab. I wasn't sure these guys could keep a secret long enough to get two or three gay or gay-supportive apostles into place, but at least they weren't just lying down and letting the Church eat them alive.

Sunday after Sacrament meeting, the bishop called me to his office. "Any luck?" he asked.

"Well, I put myself on the Affirmation email list," I began, "but I haven't heard anything yet. And I've gone to a couple of gay meetings. But you know me. I'm shy. I haven't gotten any names so far." I wondered how long I could keep putting him off. A few weeks, maybe, but surely not ten years. If he released me from the calling for getting no results and then called someone else, what would *that* person do?

"Now, you're allowed under the circumstances to go without your garments," the bishop said, referring to our long Mormon underwear. "You should wear shorts and show off your legs. If you participate in some outdoor activity, you can take off your shirt."

"Um, okay."

"Sometimes, you have to take drastic measures to fight against the devil."

I nodded.

Mark called me later that afternoon. "James, we need to meet one-on-one. Can you come over in an hour?"

I drove to Mark's house. There I met his wife and baby daughter. I felt immensely uncomfortable. "Let's meet in the study," he said.

I couldn't help but notice there was a twin bed in the spare bedroom which had been set up as an office. I pointed. "Initiation rites?"

Mark grinned. "Forging bonds."

"Your wife really doesn't mind?"

"Brigham Young had fifty-five wives. Even good Mormon girls accept additional sexual relationships fairly easily once they open their minds a bit."

"I suppose." It sounded a bit oppressive for the women regardless of the gender of their husband's "extras."

"Would you like to forge for a while?"

"I'm a virgin."

"You didn't answer my question."

I wasn't sure having sex to keep my cover was an acceptable part of the calling. At the same time, I felt more and more compelled to help gays infiltrate the Church rather than help the Church infiltrate gays. Of course, either way, I was a traitor.

"I'd like you to forge my brains out."

"That's what I want to hear. I keep having these visions of the Church trying to sneak an agent into our group. I know the Nazis would kill one of their own to convince other underground members they were legitimate. But I think a traditional Mormon man would rather kill one of his own, too, than be fucked like I'm about to fuck you."

My first time was wonderful. Mark was gentle yet strong and masculine, and he made sure I got as much out of the experience as he did. We'd just finished dressing when there was a knock on the door. Mark opened, and his wife handed him a plate with two muffins.

"Thanks, Millie."

Mark shut the door and handed me a muffin. "I guess we'll need to work off some more calories later."

"It *is* a commandment to respect our bodies as temples." I bit into a blueberry.

Mark nodded. "I really liked going into your Celestial Room."

"And I enjoyed your Holy of Holies."

Mark groaned. "Yes," he said, "you're the real thing."

"Well, I may as well tell you. The bishop did call me to be a spy."

Mark raised his eyebrows. "And?"

"I prefer to be a double agent."

Mark reached into a cabinet and pulled out what appeared to be a double-ended penis. He waved it at me like a Catholic priest sprinkling holy water and put it back in the cabinet.

It had been a long time since I'd accepted a calling I ended up enjoying this much.

"I'd love to have a time machine," Mark said, "and see just how long it will take for the Church to treat gays fairly."

"If gay marriage was accepted, would you still be having sex with other guys besides your husband, or would you be monogamous?" I took another bite of my muffin.

"You're asking if I want it both ways?"

"Well, straight Mormon men as a rule aren't having sex with other women as a form of religious struggle and political protest."

Mark shrugged. "At one time polygamy was a commandment. Now it's a sin. Rules change under different circumstances." He tweaked my nipple through my shirt. "And it's not as if we require our wives to be monogamous while we bond with others. If nothing else, we understand double standards."

I wasn't sure he wasn't just rationalizing, but I realized with a bit of surprise I had a clear conscience myself.

I didn't have that much time to think about it, though. Mark pulled out a folder with the photos of five young women. A sheet of paper accompanied each picture. "Look through these and decide if anyone interests you. If you like someone, we can arrange a meeting to see if you have any chemistry in person."

"Arranged marriage?"

"Oh, no, it's completely voluntary. If there's no spark, we'll bring out some more profiles. The trick, of course, is to have the woman you're interested in find you interesting, too. That's the case for any relationship of any kind. These young women are dedicated to bringing change within the Church, but they don't want to be unhappy for the next thirty years, either."

I nodded and started looking through the profiles. There was a young woman named Karen just getting her start in TV journalism. I wanted to be a reporter myself and had a low-level job at the news station now. If Karen and I had similar career interests, however, I realized it could work both ways. We could have a lot to share, on the one hand, but on the other, one of us might get a good job in another state and the remaining spouse might not be able to get a position with the same station or even with a rival station in the same city. Still, it was worth a second look.

"Can I meet Karen sometime?"

Mark grinned. He called her on the spot, and Karen and I arranged a blind date for the following Friday evening. For the first time ever, I felt excited about the prospect of meeting a woman.

"Any more questions?" Mark asked.

I shrugged. "What am I going to give the bishop to show I'm doing my job?"

Mark raised a finger. "We have a long list of volunteers, men and women willing to be excommunicated for being gay or believing in gay rights. We can give the bishop a new name every few weeks and then taper it off to every couple of months. Personally, I disagree with voluntarily leaving the Church, but these are people who are just too disgusted to remain. So we've worked out a way to take advantage of their position, too. It's a two-pronged attack."

That night, I looked up spies in both the Bible and the Book of Mormon. There seemed to be a long tradition. I remembered my dad revealing once that his bishop had asked him to follow a member whose husband suspected her of cheating. As a teen, I was shocked at the Big Brotherliness of it, but I learned on my mission to Paraguay that the purpose of keeping missionaries in groups of two wasn't so much so that one could give the other emotional support as it was that each missionary instead always knew there was someone to report on him if he ever stepped out of line.

I met with the Single Adult Family Home Evening on Monday night, and then on Tuesday night, I attended a planning meeting to develop a fundraiser for the Human Rights Campaign. The group decided to organize gays all over the city to mow their neighbors' and relatives' lawns on one specific day and donate the money. "I know we usually just sell tickets to a dinner or a show," said one of the women at the meeting, "but I think when you work for something rather than just give money, it creates a stronger bond. That's why Mormons have volunteer missionaries, and volunteer

Sunday School teachers and volunteer organists. Working for something for free creates a more loyal base."

It made me think of the Morlocks again. They were the workers in the future envisioned by H.G. Wells, but they were also the ones considered the bad guys. The effete Eloi who just sat around all day enjoying the work others had done were the good guys. It reminded me of the saying, "The winners write the history." Whether or not gay activists of our time were seen as heroes in the future depended on whether we ever won our rights. If we didn't, we'd be viewed forever as spiritual terrorists. If we won, we'd become freedom fighters. It wasn't that there were two sides to a coin. There were two ways of seeing the exact same side of a coin.

The next couple of evenings, I watched *Latter Days* and *Milk*, movies I'd avoided while trying to remain "pure." I still wanted to stay pure, of course, but had simply changed my ideas about what purity meant.

Finally, though, it was Friday night, and I met Karen at her apartment. "It's so you can realize from the start I have my own personality," she said. "Our house will have modern art. I'll have the final say in decorating. Are you okay with that?"

"I like Pollock," I said.

"You didn't answer my question."

"Well, I'd prefer you offer a choice of things you enjoy and let me pick which items out of those I happen to like as well."

"Fair enough."

We sat down to dinner and related our personal histories. Karen grew up the youngest child of a stake president. Her great uncle was a mission president. Her aunt was lesbian and had been driven to suicide by the treatment she received from the Church and her family. Karen had vowed as an eleven-year-old to find some way to make life better for gay and lesbian Mormons.

Her first project was to convert her father, a process which had taken ten years. But she'd finally convinced the man that equality was the wave of the future, and he'd better get on board. During that same time, her father had continued moving up in the Church, and rumor had it that the next time a vacancy appeared in the Quorum of the Twelve, he'd be given serious consideration for the job.

"So it's vital that if you marry me, you keep your nose clean. It's bad enough that I'm a working woman. Dad will have no credibility if his son-in-law is known to be gay."

"All right."

"My second oldest brother is gay, and so is one of my cousins. They're both in this, too. Both married with kids and trying to work their way up. You always hear about gays who are ex-Mormons, and there are a lot of them, but they're just the tip of the iceberg. If one out of ten people is lesbian or gay, when we hit the ten million membership mark a few years ago, that meant a million of us were gay. Certainly, lots of those people are excommunicated and disaffected, but that still leaves tens of thousands or more closeted gays and lesbians *and* their supporters who are being called to prominent positions. Sooner or later, we'll be able to influence decisions."

There'd been zero movement of the needle so far, so I assumed "later" was the option we were pursuing. I hoped we were doing the right thing, but I was also glad there were others who wanted to "burn it all down." Without a time machine, there was no way to know for sure which method would turn out to be more effective.

"I had no idea any of this was going on."

"That's the point." Karen paused a moment. "I do have another issue to raise," she said, "and that's about extramarital sex."

"They've already told me you're free to have sex with other men."

"Some of that sex will be without condoms," she said. "You need to be able to accept not all 'our' children will be biologically yours."

That wasn't where I'd expected the conversation to go, but I nodded. "All right." Perhaps every couple, I thought, Mormon or not, gay or not, should be deciding the specifics of what worked best for *them*. It was ridiculous to expect everyone on the planet to have identical thoughts on the subject.

"And you can't have sex in parks or bathrooms or anyplace you may be arrested."

"I can live with that."

We talked long into the night, about politics, and our favorite ice cream, and global warming, and what kind of pet we'd like our kids to have. We talked about our favorite callings at church, our favorite Book of Mormon stories, about universal health care, what music we liked, and our career goals.

It was the first date I'd ever been on where I felt completely comfortable.

The next couple of months passed quickly. We had a Single Adult talent show at which a lesbian and a gay man sang, "We Kiss in a Shadow." When Daniel, our Elders' quorum president, moved out of ward boundaries, I arranged for a regular Affirmation chapter to help clean his yard, pack the house, and load the truck. After he expressed his genuine appreciation, someone deliberately "let slip" that this was a group of gay Mormons. Daniel looked shocked but appropriately thoughtful as well. When I asked if he disapproved of their participation and would rather unload the truck himself at his new place, he said, "No, no! I don't have a problem."

The next Sunday, I gave the bishop my first "intelligence." As soon as I handed him the slip of paper with the name of an inactive member, the bishop looked disgusted.

I was afraid Daniel had reported the Affirmation moving team, and I was prepared to offer a reason why I'd enjoined their services. While I had hand-picked people who'd already been ex'ed, I would say I just wanted good members to help identify the wicked.

But the bishop never mentioned the incident. He just said, "So you're having success with your calling" in a kind of weary tone.

"Yes," I agreed a little nervously, "but seeing all these gays wasting their lives has spurred me to move on with mine. I'm getting engaged."

"To a woman?"

"Well, of course."

The bishop looked even wearier. "James, the whole reason I gave you this calling was to help you come out."

"What?"

"I've known you were gay for years. I could see how unhappy you were. I wanted to help. But now…"

I stared at him for a long moment. "Bishop, are you working with other Mormons on things like this?"

Bishop Olsen looked surprised. "There are no other Mormons interested in things like this."

I didn't want to be tricked into revealing any secrets but decided to share at least the overview of what I'd discovered. The bishop's smile grew wider the longer I talked. When I concluded, he held out his hand and said, "I'll have to consult my counselors, but I'm pretty sure we'll be setting you apart as the new Elders' quorum president next week."

I went to see Mark that afternoon. "That's wonderful," he said. "We know there are lots of other supporters out there, but they're isolated and usually too afraid to say or do much. We still try to keep contacts limited so we don't all get ex'ed in one big witch hunt if the Church ever discovers what's going on, but I'll pass your bishop's name on to the appropriate people."

"Shall we celebrate?"

"What do you mean?"

"It seems to me every time we forge a *new* bond, we ought to, you know, forge a *stronger* bond." I looked toward the twin bed.

"Well, I'm forging with a new recruit this evening, but I think I'm up to forging two bonds in one day. Lean over."

As I dropped my pants and leaned over the bed, Mark entered me. I could hear his wife in the living room playing with the baby, and I wondered if maybe we were in fact altogether as subhuman as the Morlocks.

I remembered a scene in the film version of *The Time Machine* when an Eloi woman is drowning while other Eloi sit idly by, eating fruit and ignoring her. Was it really the Morlocks who were subhuman, though, or these privileged elite who lived oblivious lives and wouldn't lift a finger to protect their own? I thought about how many Mormon parents no longer talked to their gay children, casting them aside as glibly as the Eloi watched Weena being carried away by the current. When monsters showed more humanity than the superior race, one had to wonder just what qualified as superior.

After we finished, I kissed Mark and then headed over to Karen's apartment. We watched *The Howling* and cuddled on the sofa. Since I knew I didn't need to fulfill her fantasies and she didn't have to fulfill mine, we could be affectionate without pressure.

"Where shall we go on our honeymoon?" I asked after the movie was over.

"It ought to be someplace fun rather than romantic," Karen said thoughtfully. "Maybe New Orleans or Branson."

"Those are two different ends of the fun spectrum."

"Is there anywhere particular you'd like to go?"

I rubbed my chin. "I've always wanted to see Orlando," I said slowly. "In Disneyworld, there are tunnels underneath each of the parks. All the service personnel use the tunnels, so the guests at the park won't see them working."

"Yeah?"

I shrugged. "I'd like to talk someone into letting us inside one of the tunnels."

"A romantic walk underground?"

"A *fun* romantic walk. We'll have to combine the two."

Karen nodded. "Disneyworld's a good place for a wholesome, white-bread couple." She paused a moment. "Perhaps we can ask my brother and his family if they want to come along. That way you could have some hot sex on your honeymoon. And I can always try to get Mickey or Pluto for myself."

I realized yet again my life wasn't going to turn out even remotely as I'd planned. Was it worth the sacrifice, to give up looking for a man I could share my life with exclusively, to work toward helping others achieve that dream?

"It's getting late. We both need to get up early." Karen stood and removed her pants and garments. Then she sat down on the edge of the sofa and spread her legs. I kneeled in front of her and pushed my face into her crotch. "Yes, eat me," she breathed.

It did nothing for me, but it didn't have to. I was okay with it.

Maybe I was playing for the wrong team. I wondered what the Time Traveler would have seen if he'd gone another twenty thousand years into the future. Would the Morlocks have taken over? Would the Eloi and Morlocks have learned to live together? Would there ever finally have been peace?

I looked up at Karen and she smiled down at me. I smiled back and kept working. My parents would not be happy to learn I was gay. I wondered if they'd be any happier knowing I was having premarital sex with my girlfriend before we married in the temple. Which team would they be rooting for? The good Mormon boy or the evil apostate?

Then I wondered for just a second if arranging my involvement in the infiltration program was all simply a trick by the Church to get me to marry heterosexually.

Double double agents? Well, if so, I'd just have to be a double triple agent.

When we finished, Karen tousled my hair. "Cliff from work is coming over Tuesday night. Could you come and show him how you do that? You're so much better at it than he is."

"So now I'm training heterosexual cunnilinguists?"

"It takes a village."

I smiled. "Happy to be of service." We kissed, and I stood up. "Will you teach him how to suck me efficiently?"

"He's straight."

"You didn't answer my question."

Karen laughed. "We'll see." We kissed again, and I started for home. It was certainly a brave new world we were moving toward, and there was no telling what lay ahead. But I knew it would be a society where love of all kinds was celebrated, even among the purest of the pure.

Because even Morlocks fell in love.

It was almost 11:00 when I walked into my apartment, but I took out my old missionary album and beat off to a picture of my favorite companion. In a perfect world, I'd be with him right now. I sighed and cleaned up. Then I turned out the light and climbed into bed, dreaming of a bright future I wasn't sure would ever come.

Garbage Balls

Henry thrust the pool cue forward savagely. The number three ball rammed against the side of the table, crossed to the other side at an angle, rebounded again, and stopped just short of the corner pocket. "Damn!" Henry scowled. "Another garbage ball." He wanted to hit the table but stopped himself.

"Your game's a little off tonight," Curtis said, lining up his next shot. "What's wrong?"

"You know what it is," Henry replied. He stopped then to let Curtis shoot. His jaw tightened as he watched the ball Curtis had pointed out disappearing into a side pocket.

"No, what?" asked Curtis after missing his next shot.

Henry didn't know if he could bear to say it, but he knew he'd have to give some reason for his poor performance. He might as well tell the truth. "It's those guys," he said, nodding over his shoulder in the general direction of the bowling lanes. "I can't concentrate with them here."

Henry took his turn, pocketed a ball, and tried again, missing. "We've been shooting pool here all summer," Curtis said. "The bowling never bothered you before."

Curtis only had two more balls and so won on this turn. "Good game," Henry said tightly.

"You want to play again?"

"Oh, man, let's take a break," Henry suggested, stretching. "You mind? I'm hungry, anyway. How about a hot dog?"

Curtis shrugged, so Henry ordered two chili dogs at the counter and brought them over to a small table. From their seats, they could watch the players in the first six lanes of the bowling alley. A man about thirty-five, with a large nose and a receding chin, wearing tight green shorts and a tight green T-shirt, threw his green bowling ball down lane four. There were only two pins still standing, and the ball knocked them both down. The man turned toward his team, put his hands below his flat breasts, and lifted them upwards as if he really had breasts.

"Oh, God," Henry groaned. "*That's* what I can't take any more. How can you concentrate knowing there's a team of faggots playing right behind your back?" Curtis looked off to inspect the players at lanes three and four while Henry continued. "I mean, every time I lean over to shoot, I can feel their eyes on my ass, imagining who knows what." Henry closed his eyes and swallowed. After a moment, he was able to resume eating. "Doesn't it bother you?"

"I guess I just haven't felt them staring at me." Curtis laughed. "Maybe I'm not attractive enough for them."

"You're too attractive is more like it. They know they could never have you." Henry paused then to take another bite, wondering if that had come out the way he'd meant it to. It was true that Curtis's physique was another reason Henry had chosen to play with him. Curtis wore blue jeans and usually either a tank top or T-shirt, all of which showed his clearly defined muscles.

The tank top, in addition, showed the tattoo of an eagle on Curtis's upper right arm. It was starting to turn green with age, though Curtis couldn't be much over thirty, probably only five years older than Henry. The guy had a deep tan from working outdoors as a carpenter, and that probably helped age his skin, but he was still a young, strong, handsome man. Anyone could tell Curtis was a real man just by looking at him. Henry sure could, which was why he'd first approached him here one night when he was in the mood to play pool.

In high school, Henry hadn't been terribly athletic, much to his father's disappointment, and had been close friends for a while with another undeveloped guy named Preston. One day after school, several of the jocks had ganged up on them, thrown rotten fruit at them, and dumped them both in a huge garbage bin. Henry had begun exercising after that and refused to ever befriend anyone else who wasn't masculine.

When he was working as a missionary in Los Angeles, Henry eventually became a zone leader over three districts, and he instituted a mandatory exercise rule to get his men in shape. One elder in particular, Elder Wynn, had seemed very wimpy, always looking at his nails.

Henry had done a work visit with the missionary once, taking his companion's place for the evening, but instead of doing actual missionary work, Henry had forced Elder Wynn to do sit ups and push-ups all evening. The pussy had called the mission president the next day and gone home early, in disgrace, rather than try to be the man God had meant for him to be. Henry had few friends on his mission, but he weeded out those who weren't up to the task of being true elders of Zion. He'd had very few friends at all over the next several years. Even now, he only associated with a select few in the Single Adults program or in the Elders' quorum. But all his friends these days were muscular and talked either of ball games or camping or fast cars.

Henry worked at Louis Armstrong airport loading baggage and was friends with a few other baggage handlers. They were fun because they talked of the girls they laid regularly. Henry was as horny as any of them, but he was still a virgin, of course, since he hadn't yet found a Mormon girl he really wanted to be with. Other friends he'd met at a local Kenner bar, mostly guys who worked at the oil refinery in Norco.

Henry only drank Cokes when he went out, but he enjoyed the camaraderie that drinking guys had. On Mondays, Henry liked to go into New Orleans, and he'd found a bowling alley in Mid-City, on the second floor over a Thai restaurant and a thrift store where he sometimes shopped. Sometimes, he bowled, but often, he played pool and just enjoyed being around other men.

But with the approach of fall, several new teams had signed up, and it looked like half the alley was filled with gays tonight. Henry had no choice but to watch that team of weak, effeminate men trying to act tough. It was nauseating. He had to admit, though, the one who thought he had breasts wasn't bad. He often got spares and even an occasional strike, but he threw the ball just like a woman. It was simply too much. These people were scum.

"Well, aren't you attractive?" Curtis asked.

"What?"

"Why are they looking at you, if you don't think they'd look at someone who was too attractive?"

Henry felt his face flush and immediately lifted the last of his chili dog to his mouth, hoping to shield the pink rise in his face. What a thing to say to another man. Real friends should be able to say anything to each other, but still. "Maybe they aren't looking at me," he finally managed. "I just *feel* they are." He got out a short laugh. "Just paranoid, I guess. Wondering how I'd react if one of them ever made a pass at me."

"God, you *are* paranoid," Curtis said, laughing too.

Henry smiled but wondered just what Curtis had meant by that. Henry knew he was good looking. Why wouldn't a gay man be attracted to him? He was sure he looked masculine enough, too. He wore a tight T-shirt, like Curtis did, which showed off his muscles, and while he'd never wanted a tattoo, which was forbidden by the Church, he had a big cock and a big sack with big balls, and the combination always had women's eyes focused on his crotch when he went out. He could see other guys looking sometimes, too, and knew they were jealous.

Over the past couple of years, Henry had checked out all the other baggage handlers he'd had to work with. Sooner or later, each had to go to the bathroom when he did, and Henry always used the urinal so he'd have a chance to look at the other guy. The other guy, too, would almost always use the urinal. It would be admitting you had something to be ashamed of to use the stall. Of course, neither man could ever just look at the other one. It had to be done carefully, accidentally, out of the corner of your eye. You couldn't let on you cared enough to look. You had to assume there wasn't any competition.

But Henry always looked, and he could tell the others did, too. Henry could never really relax around a new worker until they'd gone to the bathroom together and Henry could see that the other guy was smaller than he was. Only once was the guy bigger, but even then it was only by a little, and Henry had tossed heavy bags to him several times without much warning until the guy twisted his back and decided to get another job.

And only one time had Henry found another worker so small that he tried to get rid of him. After seeing how tiny the guy's dick was, Henry felt downright embarrassed to be seen working with him. He somehow imagined that everyone else either knew or could guess how little of a man he was.

So one day Henry went down to the French Quarter and roamed around the trashy gay neighborhood until he found a sex shop. He went in and browsed among the dildos until he found the biggest strap-on there. It cost more than he expected, and he tried to hurry through the transaction, knowing everyone there thought he was buying it for himself. Going in had taken a lot out of him, but it was for a good cause.

Back home, he carefully wrote out a note, disguising his handwriting, which read, "Just in case you ever go on a date." Then at work while he tried to look too busy to have time for pranks, he slipped the wrapped dildo and note in the drawer where his coworker kept his lunch.

It was all Henry could do to keep looking normal the rest of the workday, waiting and waiting for a reaction. But the guy ate lunch and never said a word. He came back the next day as if nothing had happened and never made any mention of it. It had irritated Henry to no end.

Then about a week after Henry left the dildo for the other guy, they both ended up together in the bathroom again. Though he already knew how small the guy was, out of habit Henry glanced over. His mouth fell open and he swirled toward the guy, almost spraying him. He was wearing his strap-on dildo.

"Wh-what?" Henry had spluttered, staring.

"Thanks for the gift," the guy replied. "But you'd be surprised how few women care about the size of a dick. Men seem much more fixated on it."

"Huh?"

"Oh, it's fun to wear sometimes. I have to admit that. My girlfriend even wants to try it out. Thanks again." Then the guy walked out.

He never did say a word about it to anyone else as far as Henry knew, but thank God, thank God, he accepted a transfer to another city two months later. Henry had been about to go crazy seeing how little the guy cared about not having a man-sized dick. For brief moments, Henry realized he felt impressed, but then he understood the guy was just trying to save face. Of *course* everyone cared about the size of a dick, especially women, but even more the man whose dick size was in question. His coworker had made a noble effort, he had to admit, but it was still pitiful.

Curtis moved his leg then, accidentally nudging Henry, and Henry looked back over toward the lanes. He felt his stomach compress slightly.

"Watching that little, wimpy guy doesn't bother you?" Henry asked.

Curtis shrugged. "I guess he makes me a little uncomfortable, but live and let live, huh?"

Henry turned again to watch the man now bowling in lane three. He was blond, with straight hair parted on the side. He wore neat, pressed shorts that came down almost to his knees, with little cuffs on them, and his shirt was pressed as well. He was good looking and reasonably masculine. Henry wasn't sure he could have spotted him outside the bowling alley without his gay teammates, but now that he looked, the guy did seem awfully prissy. The way he squatted when he threw the ball, it was as if he was afraid he'd get dirty. The guy got a strike, smiled briefly, and sat down.

"He wasn't so bad, was he?" asked Curtis.

"Could you imagine him changing a tire?" Henry returned, rolling his eyes. "Or, God forbid, changing his oil?" He looked back at the man and had to cover his mouth to keep from laughing out loud.

"Well, what about that other little guy? Yeah, him." Curtis pointed to lane four. "Doesn't he have enough balls for you?"

Curtis was right about this one. Henry had noticed him as soon as he'd arrived tonight. The man was at the bar then getting a drink. He looked very like the guys Henry usually played pool with, and Henry had wondered if he'd end up playing with him before the evening was out. It was when he'd seen the guy go over and kiss the man who thought he had breasts that Henry's game with Curtis began to veer off course.

"His tattoo isn't quite like mine, is it?" asked Curtis, straining to see.

"No. His is of a crawfish."

Henry watched as the man picked up his ball. The guy was short, probably only 5'5", but he did have muscles and that tattoo. He also either had a big dick or big balls because his crotch was immediately noticeable. He was wearing black jeans and a tank top, but he was just ever so slightly pudgy around the waist.

Henry had barely noticed at first. The impression was hardly one of softness. The straggly, lightly greasy brown hair that fell to his shoulders helped. And he had a slight moustache with a frail little goatee. Henry was sure he worked in a warehouse somewhere.

But now that he knew, he could see that the man was gay. He smiled too much. He was too friendly, patting the other guys on the back after they'd bowled, or meeting their hands in a congratulatory slap. And when the man with the invisible breasts had playfully pointed a beer bottle at the man's ass, and he'd backed into it with a smile, Henry wondered how he'd ever thought the man was straight.

He remembered how mortified he'd been when his doctor had suggested a prostate exam three years earlier. Henry had balked, but his doctor had put his hand on Henry's shoulder and said, "Every man has a chance of getting prostate cancer. For now, this is the easiest way to check. Will you feel better for having died of a completely male cancer?"

Henry had given in and leaned over, and he still remembered the sensation of having another man inside him. It wasn't only a physical feeling but touched him somewhere else, too. He somehow felt this man now knew him emotionally in a way no one else did. He changed doctors after that and never allowed anyone to test him for prostate cancer again. He'd heard that now there was a blood test for it. That might be acceptable. That didn't feel too intimate. And besides, the nurses who drew blood were usually women.

Henry wondered how a man could want to feel that close to another man. Wouldn't he feel vulnerable? He looked again at the man with the tattoo, wondering what it would be like to really know another man. Of course, knowing another *man* might be okay, but by definition, that could never happen to gays. Maybe it could only happen for doctors, and for women.

He tried to see into the face of the man with the tattoo, frowning. What was there to know, anyway?

The guy stared down the lane for a moment, pushed his hair back, and stared a moment longer. Henry put his hand on his stomach and swallowed.

The man released his ball well enough, but it veered a little to the side before reaching the end of the lane, knocking down only four of the pins. His second ball knocked down only four more. Two garbage balls, thought Henry. It figured. The man shrugged, still smiling, and sat down. Henry turned back to Curtis.

"It's kind of scary, isn't it?" Henry asked, laughing. "I'd almost have believed he was a normal guy."

"A guy like everyone else who's here tonight?" Curtis asked. But Henry noticed the corner of Curtis's mouth turn up in a smile.

"Right."

Curtis grabbed his upper arm and pulled his tattoo over so he could see it more clearly. "Does this tattoo make me a man?" he asked. Henry couldn't tell if Curtis was asking him or just asking himself. "Cher has a tattoo. So does Julia Roberts. Maybe a tattoo is like wearing a flower in your hair. Maybe it's like jewelry, like a necklace or a pin. Maybe it's a womanly thing to have."

Henry shrugged. "Okay, okay. I get it. But still, there are some things that are masculine and some that are feminine. You can't deny that." He reached over and squeezed Curtis's biceps. "That's masculine, isn't it?"

"Seen Linda Hamilton's arms in *Terminator 2*?"

"Aw, give me a break, man. You can't tell me you think that guy in green over there is a real man. Look at him."

It was the green guy's turn again, and when he got another spare, Henry waited for him to lift his breasts, but this time he smiled sweetly and grabbed his crotch. Henry groaned. Trash, he thought. These people were trash.

"I see a lot of guys grab their crotches in music videos," said Curtis.

"But it's the way he does it," Henry insisted.

They were silent for a moment, watching the next bowlers. Then Curtis asked, "Are you attracted to that guy in green?"

Henry whirled to face Curtis. "Of course not! Don't be disgusting!"

"Then he isn't woman enough for you? That must mean you find something masculine about him."

"Why are you defending this guy?" Henry demanded. "Are you queer, too?" Curtis didn't reply and Henry knew he'd taken a cheap shot. He didn't want to lose Curtis as a friend. He played well. "Look, I'm sorry, man. I didn't mean that."

"What if I were?" asked Curtis, looking Henry straight in the face.

Henry turned away. "Don't say that just to tease me. It's mean." He looked back at Curtis and smiled ruefully. "But I guess I deserve it." This was the first time the two of them had ever discussed anything other than sports. Men weren't supposed to talk about their feelings, and the one time he was doing it, he was only adding tension to their relationship.

He was *not* going to allow that gay part of him ruin what he had. His eyes narrowed as he stared at the pool table.

"Come on," Curtis said, standing up. "Let's play another game. And concentrate harder this time. Don't worry about those guys watching your butt. I promise I'll guard your ass." Curtis slapped Henry lightly on his behind as they walked back to the pool table, and Henry laughed. He knew that when Curtis slapped his ass, it was done in a manly way, like professional ball players did, not like the guys on those first several lanes did.

Henry believed that Curtis had been teasing earlier about being gay, but he kept wondering as they played. He watched how Curtis moved, how he held the cue, how he leaned over the table, how he stood while waiting for Henry, but there was nothing wrong with any of it. Because he was distracted, though, while Henry did play a little better this time, he still lost.

Two in a row was a bit much. He smiled, tight-lipped, and said, "Good game." Then he excused himself to go to the bathroom. As he stood at the urinal, thinking he might just go on home and call it a night, he realized that the short man with the tattoo and the goatee was standing at the next urinal. Using great self-control, Henry managed not to flinch.

He was sure the man would be leering at his cock, big even while flaccid, but Henry, watching out of the corner of his eyes, saw that the man was just looking at himself. Henry looked, too, and was surprised to see just how big the man's dick was. It looked even bigger because the guy was short, but it was respectable even by itself.

As the man zipped up, he noticed Henry staring. The guy smiled and offered a slight nod before heading out of the bathroom.

Henry didn't know what to think. At first, he was relieved the man didn't try anything. Then he wondered what was so bad about his cock that the guy hadn't even bothered to look. Next, he began to feel the condescension of the man's smile, as if the guy felt *superior* to him somehow. The more he thought about it, the madder he felt.

When Henry went back out onto the floor, he found Curtis standing by the waist-high wall dividing the pool table area from the bowling area, watching lanes three and four. "Let's get the fuck out of here," Henry muttered, slapping Curtis on the arm.

"What's wrong?"

"You should have seen the way that guy was looking at me in the bathroom."

"What guy?"

"The guy with the tattoo," Henry said, nodding.

"He made a pass at you?" Curtis asked, incredulous.

Henry looked at the guy for a moment. "Well, not exactly, but it still made me awfully uncomfortable."

Curtis didn't say anything but began watching the game again. The guy in green was bowling.

Turning away, Henry noticed a man at a nearby table finishing some French fries. He was not overly muscular, but he was trim and firm, with a self-assured air that made him masculine enough to be acceptable. The man tossed his French fry carton into an open trash can and headed off to lane eight to join his team.

Henry stared a moment at the trash can, remembering that awful day in high school. His and Preston's clothes were wet and stinking from the fruit and the cafeteria trash, and after the jocks had left them, Henry felt he was about to cry. He didn't want to, but he couldn't help it. He'd cut his hand on a can when they'd dumped him in. He fought it, though, and sniffled just once.

Then Preston had put his hand on his shoulder and pulled him close. "It'll be okay," he said. "It'll be okay."

"Get your fucking hands off me," Henry had shot back. "What are you trying to do? You *are* a faggot, aren't you? That's why those guys did this. They could tell. This is *your* fault."

"Henry, I—"

Henry remembered the shocked expression on Preston's face, the dawning awareness of pain. But he also remembered what he'd done to erase that look. He'd reached over, grabbed Preston by the balls, and squeezed as hard as he could.

"We'd better change our pool night," Henry said to Curtis. "I can't deal with this every week."

"Oh, come on, Henry. Don't let it ruin your night. You have as much right to be here as anyone else. Just—"

"You're right," Henry said suddenly, straightening. "I do have as much right. *More* right. It's not fair for them to make me leave." He stared at the pool table a moment. Then he whirled and stared at the players on lanes three and four. "I'll make *them* leave."

"Why are you smiling?" asked Curtis. "What are you going to do?"

Henry had to put his hand over his mouth to keep from laughing. When he felt under control, he said, "Those guys finish around 9:30 or so. I'll wait out in the parking lot and jump one of them." It would have to be the one with the tattoo, he knew. The one who thought he was such a man. The guy looked strong, but so was Henry, and Henry was bigger.

There were tons of stories in the Book of Mormon about the Nephites defending themselves against the Lamanites. This was no different. Those degenerates hurt the entire human race. The Church insisted they were abominations and shouldn't be allowed to influence children. What Henry was doing wouldn't be a sin. It was a good deed. Looking at those perverts now, Henry saw just what damage popular culture did to society, allowing these people to start feeling good about themselves and accept their depravity. Henry would give them a reality check.

Henry smiled at the thought but then remembered an incident when he was about five or six. He'd been playing catch with his father, and his father had thrown the ball so hard against Henry's chest he'd fallen in the driveway and skinned his hands. He'd started crying just a little, and his father had come over and slapped him.

"Boys don't cry!" he'd shouted. "Stop that sniveling!"

That had made Henry cry even more, and his father had slapped him again and again until he stopped. He'd never cried since, not even that day with Preston. Henry was glad his father had made a man of him at a young age. It was clearly what was missing from these guys' lives.

"There's a policeman outside in the parking lot, you know," Curtis pointed out.

"Hmm." Henry looked down at the floor for a second. "Maybe I can lure the guy around to the back first so no one sees."

"Think you're man enough to beat up a faggot?" Curtis asked.

"Are you kidding?" Henry laughed. "But you're certainly welcome to join me if you want a little more fun before the night is through." Henry felt his cock hardening, just thinking about the pummeling to come. He wouldn't really hurt the guy, of course, just give him enough bruises to keep him from coming back, enough to scare his friends away, too. A good kick in the balls to finish him off would do it.

"I've got a better idea." Curtis pointed. "See those guys down there, the ones in lanes seventeen and eighteen?"

"Uh-huh."

"I know those guys. We play volleyball together on Wednesday nights."

"Yeah, so?"

"I think I can get them to help us. Maybe together we can beat up a couple of gay guys." Curtis smiled and gave a little shrug.

"Hey, you're a pal," Henry said. He punched Curtis on his tattoo and then looked down to the far end of the building to look at the bowlers Curtis knew. They were a bit too clean cut, obviously a little educated, but they were the kind of friends he could believe Curtis might have. Every one of them looked reasonably fit. That was about all Henry could make out from this distance, but they looked like the type who wouldn't want to put up with little fairies taking over the bowling alley.

Henry looked at his watch. "How about another game of pool, my man?"

By 9:15, Henry had finally won a game. He was feeling good when Curtis went off to talk to his friends. Henry stood at the half wall, smiling in anticipation as he watched the guy in green roll his green ball down the lane. He noticed the guy with the tattoo looking at him with a little smile, so Henry smiled widely in response, returning a nod as well. The man with the tattoo also nodded before turning back to the game.

A few minutes later, Curtis returned. "Everything's set," he said. "They'll be finished in just a few minutes. Then we can all leave together."

"This is gonna be good."

"If you say so. Are you sure you want to do this? I mean, I'm willing to help out, and my friends thought it was a good idea, but I really don't see those guys causing any trouble. Can't we be big enough to leave them to themselves?"

Henry looked at Curtis, his eyebrows furrowing. "It's the way they make me feel," he said. "They're sickening. They're human refuse. They're humiliating to the male sex.

The Bible says they should be killed. I'm just going to beat them up. They're getting off easy."

Curtis shrugged, and they both watched the players in lanes three and four, the worst of all the gays in the first few lanes. The players had two frames left. Henry hoped the guys at the far end would be through soon. He looked at the guy with the tattoo, and he again felt his cock harden a little as he thought of kicking that man's ass. He'd never realized before that violence could be sexual. It was kind of thrilling.

"We better stop staring," Curtis suggested after a while. "They might get suspicious."

Henry reluctantly agreed, and they walked slowly over to the friends finishing up on lane eighteen, just tallying up their final scores. One of the two teams left, but Curtis's friends greeted Henry warmly, smiling and shaking his hand firmly. There were no tattoos or muscle shirts, but all five men exuded a calm, secure sense of maleness. Henry hoped he and Curtis might go out drinking sometime with them.

They picked up their balls and headed down the stairs and out of the building. Henry nodded to the policeman in front of the door, and then the group strolled around the corner to the back of the building to make sure it would be, as Curtis put it, "a safe place to beat up the fags."

"Yeah, this is great," Henry said. There were trees on one side, the back of the bowling alley on the opposite side, and off on the far end was an on-ramp for the expressway, at such an angle that no one was likely to see what was going on in this dimly lit area. The only real danger was a row of houses on one side, but they were across the street and shielded by several trees as well. Plus, at this time of evening, there were few people out. Someone might pass down the street at a critical moment, but then again, they might not.

"Okay," said Henry. "You guys wait here, and I'll go up front and see if I can get one or two of those guys to come back here with me."

"Take off your shirt," one of the men suggested, one with short, smoothly blond hair and a blond moustache.

"What?"

"Sure," another of the guys said. "You've got a nice chest. It'll turn them on. It'll be easier to get them back here."

Henry felt awkward at first, but it did sound like a good plan. As he pulled his shirt up, he heard the guys admiring him, and he was smiling by the time he'd finished pulling the shirt over his head. Curtis held out his hand, and Henry gave him the shirt, grinning.

But as Henry turned back toward the guy with the moustache, he suddenly felt someone pulling a cloth against his face, against his mouth. Was that his shirt? He tried to talk but felt the cloth press more firmly against his mouth.

Suddenly, hands forced him to the ground. Someone took his shoes off. What the hell were they doing? He tried to kick, but someone held his legs down. Then he felt a hand unzipping his jeans, and more hands pulling his pants down, pulling his underwear off, too. He tried to kick and squirm, but he couldn't move. *What the fuck was going on?*

"You stupid moron," Curtis hissed in his ear. "These guys are gay, too. Every team there tonight is gay. This is a gay league, you dolt."

Henry tried to shout. He tried to move. He tried to grab something, anything. But after a couple of useless minutes, he slowly quit thrashing. Maybe it was all a joke, he thought. Maybe it was some kind of initiation into their circle or something. He'd often fantasized about a certain type of hazing. But these guys didn't seem to be playing.

"I'm going to let you go now," Curtis said, "but if you yell, I've got a knife I'm going to put in your hand, and I'm going to tell the policeman you tried to rape me."

Henry felt the pressure on his face slowly lighten. Then the hands holding him down finally moved off as well. Henry looked up at the six men staring down. They didn't look gay. They looked mean and threatening. Henry wondered if they'd start kicking him in the ribs. He'd have to tell the guys at work a gang of black muggers had jumped him.

"We ought to gang rape him," one of the guys suggested.

Henry gasped. In horror, he realized his cock was half erect. These men wouldn't be able to resist.

"No," said the blond with the moustache. "He'd probably like it too much. Besides, there's no telling what we'd catch. Let's just leave him here without his clothes. Maybe we'll tell the policeman there's a pervert back here. Maybe we'll get him arrested on a morals charge."

"That's good."

"Get up." Curtis offered his hand.

Henry refused it but did stand, noticing that four of the six guys were taller than he was. He put his hands over his crotch and turned to Curtis. "You faggot!" he spit out. "It's just like a queer, isn't it? You get your jollies looking at real men, don't you?" He wondered if he should taunt them while he was so outnumbered, but then he realized they weren't about to fight him. They were wimps, after all, afraid to fight the way someone with real balls would.

Curtis laughed. "I'm no gayer than you are. Probably less. It's just that this guy here," he pointed to one of the shorter bowlers, "is my cousin. And I also know the guy with the tattoo, from work. He isn't gay, either. His brother is. He just isn't afraid of them. Only weak assholes are afraid."

"My asshole isn't weak!" Henry frowned and tried to clarify. "I can take any one of you!" He looked at the tall blond with the moustache and wondered, but he knew he'd never have to prove it.

"I don't think this jerk is getting the idea," said the cousin. "Maybe we ought to show him what we really mean."

The cousin took one arm while Curtis took the other. The others surrounded him and led him across the debris-ridden back lot to a large metal bin. "Oh, God," Henry whispered.

"Let's toss out the garbage," said the man with the moustache. Two of the men lifted the lid, and the others joined together to hoist Henry up. One man's hand was on his ass, one of his fingers dangerously close to his crack.

"Please," Henry begged. "Please."

They tossed him over the top and then lowered the lid.

"What'll we do with his clothes?" Henry heard one of the men asking.

"Let's throw them in the other dumpster so he can find them if he digs enough."

He heard something rip followed by a receding voice. "Well, he's not getting his shirt back. We're letting him off too easily." The reply was too distant to make out.

Henry heard a few more noises Then the back lot was quiet. He stood up carefully, his foot cut, and peered through the crack at the top to see if anyone was nearby. The place was deserted. His car was out front, so if he could at least find his pants and keys he'd be okay. He was glad they didn't beat him but somehow felt even worse because they hadn't. Maybe that one guy would come back alone, though, and try to rape him.

Henry thought about calling the policeman for help, but he couldn't face the thought of being seen naked. It was so cold now he'd shriveled down to nothing. He tried to think if there were any friends he could call to come down, but he couldn't think of one single guy he could trust enough. They'd all tease him and make his life miserable. He'd never live it down. They'd probably never believe the men hadn't all fucked him. Could he face them thinking that forever?

Henry remembered the guy with the tattoo, the one who had *joked*, in *public*, about getting fucked. Even when Henry had thought the man was gay, he'd been amazed at how manly he still seemed. And now, knowing he was straight… well, there was something a few of these men had that was genuinely masculine but which Henry didn't have. The jocks in high school had had muscles. That was easy enough to imitate. Missionaries had the priesthood. But these guys… How could he ever get his masculinity back after tonight?

Henry heard something rustling outside the bin, but he was too tired to care. If he could just get home, he could put this night behind him. He'd never come back here, never run into Curtis again, and none of his other friends even knew Curtis. No one would ever know. In a few days, he'd be his old self again and things would be all right.

Maybe he'd come back here next week, though, and beat someone up. That'd show them.

And it would be interesting to look at all those bowlers playing, if most of them were gay. He'd had no idea. If they could be gay and still be men, at least some of them, maybe there was something…maybe…

No. They were the whole reason men like Henry felt insecure in the first place. There was something wrong with men who only wanted to be around other men. They sucked each other's masculinity away. Even the sons of Ammon had eventually taken wives. Or was he just remembering the story wrong?

He wondered, though, if he'd met the guy with the tattoo somewhere else, if they could have been friends. He wished he could have played with him just once. He wished Curtis would at least have told him his name.

The rustling sound died away, and Henry looked about the back lot again. He could see one of his shoes by the back of the building, but he couldn't see any of the rest of his things. Maybe his car keys had fallen out of his pocket over there, though. He'd heard the guys lift the lid on the other bin but wasn't sure they weren't trying to trick him. He ought to at least look.

But he sat in the rotting restaurant food instead. He wished he was back home. He wished he could go back inside the bowling alley. Mostly, he wished he'd never come tonight. Or that he could have gone home earlier as he'd planned after that second game. He wished he would've stayed home altogether and watched football on television. He wished he were back in his apartment right now safe in bed.

His throat ached. It felt swollen and sore. He felt like he couldn't breathe. He blinked to keep his eyes dry, hugging himself in the stifling trash. He wished he were upstairs with those other men, safe inside, having fun.

He heard rustling outside the trash bin again and closed his eyes. He wished he was home. "Oh, man. Oh, man," he whispered. What was he going to do? He wished he were a stronger person. He wished someone would come help him. He wished he didn't need any help. He wished he could really wish for what he wanted.

He stared ahead at the dark wall in front of him. He wished more than anything that his school friend Preston were here to comfort him.

And he wished he was able to comfort Preston in return.

Sex Organs

"Oh my god."

"Larry, we'll do everything we can to fight."

"This can't be real."

"Don't give up. We'll overcome this. It's not the end of the world."

Larry smiled. It *was* the end of the world. He hadn't been so happy in all his life, in all his seventy years. Pancreatic cancer. He wanted to get down on his knees right there in Dr. Kramer's office and praise God for His goodness.

"Is there any treatment that will cure this, or will it just prolong my suffering?"

"There's always hope."

Larry smiled again. There clearly was no way to survive. Tears came to his eyes. Ten years ago when he'd had his heart attack, he'd submitted to having a stent placed in his heart, and he'd suffered some unappetizing changes to his diet. He'd *wanted* to die of a heart attack, but not fighting to survive would have been suicide, and that was as terrible a sin as homosexuality. If he'd managed to stay a virgin his entire life, he wasn't going to ruin his chances for the afterlife by losing points at the very end.

But terminal cancer to a vital organ. There was nothing he could do about that. His test was finally over. His trial. His torture.

"Please don't cry, Larry."

"How long do I have?"

"You know we can't say."

"How long?"

Dr. Kramer shrugged. "Six months."

Larry nodded. "Thanks, Doc."

Larry drove home slowly. The trees looked greener, the flowers redder and yellower, the sky bluer.

Back home, Larry got on the internet and booked a flight for Atlanta. His favorite destinations were San Francisco, New York, and Toronto, but he thought he'd start out with a tamer city. The Pole Vault in Atlanta was a reliable first way to celebrate. Larry made a reservation at the Marriott. He liked Marriott because he was Mormon, too. And Marriott had shown himself to be sensitive to gay issues, though of course he couldn't be too supportive or he'd risk excommunication.

Larry had longed for sex almost sixty years, but his longing for the Celestial Kingdom was even stronger. He'd prayed at first to be made heterosexual. When that didn't work, he'd prayed for paralysis or coma. Those hadn't happened, either. Finally, he'd begun praying for death, but after thirty years of unanswered prayers, hearing the doctor's diagnosis was like seeing a vision of Jesus Christ. A miracle.

"Cole, this is Larry from Salt Lake. How are you?"

"Hi, Larry. You coming to Atlanta?"

"I want to arrange another 'date.' On the 17th. Around 6:00, so you still have time to dance at the club later."

"Sounds great. I'd love to see you again."

"And can you find someone else to come along? You know my type and what I like."

"There's a new guy. Cliff. He'll be perfect. Want me to send you a picture?"

Larry considered. He loved looking at naked men, but he'd worked hard over the years to avoid addiction to pornography. There was no sense risking it now. "No, surprise me."

Larry gave Cole the address of the Marriott and his cell number, and he started packing. Normally, he planned trips weeks, even months, in advance. He already had one set up for San Francisco five weeks from now. But this diagnosis called for immediate celebration. He was willing to pay extra for a last-minute ticket.

After he packed for his flight the following morning, Larry sat on his bed, wondering what to do. He had no friends to call. He'd stopped attending Single Adult activities decades ago. It was too painful to see everyone else pairing up. He never accepted callings at church because it meant involvement with people who talked incessantly about their happy families. Larry went to Sacrament meeting, Sunday school, and Priesthood. He didn't volunteer answers. He didn't ask questions. It was too agonizing to have human contact that was never quite enough.

Larry remembered the interviews with the bishop when he was in his twenties. Why aren't you married? When are you going to settle down and raise a family? It started getting serious, the bishop almost threatening him if he didn't do his duty as a man. Finally, Larry had to "admit" to having sustained an injury while serving in the army. It was during peacetime, so he described it as a "training accident," but thankfully, the bishop left him alone after that.

The problem with this story was that it meant Larry could never confess his sin of masturbation to the bishop. He could therefore never fully repent and be forgiven, and that might affect his salvation. Of course, true repentance meant giving up the sin, and Larry had never been able to do that, either. He figured it was a compromise. "I won't have sex with another man. I won't ruin a woman's life. But in exchange, You'll have to grant me the right to touch myself."

He knew it was still a sin, but he watched TV. He watched movies. He knew perfectly well there wasn't a man in a million who had *never* had sex, not even Catholic priests or Buddhist monks. He wasn't sure he qualified for the lower part of the Celestial Kingdom, the part set aside for ministering angels who would never be gods, but he hoped at least for the Terrestrial, where "good, decent people" were to go.

In his heart of hearts, though, he still hoped for a bell curve. For a gay man, he'd done exceptionally well. He deserved amnesty and admittance to the top kingdom. He wanted it. He'd earned it.

Larry looked at the phone again, wanting to talk to *someone*. He'd never had a roommate, of course, or a best friend. It would have been too difficult not to confide, not to want a comforting shoulder.

He smiled. Soon he'd see his mother again. He could talk to someone then.

Larry lay back on the bed and rubbed his crotch through his pants. He smiled as he felt a hardening under the thick cloth. Not bad for an old man. It would be even better once he had a resurrected body.

Larry started fantasizing about what would take place in Atlanta. He always hired two escorts at a time. He had them act out various scenarios. Perhaps one of them would play a Roman slave dealer who had to show Larry a prospective slave to purchase. The slave dealer would slowly unrobe the slave to let Larry see the entire piece of merchandise. He'd get the slave hard to show how well he'd be able to service his new master. The dealer would kiss the man to gauge how passionate he could be.

But Larry would never let the two escorts have sex. It was a sin to commit homosexual acts, and Larry couldn't allow asking others to sin be on his conscience. He just needed to see beautiful men, sexy men, impassioned men.

But no sex.

Larry unzipped his pants and pulled out his penis. He stroked it lovingly and closed his eyes.

No, he was not going to do this. He was going to be strong.

Yet he needed *something*. Larry walked to the kitchen and ate a peach. Then he ate a banana. Somehow, he still wasn't satisfied.

He paced back and forth across the living room for twenty minutes. He looked at prints of the famous Arnold Friberg paintings on his walls. The stripling warriors, Samuel the Lamanite, Moroni burying the gold plates. He rubbed his crotch again.

Larry sat at the kitchen table and thought. He'd never hired an escort in Salt Lake before. It always seemed too risky. But he needed to see another human being. Maybe touch his arm or chest. He always picked up the gay paper and knew there were ads.

He nodded. He was going to do it.

Around 3:30, Jeffrey knocked on his door. Larry smiled when he opened it. "You're perfect," Larry said.

Jeffrey smiled and came inside. "Nice house. You have money."

"Not really. I just don't have kids."

"What do you want to do?"

"I want to see you look hot and bothered. I want to watch you slowly, very slowly take off your clothes and rub yourself all over. I want you to look like you've just got to get off, but I don't want you to actually do it."

Larry didn't know why he couldn't allow himself to ask an escort to masturbate for him. If it was a small enough sin that he could do it himself, what would be the harm in ordering someone else to beat off? Larry didn't really know. He just understood it would be a sin, and he didn't do it.

"Right here?"

"This way."

The two men walked into Larry's bedroom, and Larry sat on the edge of his bed and licked his lips. Jeffrey walked slowly about, pulling at his collar a little, wiping his brow, and finally ripping off his shirt. He caressed his stomach and his nipples, traced a line up and down his chest, and let the line go down to his crotch.

He rubbed his crotch lightly for a moment, sighed, and then squeezed. He moaned and slowly unbuttoned his jeans. With each button he undid, Jeffrey would moan and squeeze again. Finally, the pants fell around Jeffrey's ankles, and Larry watched in delight as the escort's huge penis throbbed against his underwear. There was a little drop of pre-cum on the fabric. Larry rubbed his own crotch for a second, too, but quickly stopped. He was not going to masturbate while with another man. That would be sex, not masturbation.

"I need you," Jeffrey said.

Larry smiled and nodded for him to go on.

"I really need you." Jeffrey moved up to the bed and put his hand on Larry's chest.

"No. No touching."

Jeffrey removed his hand but still stood right next to Larry, his bulging underwear only a centimeter away from Larry's leg. Larry closed his eyes. The pain was almost unbearable. But he smiled. Soon he'd feel the pain of his cancer, and then everything would be fine.

When he opened his eyes, Larry saw Jeffrey's face only inches from his own. He could feel the warmth across the brief space between them. He tried to move backward, but Jeffrey moved forward. "Just a little kiss," he whispered. "I don't usually kiss my clients, but I want to kiss you. You're different. You're special."

Larry's first instinct was to say no. He'd never kissed a man before, and while kissing didn't sound like a serious sin in itself, he was scared to cross the line into physical contact.

But he was about to die. What if there was no kissing for celibate angels in heaven? Maybe this was his only chance in all of eternity for a kiss.

"Yes," he breathed.

Jeffrey leaned in closer, and his lips met Larry's. It was the most glorious thing Larry had ever experienced in his entire life. Something so wonderful *couldn't* be a sin.

Jeffrey pushed Larry gently onto his back and climbed on top of him, his lips still latched onto his. Larry protested weakly, but he was fully clothed, wasn't he? It wasn't as if he were guilty of petting. Then he felt Jeffrey's hand on his crotch, and he moaned in protest. Jeffrey seemed to think this was a good moan and squeezed harder. Now he forced his tongue into Larry's mouth. Larry tried to pull away, but Jeffrey was too heavy.

And yet that weight seemed altogether heavenly. Larry couldn't bring himself to push Jeffrey away.

Gravity, after all, wasn't a sin.

Jeffrey started unbuttoning Larry's shirt. He moaned in protest another time. Then again, it wasn't as if a man's chest was a sex organ. There was no real sin in letting Jeffrey touch it. He reached up to feel Jeffrey's chest as well.

Jeffrey got out of the bed and pulled off his underwear. Now he was completely naked in front of Larry. Larry could see something glisten on the end of his penis and stared. Jeffrey touched the tip of his penis and then brought his finger to Larry's lips. Larry kept them pressed firmly shut, but he couldn't resist the curiosity. In seventy years, he'd never tasted semen or even pre-cum. It was a sin to find out, but he licked his lips and felt a warmth spread through his chest.

It tasted good.

Jeffrey reached over and started unbuckling Larry's belt.

"No. I have to draw the line. We can't do any more."

"I just want to look at you. That's fair, isn't it?"

Larry considered. Just looking wasn't a sin. Or much of one, anyway. It's what he hired these men for, wasn't it? He took off all his clothes and lay on the bed. Jeffrey climbed back onto the bed, prying Larry's legs apart. "No sex. Just looking," Larry reminded him.

Jeffrey smiled. "A touch won't hurt." He put his hand gently on Larry's penis.

"No. Don't touch my penis. It's a sex organ. I'll go to hell."

Jeffrey giggled. "Okay, okay." He took his hand off and knelt, looking at Larry. Then he smiled again and wet his finger. He reached under Larry's balls and found his asshole. "Your ass isn't a sex organ, is it?"

Larry frowned.

"Is it?" Jeffrey repeated.

"It is if you put your penis in it."

"Then I won't put my penis in it." He pushed his finger forward, and Larry felt it bearing past his sphincter.

"No."

"A finger isn't a sex organ."

Larry frowned again. That was true enough, too, wasn't it? Even the General Authorities got prostate exams.

Jeffrey pushed his finger in deeper, pulled it almost all the way out, and pushed it in again. Larry had never felt anything so wonderful in his life. He relaxed and enjoyed it for a moment but then understood that despite the rationalizing, it *was* still a sin. He was almost finished his test. He couldn't allow himself to fail now.

"Okay, thanks," said Larry. "That's enough."

"I want to make you come."

"Oh, God, no."

"I can do it without ever touching your penis, I swear."

This thought intrigued Larry, and he considered again, but then he shook his head.

Jeffrey's eyebrows furrowed. "Old man, you are a real pain in the ass. I get so sick of the role playing. We all know the game. But I've got places to be." He lifted Larry's legs in one quick motion and in seconds had thrust his penis deep inside Larry.

Larry yelled from the sudden pain, but then Jeffrey clamped his mouth on top of his. He began pumping away, pumping away, and Larry could feel that enormous penis sliding back and forth against his sphincter. After a few moments, it stopped hurting and began to feel good. But he was scared. Scared of Jeffrey, scared of his penis, scared of enjoying what he shouldn't be enjoying. He tried to push Jeffrey away, but Jeffrey was too young and strong.

Then something horrible happened. Just as Larry heard Jeffrey's panting reach a crescendo that told him the young man was getting close to climax, Larry felt his own penis burning. With one last, deep thrust, Jeffrey came, groaning heavily, and a second later, Larry came as well.

But he'd been raped. It wasn't as if he'd done anything voluntarily. He was still innocent.

Jeffrey pulled out and got dressed while Larry lay there stunned. "That'll be $200, grandpa." He held out his hand.

Larry continued to lie there.

"Come on, geezer. Pay up."

Larry sat up, his semen dripping off his stomach, and went to gather his wallet. He pulled out some twenties, and Jeffrey stuffed them in his pocket and left. Larry sat back on the edge of his bed.

He'd liked it. He could confess and repent, of course, and hold out without repeating the incident another six months. Six months wasn't forever. He could do it. And it wasn't technically deathbed repentance. He still had time to prove he was sincere.

But he'd crossed the line. Could he see Cole in Atlanta without touching him? What would it be like to have a man come in his mouth? What would it be like to enter another man?

What would it be like to love someone?

No. He was going to be pure when he died. His parents and grandparents had all lived well into their nineties. God was merciful to let him die at age seventy. Larry would show his appreciation and be a good boy. The brain was the biggest sex organ, and he was going to keep it under control.

The phone rang. Larry looked at his watch. It was almost 5:00. Probably a telemarketer. No one else ever called him. But maybe it was a survey. He needed to do his civic duty. Larry sighed and picked up the receiver. "Hello?"

"Larry?" said a breathless voice. "It's Dr. Kramer. I had to call right away." He paused just a moment. "There's been a terrible mistake. Your lab results got mixed up with someone else's. You don't have cancer. Do you hear me? You're perfectly fine. Healthy as a horse. I wanted to let you know as soon as I found out. I didn't want you to suffer needlessly."

Larry sat holding the phone in silence.

"Larry? Larry? You okay?"

"That's…wonderful news," Larry said dully. "Thanks for calling." He hung up the phone in a daze. He sat there motionless for fifteen minutes, and then for another twenty. Finally, he blinked and looked about the room.

He needed to talk to someone.

But who? Larry didn't even own an address book.

He sat staring at the floor for another quarter of an hour. He needed human contact. What was he to do?

His eyes fell upon the gay newspaper again. He picked it up listlessly and turned to the back. Sighing, he picked up the phone and dialed. "Dallas, can you come to my place in an hour?" He listened a moment and then continued. "Yes, I have the money here." He nodded silently. "See you soon."

Larry sat naked on his bed for a few minutes longer. Then he licked some flakes of his dried cum, while a single tear caught on his cheek.

He put some bills on top of his dresser.

He brushed his teeth.

And waited.

Alien Dick

My first taste of alien dick came when I was eighteen and attended a science fiction convention in Denver. I met a twenty-six-year-old black Klingon, and he had his way with me in the convention center bathroom. From that moment on, I've always wanted more alien dick.

My quest was put on hold for a time while I served as a Mormon missionary in Germany, but then I saw some leathermen who reminded me of the Borg, and I ended up being sent home early. My excommunication was a terrible disgrace to the family, and I briefly wondered if there was a place for me in the universe any longer, but before long, I discovered gay science fiction novels and began feeling more alive than ever. It was romance by proxy, but as a former Mormon, I understood that proxy work had its place.

My parents no longer supported me, so I found a job at Leather Life, a sex shop in downtown Salt Lake. I got a lot of phone numbers and had a good deal of sex, but most guys weren't into role playing the part of ET. They wanted to be tough, super masculine men, but not a creature from another planet. After a few years, the exotic smell of leather started to lose its appeal. Being fucked by a man in chaps and a harness began to feel very vanilla.

I tried joining a couple of Dungeons and Dragons games during this period, the ones where the participants dress up as their character. But sucking an elfin dick wasn't the same as sucking off an alien. I read the ads on craigslist and various sex sites, but mine was a hopeless pursuit. While I found many of the ad writers far too specific ("Seek man with size 8, E width feet to suck his toes"), I realized my own desires were even narrower.

Was there truly someone for everyone? Why couldn't I just have a thing for Asians? There were a billion of them. Why not Swedes? Even they numbered more than the extraterrestrials in my neighborhood.

I had a couple of flings on Halloween night, once with Darth Vader and another time with Spock. I get hard just thinking about it. But neither guy was into prolonged alien impersonation. I was horny enough to try normal men regularly, of course. I had fat, short dicks, long, narrow ones, dicks with mushroom heads, and wide, curved dicks, but while they were mildly entertaining, I was all too aware these were average human dicks. I admit I did consider animal dick once, but it simply didn't appeal to me. I wanted sex with a humanoid, sentient species. Bestiality was just as unappetizing to me as to any other gay guy. Even furries were human. And their culture wasn't focused on sex.

I was able to save money after I stopped going to the bars and so managed to attend one science fiction convention every year. I was lucky enough to hook up two or three times at each convention. It was always tremendous fun, but not a single one of the guys I met was looking for a long-term interspecies relationship.

I sought counseling.

It turned out my therapist was also LDS, not a surprise perhaps, since we were both in the world capital of Mormondom, but worrisome all the same.

"Derek, why do you think you're attracted to aliens?"

"I don't know."

"Are you uncomfortable with yourself?"

"No."

"Do you consider being with men repulsive? Sinful? Is it easier to face your homosexuality if you aren't having sex with other men?"

"I like men. I just like alien men."

"Hmm." The therapist thought for a moment. "Do you miss planning out your life in the Celestial Kingdom?"

I frowned. "What do you mean?"

"Well, those of us who make it to the Celestial Kingdom become gods and get to people our own planets. Are you trying to compensate for no longer being in a position to create your own extraterrestrials?"

I looked at him a moment, wondering which of us was more fucked up.

The therapist pushed onward, feeling he was onto something. "Do you think maybe if you came back to the Church and could have Celestial goals again, perhaps your abnormal obsession would be replaced by healthy ideas?"

I looked him in the eyes. "I'm not here because I feel unhealthy. I'm here because I'm lonely and want to learn to relate to Earth men. Do you want to bend over for me and see if I can adapt to your human form?"

Our first session was also our last.

I watched *Close Encounters of the Third Kind* and *The Day the Earth Stood Still* so often I knew every line by heart. I found Michael Rennie intriguing, knowing he would satisfy me completely, even though he looked "normal," because deep down I understood he was in fact really an alien. It was the alien part that fascinated me, not looking abnormal. Still, if I could have both, I knew we'd have a fighting chance.

I bought a radio set and sent messages into outer space, offering my body to any extraterrestrials who wanted to slum it with an Earthling. I played the Carpenters' "Calling Occupants of Interplanetary Craft," hoping to make contact.

After months with no response, I realized I couldn't wait forever. I decided to force myself to start having more sex with "regular" guys. I found I had to be bottom, though, because I simply couldn't stay hard with a mere human. Was I destined only to be able to ejaculate with a bumpy dildo up my butt as I beat off looking at the pawn shop owner from *Men in Black*?

People wondered if being homosexual was genetic or learned. But surely, being xenosexual could not be a result of my DNA, could it? Or had God gotten me mixed up and put me on the wrong planet? He apparently had a great many to govern, after all. And with all the XXY and XXX and XYY folks out there, he clearly made mistakes.

I decided I'd have to try an arranged marriage, even if I was doing the arranging myself. If Jews throughout the centuries could "learn to love" the spouse foisted on them by others, I could learn to love a fellow human being.

The following Saturday night, I decided to choose a terrestrial mate. I prayed for guidance, wondering if God could possibly care about a speck like me in the entirety of the cosmos. I dressed in my most preppy, white bread clothes and headed for the bars. I still didn't drink, so I'd need to loosen up without the alcohol. I was going to approach the blandest looking guy there and take him home. And I was going to like it.

A couple of ugly guys made eye contact, but while ugly *could* seem alien, even I liked attractive Cardassians. And since I was after *Homo sapiens* tonight, it was an absolute prerequisite he be reasonably attractive in an Earthly sense.

But one of the ugly guys was persistent. "I know what you're thinking," he said, moving over toward me when I accidentally looked back a little too long. "But I'm going to get some plastic surgery. I won't always look like this."

"No need to bother on my account," I said.

"I've already got a tattoo."

"That's nice."

"It's in a private place." He grinned, and I nodded politely.

The ugly man leaned in close. I was surprised to find his breath smelled fresh, not like alcohol. I looked at him again.

"I can promise you a night you'll never forget."

I felt a shiver. Something told me the man wasn't lying. But was he some kind of kook? I was looking for human, not kinky. Even my encounters with aliens had always been rather straightforward. I wasn't into S&M Romulans, after all.

"I may not be able to get it up," I admitted.

"I'll get you up," the man promised. He didn't sound like a braggart. He sounded sincere.

I shrugged. "Oh, all right."

"My name's Richard."

"I'm Derek."

"Dick and Derek. It was meant to be."

I smiled politely again.

I followed Richard back to his apartment. There was a dim lamp inside, and Richard didn't turn on any overhead lights. I wondered if this was supposed to be mood lighting, or if he was in some kind of vampire cult. I wasn't into vampires. Dead or undead, vampires were still human.

When I followed Richard into the bedroom, I was surprised to see padded restraints tied to the headboard. I looked over at Richard. Getting tied up by a complete stranger was not the safest strategy in the world.

"Bondage?" I asked.

"Just the first time."

I raised an eyebrow.

Richard shrugged. "I have an unusual dick. I have to tie you up so I know you'll go ahead with the sex even after you see it."

I laughed. "Well, if you have herpes or genital warts, I certainly hope you'll wear a condom."

Richard just smiled, and I felt another chill. Part of me was intrigued, and part of me was simply feeling my sex life was hopeless in any case, so who cared what happened?

Though it wasn't always the desperate who ended up in catastrophic situations, it often was. Perhaps in Outer Darkness, I'd run into outcasts from other worlds. Mormon doctrine promised that everyone, good or bad, would be resurrected. Perhaps I'd only be able to have alien sex once I was in the next world.

I took off my clothes and lay back on the bed, allowing Richard to bind my wrists to the headboard. I was surprised, though, when he gagged me as well. *That* made me a bit nervous. I wondered if my parents would even care if they never found my body.

Richard stood beside the bed and slowly removed his shirt. After he pulled it off, he remained motionless to let me take in the sight, smiling almost sardonically. Frankly, I was rather unimpressed. He was moderately hairy but not in particularly good shape. I nodded politely, unable to smile with the rubber ball in my mouth.

Then Richard tugged off his pants and knelt on the bed between my legs. His dick was pointing straight toward me.

And now my eyes popped wide open.

Richard straddled my chest and waved his dick right in my face. This was the tattoo he'd talked about. His penis had green squiggly veins and purple circles outlined on it. But the real shock was that Richard had obviously undergone surgical procedures on his penis as well. There were two bands of large bumps under the skin, similar to the specialized dildos I owned, guaranteed to produce "extra pleasure."

"I'm from the planet Zor," Richard said. "And I impregnate Earth men with my seed. In three months, you'll give birth to a Zorian baby." I smiled, even with the gag. I liked this game.

Richard lifted my legs and applied some lube. Even aliens needed KY.

Being screwed by that wide, bumpy dick was quite the experience, far different from any dildo I'd tried. For the first time in my life, I came solely from being fucked. With Richard's chest so close to me now, I could see that what I originally thought was hair was instead a series of scales tattooed across his torso.

After he came, Richard pulled out and licked cum off my stomach. He smiled but then suddenly looked vulnerable. "Will we be able to do that again sometime?"

I nodded vigorously, and Richard removed my gag.

"Did you have fun?" Richard asked, his voice almost but not quite breaking.

"Can we do it again tomorrow?" I replied with my own question. "Wait. How about in the morning? I can stay the night."

"You don't think I'm too weird?"

"Thank *God* you're too weird!"

Richard sighed. "It's not over, you know."

"What do you mean?"

"I have more surgery planned when I save up some money. Insurance doesn't cover this, obviously."

"More?" I asked, intrigued. "Like what?"

He shrugged. "I'd like some prominent ridges on my forehead. Not Ferengi or anything. Something unique. I've designed it all myself. And if I get the nerve, I'm going to split my tongue so that it's forked. I'm a little nervous about learning to talk again."

"It sounds *fantastic*."

"Really?" Richard looked at me carefully. "It's one thing to have sex with a dwarf or a one-armed man once just to say you've done it, but…"

"You're exactly what I've been looking for," I said. "I only hope we actually like each other as people, too." I paused. "I'm sorry, I mean, as intelligent beings." I began laughing. It was like an infertile couple who finally give up trying to conceive and then adopt, who then surprisingly discover themselves pregnant six months later.

Perhaps those stories were urban legends, but this…this was the stuff of scripture.

Maybe I'd pitch a dating advice column for a science fiction magazine.

"How about if I add scales to my arms, and a few dots to my face?"

"You're planning a career in banking?"

Richard smiled. "I'm an art professor."

"You'll be a masterpiece."

Richard squeezed my leg. "Come on. Let's have some Zorian tea." His brows furrowed. "You're not Mormon, are you? You do drink tea?"

"Zorian tea isn't mentioned in the Word of Wisdom."

"Well, this will look like regular ole black tea at first," he admitted. "It only finishes a full brewing cycle after it makes its way through a Zorian's system."

"How do you sing, 'I'm a little teapot' in your language?"

Richard smiled and offered me a hand. "Come on, Earth boy. We need to stay up talking till 3:00 a.m."

We did. I found out that Richard's first outpost on Earth was in Minneapolis. After high school, he explored more of the planet by joining the Peace Corps for three years, working in El Salvador, Colombia, and Haiti. He began painting the exotic locales he'd seen after he returned and eventually ended up with an MFA.

But it wasn't till a hustler he picked up once refused to have sex with him, claiming Richard reminded him of a monster from outer space that he became obsessed with his looks and began turning himself into an alien.

"You sure you won't mind a full transformation? There's a lot to be said for the V effect, not realizing I'm an alien till the outer layers are stripped away."

"Are you okay with me looking human?"

He leaned over to smell my hair and moaned with pleasure. "I feel a little guilty spending so much on myself when plenty of people on the planet could use the money to resolve real problems. But my sex drive is pretty strong, I'm afraid."

"You're already alien enough to satisfy me. So you can put aside some money toward other causes, too, if you want. Or at least *I* can now. Instead of going to a science fiction convention every year, I could go to Peru and have a working vacation. Do volunteer work the whole time I'm there. You can fuck me by the Nazca lines."

"Leaving the country might not be so easy for me once I alter my face."

"Then you'll just have to sell some paintings and send the money to Africa or India or Nepal."

"I have sold a few," Richard admitted. "That helped with the surgery. But I don't know that I'm any great talent." He gave me an appraising look. "Perhaps we could earn a little extra by doing alien porn." He smiled. "You think there's a market?"

My sphincter clenched as I remembered our encounter. "We could have a three-way with a Bajoran. Add some guest stars."

"I hear Wookies have the biggest dicks."

"Then maybe we do need to go to another SF convention and do some recruiting." I wasn't sure if we were bantering or literally planning.

"I have a friend who teaches a film class. He could shoot it."

I gave him a thumbs up. It wasn't as if I was in banking, either.

Richard caressed my hand softly. "A fetish isn't much to build a life on."

Perhaps I'd contact a furries designer and come up with an alien costume unique to me. I wasn't prepared to navigate the world permanently with pointy ears and spikes on my elbows, but I could do it at home, if I shared a home with someone who liked spiky elbows.

Options, I thought. I had options now. *We* had options.

I looked at what before had seemed an ugly man and no longer found ugliness there. "I can't wait to bring you home for Christmas."

"So I'm just a trophy alien, am I?" Richard laughed.

I was getting an erection again, just thinking about his future forked tongue. "I think we need to practice some possible scenes for our upcoming film."

"Ready for some tea?"

I leaned over and kissed Richard on the lips.

"Are we in love yet?"

"Getting there."

"What can I do to help?"

I whispered in his ear.

He nodded. "An alien abduction with an anal probe. You didn't peek in my anal probe drawer, did you?" I grew even harder imagining what might lie in there. "But Zorian tea first." He took me by the hand and led me to the bathroom.

Three alien sex acts later, when we finally collapsed in bed around 4:00 in the morning, Richard lay with his head on my stomach. "Zorians need a breathing tube when they sleep in Earth's atmosphere." He slid my dick into his mouth.

"As long as Zorians don't grind their teeth."

But Richard was already asleep. I rested my hand on his head with a sigh. "Where no man has gone before," I said softly. I prayed, asking God to bless everyone on the planet Zor, if He had indeed created such a place. Whether there really was a Celestial Kingdom or an Outer Darkness or an afterlife of any kind at all, I was going to create my own world right here and now.

I closed my eyes and drifted off to sleep, dreaming of an otherworldly love, in a solar system at the end of the galaxy, on a little, unremarkable planet called Terra.

The Sneakover Prince

I met Alan at the Faubourg Marigny gay bookstore in New Orleans. "Any new porn?" I asked breezily, walking past the counter where he was reading a book, then heading to the porn rack in back of the store.

"Oh, I—I don't know," he said. "I don't put out the magazines. I just work the cash register."

He sounded a bit nervous, as if talking about gay porn unsettled him. I smiled. How could you work in a gay bookstore and be uncomfortable with gay porn?

Well, he was new here, I figured. I hadn't seen him in the bookstore before. Still, even to come in and talk to the owner about a job suggested some degree of comfort.

I decided to test my suspicions about his jitteriness, just for fun. After looking through the magazines, I brought two up to the counter. One was the mainstream *Advocate Men* and the other was *Leather Men.* I put the two magazines in front of the new cashier and opened both, one to a photo of a businessman in an office with his pants down, and the other to a photo of a man in leather chaps kneeling doggie-style while another man in a leather harness rimmed him.

"Which do you think I should give my dad for his birthday?"

The man grew bright red in seconds and turned quickly to fiddle with some papers. "Is—is your dad really gay?"

"Well," I said, "since the stroke, he can't remember, so I keep trying to convince him he is."

The man turned to look at me a moment, deciding if I was joking or not. We chatted for fifteen minutes. He told me his name was Alan. He was working part-time here and part-time in a used book store in the French Quarter a few blocks away.

"Nice," I said. "I'm a librarian at Tulane University. We'll have to get together to talk about books sometime."

Alan looked a little flustered at that, but I wrote down my address and phone number and told him to give me a call or just drop by after work someday.

I didn't expect anything to come of it, but I was in the habit of regularly asking strange men over to my place, so I didn't see any reason to neglect this particular young man.

Only he wasn't all that young, was he? He *seemed* young because of his nervousness, but he had to be in his late thirties. And I was forty-two myself, so I wasn't usually up for delicate schoolgirl flirtations. As a rule, I was more direct. "Want to come over to my place and fuck?" But Alan seemed to demand a softer approach, and something about that intrigued me.

Later that day, I stopped off at the bathhouse on Toulouse in the Quarter, sucked two dicks and had my own dick sucked, and then biked home to the Marigny.

By the next day, I'd completely forgotten about Alan.

I got down to my part-time job after lunch. I worked from home writing reviews for porno movies, which brought in roughly $400 a month, but it was still only lagniappe. I couldn't have gotten by without my library job. I worked in the reference section on the main floor. Despite the internet, people still needed me occasionally.

I enjoyed reviewing porn, though. First of all, I enjoyed *watching* porn. And I enjoyed the fact that since I was a reviewer, I received the new porn DVDs for free. All I had to do was write my reaction to what I saw. I tried not to let my own specific interests make me too opinionated, but I found I didn't have to say, "Oh, my god, how boring!" or "Ooh! Hot!" I could just pretend to be objectively describing a scene but simply use boring or exciting words to convey my opinion.

It was Thursday, my day off, and after watching two DVDs and beating off only at the end of the last one, I went downstairs to see if my mail had arrived.

I owned a two-story house in the Marigny I'd bought with my partner of twenty years. He'd died almost three years ago of a heart attack at the age of sixty. I lived on the top floor and rented out the downstairs as two small apartments. I had an entrance on the ground floor, naturally, and was walking down the stairs when I heard the metal squeak of the mail slot. Just in time, I thought.

But I stopped short when I realized there were eyes peering at me through the slot. I was wearing only my T-shirt and underwear, and I realized suddenly my underwear had a little wet spot from where I'd leaked after coming.

Was that the mailman peeping at me, I wondered? Well, whoever it was was going to get an eyeful.

I ran the rest of the way down the stairs and opened the door.

It was Alan, turning beet red.

"I—I was just—I mean—I—"

"What a perv," I said, laughing.

Alan turned even redder.

"You don't have to sneak a peek," I said, putting my hand on his shoulder. "I'll show you anything you want to see." I reached down to the elastic band on my boxer briefs.

"I've got to go." Alan jumped on his bike and hurried off.

I laughed, but I couldn't help but think, "Hey, we've both got bikes. We'll have to go riding together sometime." I knew I'd have to stop by the bookstore again to tease him.

A few days later, I did stop in, happy to see Alan at the register. "Hi, boyfriend," I said, smiling sweetly. He turned red. "Any new porn?"

"I don't know."

I left him alone and browsed the card rack, looking for a racy birthday greeting for a friend. When I glanced back over at the counter, I could see Alan checking out my box.

He was almost squinting, of course, since I didn't have that showy a box, being more a grower than a shower, but he was trying hard to see what he could. I smiled, and he turned away quickly to do some paperwork.

I selected a card and went up to the counter. Alan didn't say anything, but when he handed me the card, I took his hand and held it, mostly to see his reaction. I saw barely controlled panic in his eyes.

"What time is your shift over?"

"6:00. Why?"

"Have you ever seen *Under the Tuscan Sun*?"

"No. Why?"

"Do you like catfish?"

"Yes. Why?"

"You're coming over to my house when you get off work. We'll have a nice dinner and then watch a DVD."

Alan looked down at the counter. "I—I'm not really supposed to date," he said softly.

"You already have a boyfriend?" I asked. I think I let the surprise in my voice show.

"Oh, no. It's just that I'm Mormon. I'm supposed to be celibate. I've never gone on a date before."

"Well, I wasn't asking you to bed. Just to see a movie."

"Oh, I thought—I—"

"Not that I wouldn't have tried to make a move on you, but I can control myself, even around someone as good looking as you."

Alan turned red again.

"But we'll have to cuddle while we watch. Will that work for you?"

"I—I suppose."

I didn't know why I was pursuing Alan so strongly. Part of it had to be just for the fun of watching him squirm. But I also did find him attractive, and while I had a good circle of friends already, I was always open to widening that circle. Gay people had to rely on chosen family more than biological family, and I always wanted more "relatives."

Alan and I did have dinner that evening, and we did cuddle while watching the movie. There was no fondling, though, not even any kissing. I was touched at the end of the evening, however, when Alan stood up formally and offered me his hand. "I had a very good time," he said. "Thank you."

I grabbed his hand and pulled Alan close to me, kissing his ear. "Will you come back next Sunday?" I whispered.

"Y-yes," he whispered back.

Alan came over every Sunday evening for the next several weeks. His shift was only from noon to six, he explained, and he went to church with his mother every Sunday morning before work, and so, he went on, "I feel I just need to treat myself after all that." He looked guilty immediately and added, "You don't think that's a sin, do you? It's not like we're having sex or anything."

"Well, there *is* a little bit of 'anything,'" I said. "I do beat off thinking of you after you leave."

Alan turned red, but he smiled, too. "Really?" Then he looked concerned. "But if I make you sin, does that count as a sin against me, too?"

"I'm not sinning, honey."

Alan didn't say anything.

"If you think being gay is so bad, why do you work in a gay bookstore?"

"Well, I'm not *sure* anymore if it's bad. And I want to see a little of the other side so I can make up my mind. I'd like not to be alone the rest of my life. I mean, I have my mom, but…"

"I think you need to start coming over on Wednesday evenings, too."

"Really?" Alan smiled again.

"I have a lot of DVDs," I said. "You mind more cuddling?"

Alan thought for a moment. "I *like* cuddling," he said slowly.

"I get off work at 6:00 on Wednesdays. So can you be here at 7:00?"

We started doing other things besides watching movies. Sometimes, we played Scrabble or UNO or gin rummy and even games like Hangman and charades. I found Alan delightfully innocent and playful on the one hand, but on the other, I was a little disturbed to learn that at thirty-eight, he still lived at home with his mom. She was in perfect health and didn't need a caretaker, but Alan felt that after his father's death fifteen years earlier, he had to look out for her. It seemed sweet in some ways, but I wondered if he hadn't really stayed eighteen years old for the past twenty years.

Of course, *I* wasn't still just a kid, and while I enjoyed Alan's company, I was also actively pursuing the company of other men. Sometimes, I'd sit on the stoop in front of my front door and pick up guys just walking down the street. Other times late at night, I'd go to the bar three blocks away and pick someone up there.

I usually told Alan about these episodes. He looked perturbed but also always asked for details. Then he'd look at the floor a moment and think.

One day, though, he surprised me by kissing me hello. "Wow," I said, "That's a big step."

Alan turned red but then looked a little depressed. "It's pretty sad when something as simple as a kiss is a big step."

"Well, let's be happy about it, not sad."

He looked up then and nodded. "Okay. I'm sorry. I guess I'm a bit down mood because I've decided maybe there is no God. I've been praying for something for a long time and God hasn't given it to me, so I finally realized maybe he doesn't exist."

"Hmm," I said, trying to keep this light. "Maybe he *does* exist, but he just doesn't like you." I smiled teasingly.

Alan's brow furrowed. "You know, with my low self-esteem, it's a wonder that never occurred to me."

"So you'll keep the faith a little longer?"

"Why do you want me to believe? I thought you disapproved of my angst."

"Oh, there's nothing wrong with believing in God. It's just believing he doesn't want you to be loved by someone I find upsetting."

Alan nodded. Of course, I hadn't myself prayed in a very long time, but I didn't see why Alan couldn't have both faith and love in his own life.

I decided to lighten things up now, though. I'd found an old game of Twister at a rummage sale, and after dinner, we improvised a way to play with just two people. When we were sufficiently entangled already, I announced, "Left hand on right buttocks," and placed my hand on Alan's ass. He jumped, but a moment later, I felt a hand on my ass as well.

He kissed me goodnight that evening as he left, and kissing became a regular part of our encounters from then on. I tried introducing it to the cuddling sessions, and after only a brief moment of resistance to the suggestion, Alan gave in and started some respectably good French kissing. It didn't take him long to polish his technique, either.

He started staying longer after our Sunday night movie was over.

I found Alan a truly sweet man. He told me of his two years as a missionary in Tonga, where he helped teach people English as well as helped local church members build houses for some of the poorer islanders. I'd always thought Mormons just proselytized, so it was nice to hear they occasionally did something useful, too.

In the years since he returned to the States, Alan regularly volunteered with the Cub Scouts, the Sierra Club, an AIDS hospice, and with organizing local March of Dimes events.

"You think a lot about other people," I said.

"Well, to be honest, it's mostly to divert the energy I *want* to put into sex. I sometimes wonder how many great things we could do as a people if we didn't invest so much of ourselves seeking an orgasm."

"It doesn't have to be either/or," I said. "I teach ESL to Latino immigrants." I paused. "Of course, I make the men take their shirts off if they want any extra help."

"See what I mean?"

"You may have a point. But how about I make you a promise? After we start having sex, I'll begin volunteering with the Sierra Club, too."

Alan turned red but then looked pensive a few moments.

But we didn't start having sex. Soon, we'd been "dating" for five months, and I had yet to so much as grope him. He did let me rub his chest during our cuddling sessions, and he would rub mine, too, but if my hand strayed down to his stomach, he would grasp it and place it back on his chest.

We did a few day excursions, too, biking together through the Marigny or up to Audubon Park, buying fruit at the Farmers Market, walking slowly along the levee, and even going to gay bingo once. I found Alan intelligent, and we talked about the Middle East, about health care reform, about nuclear and solar and wind energy, and even about astronomy. Sometimes, we watched lectures on DVD about

Greek archaeology or Jewish intellectual thought of the 16th century.

"You know," I told him one day over gumbo, "if I could just get you into bed, you'd make a great husband."

"There's so much else we can share," Alan replied. "Shouldn't that be enough?"

"But when you love someone, you want to share yourself with them completely."

"I love my mother, but I don't want to have sex with her. And what relationship can be stronger than that between a mother and son?"

"That between a married couple."

Alan looked at the floor a moment. "Maybe," he said slowly. "Maybe."

It was on our six-month "anniversary" that I was finally able to meet Alan's mother in their Gentilly home. She hadn't heard anything about me, I learned, and thought I was a regular at the straight French Quarter bookstore where Alan worked. He'd told her months ago he also worked at a gay bookstore, and they'd talked a few times about his feelings toward men in general, but she was only okay about his "being" gay, he told me, as long as he wasn't "doing" gay things.

"Like listening to old disco songs?" I asked.

Alan glared at me but laughed.

"So you're a friend of Alan's?" his mother asked that evening, shaking my hand as she let me into her home. "I'm Sharon."

"I'm Balzer," I said.

"What an odd name." She smiled.

"It suits me," I replied. "Because I'm ballsy."

"Oh, dear. We try not to use language like that around here." Her face was unreadable. "I hope I'm not offending you."

"Oh, no. I'm a librarian. I'm used to attempts at censorship." I smiled, and she smiled back uncertainly.

But after our rocky start, I found I really liked Sharon. She was a social worker who also volunteered with the Breast Cancer Run and the Brownies. As an active Mormon, she naturally taught Sunday school every week, but she also made a point of being pen pals with three children in South America she was sending money to each month, teaching herself Spanish on the side. I suppose after fifteen years without a husband, she was deflecting some sexual energy, too. Still, there were plenty of more selfish ways to do that. She struck me as a genuinely nice woman.

"I don't know if Alan has told you," Sharon said, "but we only just got our stove working again. We had to cook on the grill for a whole week." She shook her head. "I tried hard to be creative…"

"But it's so difficult to grill those peas," I continued for her.

Sharon laughed, a hearty, sweet, good-natured laugh. "It was the red beans and rice that was the toughest."

"She's not kidding," Alan said.

We had a pleasant, cheerful meal, and I could see why Alan liked his mother, though I was still concerned she had too much control over her son's life. Not really my business, of course. Except that when you liked someone, you wanted them to be okay.

"Now tell me," Sharon said over dessert a little later. "Alan's been very secretive. But he stays out late a couple of times a week. Do you think he's got a sweetheart? Does he talk to you about these things?"

"He's been very vague," I replied, "but I think he may be seeing someone special."

"Oh, I hope so." She paused a moment. "Are you married, Balzer?"

"I was married for twenty years. But three years ago after a terrible heart attack…"

"Oh, and so young. How awful."

"Yes, it was awful. I'm sure your loss was awful for you, too."

"Yes." She nodded slowly. "But you find ways to cope." She smiled at Alan.

"I had a friend," I said suddenly, "a woman named Ann. She had a sister who left home at twenty. That left Ann alone with her parents, who hadn't gotten married till they were over forty. So they were in their sixties by then. Ann felt she had to stay home and take care of them. Of course, they lived until their mid-eighties. By the time Ann allowed herself to date, she was forty-five herself. She did finally marry at forty-eight, but naturally, she'll never have children. She felt she was doing a good thing by staying with her parents, but she gave up her whole life to do it."

"Greater love hath no man than this, that a man give up his life for a friend," Sharon said, apparently quoting some scripture.

"Then why shouldn't it be the parent giving up *their* 'life' for their child?" I asked.

There was silence for a moment. Then Sharon said slowly, "Do you have any children?"

"No."

"I didn't think so."

"I think your friend Ann stayed with her parents because she *wanted* to," said Alan, "not because she *had* to. There's a difference."

Sharon smiled again.

The dinner was over by then, and I only stayed fifteen more minutes, as I could clearly see Sharon had had enough of me for one evening. But she smiled sweetly and shook my hand at the door as I left. I couldn't read Alan's expression as he said goodbye.

Alan didn't call the next day, or the next, but he did show up again on Wednesday night. He kissed me and hugged me when he came in the door.

"Oh, what a scene you caused," he said, plopping down on the sofa. "My mother cried for half an hour, asking if she was ruining my life. It took me forever to convince her I liked things just the way they are."

"Why would you want to convince her of that?"

"Because she was crying."

"So if I start crying, you'll begin sleeping over?"

Alan looked at me.

"I took acting in college. I can be very convincing."

"My mother isn't acting."

"I think you stay with your mother because you're comfortable there. She does the cooking and the cleaning, and you don't have to face any adult responsibilities."

"Always being there for someone *is* an adult responsibility."

"What are you going to do when you're fifty-five or sixty and your mother dies? You'll be all alone in the world."

"She'll be all alone *now* if I leave her."

"I think most men with wives and children still manage to call their mothers and visit. And there's no reason she can't try to make a few friends and stop forcing you to be her only social support. Aren't there any nice people at your church?"

Alan was quiet a moment.

"I want you to start sleeping over one night a week."

"I don't want to have sex."

"I didn't say anything about sex. I just want to feel you beside me all night. Your mother still has you six nights a week. I'm not asking for the world. But I need you over here at least one night a week."

Alan looked at the floor.

"Even God needs a break once a week," I reminded him.

"What will I tell my mother?"

"Tell her anything you want."

"She'll think I'm having sex if I stay out all night. I couldn't do it."

I was growing irritated by this point and wanted to say, "Are you wearing diapers? Be a man!" but instead I said, "Can't you sneak over and then sneak back home early in the morning?"

Alan continued looking at the floor. "Maybe," he said slowly. "Maybe."

Two weeks later, on a Wednesday night, Alan stayed for his first sleepover, or as we decided to call it, his "sneakover." We had our usual evening together first, then Alan rode his bike back home, made a show of going to bed, and then sneaked back over after his mother fell asleep. We debated about whether to have the sneakover at his place or mine and finally decided it wouldn't feel like a grown up thing to do unless we did it at my place.

As we were cuddling with the lights out, still wearing our underwear—and Alan's Mormon underwear certainly took some getting used to—I said, "I'm going to tell you a bedtime story."

"Okay." Alan giggled, holding my arm tightly across his chest.

I proceeded to outline a scenario from one of the porn DVDs I'd had to review the night before. I was determined not to let this evening be just the equivalent of a preteen slumber party.

"Oh, you're mean," Alan said, but he laughed anyway.

He could feel my dick growing hard against his backside and he pressed his ass up against me, but there was no official fondling. Still, I thought it was a step forward, and I fell asleep contentedly.

I wondered over the following weeks if all this effort was worth it. Alan was clearly damaged goods and would never be "normal." Of course, who in this life wasn't damaged in some way? But even if we did start having sex, there was no guarantee we'd be compatible in the first place. Besides, there'd be so much pressure to perform well after all this foreplay it was bound to be a little disappointing.

But I liked the guy. Even if Alan were no good in bed, I could still get my rocks off with other men, as I was doing now. I just wanted to be with him. As irritated as I was with Sharon, I had to admit she'd raised a good son.

One Sunday when Alan showed up, I said, "Want to help me with some work?"

"What do you need?"

"I've got another DVD to review."

"I don't know," Alan said cautiously. "I've never watched porn before. I've heard it's addictive."

"Well, I have an endless supply. You'll never need to go through withdrawal."

"I don't know."

"If you get too excited, you can go in the bathroom and beat off by yourself. I won't take advantage of you."

Alan looked a little dejected at that, which made me smile. "If you want to understand the gay world, or be comfortable in that world, you have to at least be exposed to a little porn."

Alan looked at the floor. "Okay," he said softly.

He giggled during the first ten minutes of the movie, but then his brows furrowed as he began to concentrate. We didn't talk the whole time. I was taking notes and didn't pause the action as I might normally have done. I wasn't sure Alan would be able to take an entire DVD, but he sat on the sofa next to me till the very end. Then, without a word, he strolled off to the bathroom. I smiled.

I felt a brief flash of guilt, though, wondering if I was corrupting a pure man. But I believed in God, too, and that he gave us sex to make our lives better. What was corrupt was making people feel like dirt when they were sharing one of the few real pleasures in an otherwise difficult life.

Alan had told me a little about his theology, how sex was reserved in the hereafter only for those who'd lived the most righteous lives. When Alan came out of the bathroom now, he looked worried, so I said, "If it's okay for the righteous to enjoy their bodies for eternity," I said, "why is it a mortal sin to do it now?"

"Because we *are* mortal. The rules are different here."

"Money can be used selfishly, to buy a hundred pairs of shoes, or to feed the hungry," I said. "Books can be used to elevate the mind, like *To Kill a Mockingbird*, or they can be like *Mein Kampf* and used to hurt people. Sex can be used to degrade people or exercise power and control, or it can be used to make people feel good and loved. Anything can be used positively or negatively. But just because something *can* be used negatively doesn't mean the thing itself is necessarily bad. Don't throw the cum out with the smegma."

Alan looked at the floor, his brows furrowed. "Maybe," he said.

"How do you feel right now?"

"I don't know. I've fantasized about some of those things before, so I don't know that it's any worse to watch it." He paused. "It was oddly satisfying, and yet…"

"And yet…"

"Somehow it made me think that just getting off vicariously would be something lesser than real sex."

"Duh."

"That it would be a Telestial act rather than a Celestial one."

"You're getting too Mormon on me."

"The bottom line is it makes masturbation less satisfying than it used to be."

"Oh, don't give up jacking off. Even after you start having sex with others, it's still fun to have sex with yourself. There's no sin in loving yourself, too."

Alan looked at the floor. "I wonder."

But I felt we'd made a breakthrough, and every Sunday night thereafter, I asked Alan to "help" me with my reviews. It felt like the world's longest seduction, but we were both enjoying every minute of the attempt. Alan was perfectly aware of what I was doing, but he seemed quite willing to let me pull him slowly along.

I thought things were going pretty well, but one Thursday evening, Alan knocked on my door, on an unscheduled visit. "My mom almost caught me coming in this morning. I don't know if I can sleep over anymore. It would be too awful if she found out."

"Alan," I said calmly. "What's the worst she can do if she learns you're sleeping here?"

"She might say something about me being 'confused' rather than gay."

"So she makes some remarks. That's it?"

"Well, she also might just ignore it and keep it to herself."

"Great. She shuts up and minds her own business."

"Well…"

"None of that sounds all that terrible to me. It's not like she can disown you and move to Acapulco."

"There's another possibility."

"What's that?"

"She might feel sad."

That one threw me for a second. Then I said slowly, "Well, *I'll* feel sad if you don't sleep over. And *you'll* feel sad, too. That makes it two to one. Is it right for her to make us sad?"

"I'm not sure that's fair," Alan said. "If it makes forty million Germans happy to make six million Jews unhappy, do the numbers make it right?"

That threw me a little, too. "I just think at some point we have an obligation to live our own life. It's an absolute obligation. God gave you life, and it's not yours to throw away. You have to live while you're alive."

"Well, it's not like my life is meaningless now. I have a good job. I earn my way in the world. I read interesting books. I do good things for people. I have a good friend I really care about. That's not nothing, is it?"

I waited a moment before speaking. "I value your friendship. But I've had a partner before. And I know from experience that loving someone so much they're your best friend *and* your lover is better than having someone who is just a friend. *Or* just a lover. There's certainly a place for platonic friendship, but there's a place for sexual love, too. Adam and Eve had that. The prophet in your church has it. It's not something to toss aside like so much garbage."

"Gandhi was celibate the last couple of decades of his life."

"Are your apostles abstinent? Does your church teach that abstinence is a higher way?"

"Only for gays."

"You said that even God has sex with his wives in heaven. Are you higher than God?"

"If there is a God," Alan mumbled. "Why would a god feel the need to torture me all my life?"

"This is crippling your chance at happiness, with me or anyone else. Are you sure you're not using your mother as a gatekeeper or a scarecrow? I think maybe you're just avoiding taking responsibility for your own ambivalence about intimacy."

"I've been trying."

"Fifteen-year-old boys try harder than you. You're an adult. You can't stay a shy teenager your whole life."

Alan started crying, and though I was irritated with him, I moved over and hugged him.

"Please help me," he said, still sniffling. "Please love me enough to put up with me."

We lay down on the bed for a few moments so I could hold him close.

I decided to try a new approach over the next several days. I'd been keeping Alan to myself, a little selfishly perhaps, but I thought maybe exposing him to other gay men might help him feel more comfortable about "our world." I hoped working in the gay bookstore was helping, too. He'd gotten some propositions there, but he hadn't made any friends among the regulars. I wanted Alan to have a larger network of gay men in his life.

On Tuesday night, I usually played cards with a few friends, so I asked if I could bring Alan along. They were all anxious to meet "the Mormon." We chatted as we played, saying nothing particularly deep or meaningful. But then, normalcy was what I was hoping for.

"I'm going on a cruise this summer," said Ted, one of the guys. "But I'm telling everyone I meet there I'm fifty-five instead of forty. They'll all be saying how good I look."

"My last vacation was back in 1995," said David, another card player. "I mean, 2005," he corrected, slapping himself playfully. "I hate when I get the wrong decade."

"Well, I know the year," said Peter, the last in our group. "Jared and I just celebrated our seventh anniversary."

"How's the itch?" asked Ted.

"You have to be careful when you say that to a gay man," David countered. "That could mean so many different things in our community."

"I bought Jared an expensive new shirt for our anniversary. He likes to look good. In fact, this is one of his shirts I've got on now."

"You wear his clothes?"

"All the time. I hate to do laundry, and he insists on doing his own. So I wear his things, and he has to clean them."

Alan giggled.

"He complains and asks why I always wear his clothes."

"'So I can feel closer to you,'" Alan suggested.

We all chuckled at his efforts. I was glad he was taking part in the conversation.

"Good answer," said Peter. "You have the makings of an annoying lover."

The evening continued in much the same way, with unexceptional banter over a meaningless card game. Alan seemed to enjoy himself, and I asked the others later if it would be okay to add him to our Tuesday nights. They all consented, and soon, Alan and I were seeing each other three nights a week.

The sneakovers continued unabated, even after Sharon discovered one night that Alan was gone. She went into a fit the next day, claiming she thought Alan had been murdered and she was up the rest of the night worrying.

"But she didn't call the police, did she?" I asked. "Or call the hospitals? She didn't ask for a name, did she? She's not stupid. She knew where you were."

I was impressed Alan managed to avoid explaining where he was on his nights out and managed to keep coming despite his mother's displeasure with it.

But a few weeks later, Alan stopped by with some bad news.

"My mom has a lump in her breast," he said gloomily. "She goes in for a biopsy in a couple of days, and it'll be another week or so before she gets the results. I need to be at home with her."

"She'll be okay," I said softly. "Even if it's cancer, they'll get it in time."

"You understand why I can't stay, don't you?"

"Sure. I understand."

I did understand but was still irritated, though I felt like a heel for my reaction. Obviously, Sharon couldn't have implanted the lump to obstruct us, but it somehow still seemed calculating. Was there even a lump at all, I wondered? Or was all this just a ruse to get her boy back?

I'd wondered if Sharon might start having dizzy spells or some other minor problem if she ever discovered Alan was sleeping over, but breast cancer was another thing. If it turned out to be serious, Alan would be gone for months. While I did truly love him, I realized with surprise, I wasn't sure I was up to waiting for him.

"Do you love me?" I asked.

"What?"

"Will you come back to me later, no matter how things turn out with your mother?"

"Yes," Alan said. "I promise I'll be back."

Either I called Alan or he called me every night over the next several days, but we only talked a few minutes before I could hear Sharon calling out for him in the background.

But as it happened, my own life got busier because my friend David from cards was starting work on a calendar that would be used as a fundraiser for local HIV charities. He was a photographer and wanted to take photos of naked men.

"Charity work can be so trying."

I decided to get involved, and over the next couple of weeks, David set up three photo shoots. The first model stood in the hot tub at David's house. I got to apply the foam in the shoot.

David also had a private and jungly backyard, so he decided to use that as a setting for his second shoot with a handsome math instructor from Loyola. I got to apply the baby oil this time.

The third photo shoot took place in an out-of-the-way voodoo temple in Bywater, just down the river a few blocks from the Marigny. It turned out the temple priest was good looking enough to be right for the photos, so I was happy to attend this session as well and got to light the candles.

What with card night and the library and the porn DVDs and the photo shoots and my occasional forays to the baths and to the bars, I realized I could still lead a perfectly happy life without Alan, if it turned out he saw the cancer as divine retribution and slowly faded out of my life.

I still *wanted* Alan, though, and was pleasantly surprised when he showed up at my door one Monday evening a couple of days later.

"How's your mom?"

"She's fine. The lump wasn't cancerous."

I pulled Alan inside and gave him a hug and started kissing him. He kissed back enthusiastically.

"You need any help with your reviews tonight?" He smiled.

"Sure." I waved for him to follow.

We went upstairs and kicked off our shoes, falling down together on the sofa. "So what've you been up to?" Alan asked eagerly.

I took Alan's feet in my lap and started rubbing them while I told him in detail about the photo shoots. When I finished, he pulled his feet away and sat up stiffly.

"I don't want you doing things like that anymore," he said. "You're *my* boyfriend."

I looked at him with what I hoped was tenderness and said, "I'm not a priest, you know."

"I am," Alan said sadly. "Since I was sixteen."

"You could come along on some of the photo shoots if you like. I'm sure David would be okay with that if the models are."

Alan stared at the floor. "I can't keep living my life by proxy." He laughed rather bitterly and shook his head. "You know, in our temples, we do baptisms for the dead by proxy, and marriages by proxy. I don't want to live my whole life as if I'm not really here in person."

"So what are you going to do about it?"

"I think we're going to skip the porn tonight."

He pulled me close and kissed me slowly. Then he took my hand and placed it on his crotch. I squeezed softly, and he moaned. We pulled away for a moment and looked in each other's eyes. Then he nodded gently and pulled me close again.

Two and a half hours later, Alan rested his head on my arm as we lay in bed. He held my other arm against his chest. It was the first time I'd felt the hair on his chest without the buffer of his Mormon underwear.

"I hope you understand I'm going to be insatiable for a while," he said.

"I'll make the sacrifice," I replied. "For your sake."

Alan laughed. There was a lightness to it this time.

We lay there quietly and slowly fell asleep in each other's arms.

I was anxious to see Alan's reaction in the morning, when he'd realize more fully what had happened, but he was smiling as we ate a bowl of cereal, our first breakfast together ever, since he hadn't felt the need to sneak back home at the crack of dawn.

"My mother may have been the reigning queen all these years," Alan said, "but I'm not going to be the prince-in-waiting anymore."

"No, you're officially a queen now, too."

I got ready for work, and we went downstairs together to leave. "I'll see you for cards tonight," I said, kissing Alan as I locked the door behind us. We both climbed on our bicycles but gave each other one last long look before getting ready to take off in different directions.

"I learned something last night," said Alan.

"What's that?"

"There definitely is a God," he said. "And he does love me."

"He's not the only one." I paused and then grinned. "The Sierra Club loves you, too. I keep my promises."

Alan smiled, blew me a kiss, and started pedaling off. I smiled, too. Forty-two and thirty-eight suddenly seemed very young.

I made my way through the Quarter, heading Uptown, and watched people hosing down the sidewalks as I passed.

I had a lover now. It *was* better than just having a good friend. It *was* better to have both, and to love the man you were having sex with.

I waved at the men cleaning the rubber floor mats outside the bars and kept on, still smiling. I was going to have a good day.

And I was going to see Alan again tonight.

I started whistling an old disco tune and then, giggling happily, offered up a prayer of thanksgiving into the early morning sky.

Ronnie and Clyde

"Hey, Clyde." My lover looked up dreamily into my face after we made love. "You want to be Friar Tuck or Maid Marion?"

"I can't be Robin Hood?" I asked.

"No. I'm Robin Hood."

Ronald always liked to choose his role first. If we went out for Mardi Gras as a Confederate couple, I'd be the soldier and he'd be the belle. His brown hair came down to his shoulders, so he was really the better choice, and he practiced how to sit so that his bloomers wouldn't show. Sure, he had a moustache, but at least he didn't have a beard as I did.

Every time we'd go out together in costume, his was always larger or fancier than mine, one that would get the most attention. As dungeon master and slave, he was the slave because he got to wear more accessories. He was the sheep and I was the shepherd. He'd be the dragon's head and I'd be the tail. It didn't matter if he could be recognized. He just wanted to be seen. Even when we went as ourselves to a party or out shopping or wherever, he was the one who wore the T-shirts saying, "We are not just good friends" or "Nobody knows I'm gay."

We'd met while walking in opposite directions on Royal Street in the French Quarter. Ronald wore a National Coming Out Day T-shirt and strode right up to me. "I have a family reunion this weekend and refuse to go alone. They're all Mormon. Will you go with me?"

"I'd love to." I was Mormon, too, had recognized him from one of the last Single Adult events I'd participated in, though he didn't remember me. Ever since the reunion, I saw Ronald do whatever popped into his head, especially if it was showy. And now a new idea had just popped in.

"So, Robin," I said, "when do we start stealing from the rich?"

"Next Friday," he said. "I overheard two women while making groceries at Schwegmann's. One is leaving town next weekend. I followed her home."

"Not at all creepy, dear."

"There's a sign that says 'Beware of Dog,' but she didn't buy any dog food, and I didn't hear any dog when she opened the door."

"Just the same, you go in first."

"Don't you trust me?"

"Well, there was that time your brother came to town…"

"That's not fair. How was I supposed to know you couldn't tell us apart in the dark?"

"Maybe if you'd just remembered to tell me he was coming to visit—"

"Okay, okay, so you got a black eye. I'm sorry. But this is different. And you know how much we need that money."

I sighed and pulled Ronald closer against my chest. "All right," I said. "But I'm scared. I know people get away with this all the time, but this is *us*. I don't want to go to jail."

"Maybe they'll put us in the same cell together. Think of the fantasies we could act out."

We'd both lived sheltered lives, but we weren't *that* naïve.

The first burglary went well. The occupants were gone and had either taken their dog with them or didn't have one after all. We took the stereo, the VCR, the microwave, and a radio, leaving the TV. We certainly didn't want to be mean or anything. Just as we were leaving, though, Ronald gasped.

"What?" I whispered. "What's wrong?"

"Look!" He pointed to a glass cabinet filled with china and crystal.

"We can't sell that stuff, can we?" I asked doubtfully.

"Oh, I don't want to! I want to keep it!"

"Ronald! You know we're not doing this for us. I only agreed because we said all the money would go to charity."

"You're right." Ronald looked a moment longer at the case. "I'm sorry." But still he looked.

"Come on. Let's get out while we can."

"We couldn't take just one piece of crystal?" he asked. "Kind of as a commission?"

We sold the appliances without any problem and immediately divided the money into three piles. We sent the first of it off to North Carolina to fight Jesse Helms, the second pile to the ACT UP group in New York, and the last of the money to Greenpeace. We sent it anonymously, of course, not wanting to take credit for money that wasn't ours. We also didn't want to attract attention. My tips as a waiter at La Peniche weren't sufficient to justify large donations, and Louisiana wasn't the place to be if Ronald wanted to earn much as an elementary school teacher.

Besides, we were still saving for Ronald to go to law school. He'd graduated with a 3.9 in English before getting his teaching certificate and had become more interested in law over the three and a half years we'd been together. Something about knowing merely having sex with each other could put us in prison for five years kept him continually thinking about the justice system.

Our next three burglaries, every two weeks apart, were in different neighborhoods since we didn't want the police to start patrolling any one area too heavily. We again stuck to things we could sell easily, and we divided the money three ways each time, sending the money to different organizations for each burglary.

The soup kitchen Uptown got some money, as did the Project Lazarus hospice, Amnesty International, the NO/AIDS Task Force, a national cancer research organization, the NAACP, a "foster parents" group helping children in Central America, the Helen Keller institute, and

ACT UP/San Francisco. We also put aside eight dollars of our own money each week, but that didn't go very far toward our donations. I started to accept we *had* to steal if we were ever going to make a difference.

I remembered when I was seven, I'd wanted to do something special for my dad's birthday. I saved up for two whole months, picking up pennies and nickels I found on the street, watering the neighbors' flowers for a nickel, saving up my tooth fairy money, and anything else I could think of, and I bought my daddy the best collection of bubble gum baseball cards available for $1.14. I knew my daddy watched baseball all the time. He'd not only like the cards, but he'd see how much I loved him since I wasn't just letting Mom write my name on her gift.

When I saw the cards in the trash the next day, I realized people lied when they said, "It's the thought that counts." I knew my daddy could never be satisfied with a $1.14 gift. It took real money to make people happy.

When I was twelve and started earning a little of that real money, I of course immediately began paying tithing. I was so proud at the end of the year to make an appointment with the bishop to discuss my tithing settlement. It amounted to $67.

I'd read the promises in the Bible to those who tithed, and I was shocked to hear the bishop tell me, "This is a busy time of year for me, son. You shouldn't be wasting my time over this trifling amount." Even charitable institutions, even *God*, wasn't impressed with paltry figures.

I'd learned more about giving in the years since but had seen little to change my mind. A few select people could be easily satisfied, but to give anything worthwhile for most people truly did take money—money I never had. Just once I wanted to give something meaningful.

Hopefully, we wouldn't be caught for a while.

A week after our last burglary, I woke up in the middle of the night and found that Ronald wasn't in bed. I saw a light on in the kitchen and went to see if he was feeling okay. When I reached the door, I stopped and stared.

"What's that?" I demanded. Ronald was sitting at the table with his chin on his hands, leaning forward and staring at a crystal goblet.

"Isn't it pretty?" he asked.

"Where did you get that?" I snatched it up and looked closely at it.

"I slipped it in my jacket pocket at the last house." He looked at me pleadingly. "It was just too pretty."

I threw the goblet into the sink, where it crashed with a crackling roar in the 3:30 a.m. stillness.

"Why did you do that?" Ronald shouted.

"No stealing for us!" I said, trying to keep my voice low. "We won't steal for us!"

Ronald shut his mouth firmly and headed for the bathroom. I heard the lock click.

There was an "I'm sorry" card on my pillow the next evening, and Ronald set aside an extra ten dollars that week of his own money. The next two houses we burglarized let us contribute to research for autistic children, the Sierra Club, the National Gay and Lesbian Task Force, multiple sclerosis research, the Louisiana Gay Political Action Caucus, and Covenant House for teenage runaways. We both compiled a new list of possible organizations to donate to, and every day the list grew longer.

"We'll be breaking into houses for another year just to give to each group *once*," Ronald moaned.

"Should we stop spreading out the money and focus on helping maybe *one* group achieve something?" I asked.

"But which one?" he moaned. "Does a child in Sri Lanka deserve to eat, or does a blind woman in Morocco deserve to see? Does a child in Kentucky deserve to read, or do two consenting adults deserve to love each other?" He huffed in frustration. "How do we make a decision like that?"

We decided to keep splitting up the money. We almost decided to burglarize more homes, but though we were getting better and faster at it, we realized we were still very much amateurs, and we continued getting more and more nervous at every siren we heard, even when we didn't have any stolen goods in our possession.

I remembered another time I was a kid, and the son of a school board member used to steal my lunch money once a week. He said he was saving to buy a larger tank for his fish. One time, the creep was facing me with his hand outstretched. Looking over his shoulder, I could see the teacher approaching.

I stalled as long as possible, hoping the teacher would catch the bully in the act, but another kid called to her at the last second, and my money was soon in the guy's pocket. He realized then what I'd been up to and punched me in the stomach, but he never did get caught. His luck kept on throughout that long, miserable year.

Ronald and I had also been incredibly lucky, for a good while now. I knew it couldn't last much longer.

But it did for seven more houses and twenty-one more contributions. We doubted any of these groups would condone our methods, and I began wondering if it was fair to force our "targets" to make these donations. In a free country, didn't people have the right not to be nice? Over three years Ronald and I had contributed $1,100 of our own earnings to various groups and donated many hours to mailings, protests, letter writing, and a walkathon.

We tried to encourage others to get involved, but if they didn't, that was their right. Were they *obligated* as people owning fifteen movie videos to help a twenty-three-year-old woman enter a drug rehabilitation program before she gave birth to another baby?

But people were going to be robbed anyway, I told myself. At least we were using the money for good causes.

One evening, I found myself unable to concentrate while we watched a movie at the Pitt. We hadn't bought any popcorn, but a viewer during the previous showing had left a partially filled box on the seat that staff hadn't cleared away.

I'd reached in to grab a few pieces before I realized what I was doing.

On the way home, Ronald tried to talk about the movie, but I didn't respond.

"You okay?" Ronald asked.

I couldn't answer.

"Clyde?"

"How can we justify going to see a movie if we're stealing other people's VCRs?"

"It was only a dollar movie."

"Still."

We were quiet the rest of the way home, but we stopped going to dollar movies and to the bars once a week to meet friends. We increased our personal donations by $5 a week, plus put a little more aside each week for law school. The sooner Ronald became a successful attorney, the sooner he'd have more legitimate money to donate.

Yes, we knew what people said about lawyers.

Two more burglaries and six charities later, even though we were only eating generic food and no treats, were watching TV in the dark, and were keeping the air conditioner off completely despite the increasingly warm days of late spring, I felt guiltier than ever about stealing. When another waiter at the restaurant told me his house had been burglarized, I felt so angry I almost yelled at a customer who took too long to make up his mind.

"Let's lay off for a while," I told Ronald that evening, intending to stop completely but afraid he wouldn't go for the idea without a little weaning first.

"We still have two whole pages of charities we haven't gotten to yet."

"They can wait."

"But what if someone dies of leukemia because we waited? What if—"

"They can wait. Let's lay off for a while."

But I wondered. What *if* we could help by giving just that last tiny amount needed to make a breakthrough somewhere?

If it were that close, I told myself, within a week other people would have made up for our small missing donation. And yet it didn't feel fair for me to put the burden on others and just wash my hands of it. I felt guilty no matter what I did.

I escaped my thoughts by reading two used paperbacks I indulgently bought at a garage sale for twenty-five cents each. I'd found a quarter on the sidewalk and felt I could splurge.

Three weeks passed without any burglaries. On one of the nights we'd normally have broken into someone's home, we felt so restless we had to get out and decided to take a walk through the Quarter, looking in the windows of antique shops on Royal Street.

"Look at that crystal," Ronald said, pointing.

"Nice." We looked at the set of glasses on a dark wooden table. "And look at that oil painting." I pointed.

"Ooh."

We walked to another shop. And then to another. And to yet another.

"$2000 for that little table." Ronald pointed.

"I see it."

"How can people pay that when others are starving?"

"They're preserving history," I said. "Isn't that important, too?"

"Yes, but look at that bed. $10,000. Think what we could do with $10,000."

"If I have to think of money another minute, I'll scream."

We walked home through the Quarter and into the Marigny, crossing the street once when we saw a suspicious looking guy, and then watched TV until we fell asleep.

Another month went by during which I tried not to think at all and was surprisingly successful. Before I knew it, our fourth anniversary was approaching, and I had something positive to occupy my mind.

What should I give Ronald for our anniversary? A piece of crystal? Maybe he'd like a contribution made in his name. An agreement to start up with the burglaries again.

What would he want, that I could live with as well?

Most of our friends had stopped seeing us over the past few months. Since we wouldn't allow ourselves luxuries like popcorn or movies or going out dancing, we'd become boring. Maybe we were already boring before but had been able to mask it.

Perhaps we were only boring now because we couldn't talk about TV shows or what Ricky Graham did in his latest skit at The Parade. Maybe it was because we were no longer planning new Mardi Gras costumes as they were. Or maybe it was because we couldn't even talk about the weather anymore. All we could talk about was supporting causes.

We didn't have to worry about the cost of including friends in our anniversary celebration.

About a week before the big event, I was working at the restaurant when a group of six guys from the Gay Men's Chorus came in after rehearsal for a late dinner. They laughed and joked and talked loudly, attracting the attention of the other patrons. When I set a dish down in front of a man dining by himself, he smiled up at me and motioned toward the table of six men.

"I love coming here on Tuesday nights," he said. "Those guys always look so happy. It makes me feel good."

I nodded briefly in response and returned to the kitchen, unable to get the comment out of my mind.

My shift ended too late for me to dare walking home, but recently I'd begun feeling so guilty for spending money on cab fare that I risked it anyway. Ronald was already in bed when I got in, of course, and as I crawled in beside him, I whispered, "It is you, isn't it, Ronnie? You're not your brother, are you?"

"No, but I'll give you a black eye anyway for waking me up."

"Oh, I'll make it worth your while." I started rubbing his thigh.

"It's too late. Can't we do this in the morning?"

But I knew what to do and kept him up for another hour. He finally rested in my arms with a contented sigh.

The next day, I bought an "I love you" card for Ronald and left it on his pillow.

"What's that for?" he asked. "You could have just told me. You didn't have to spend a dollar fifty."

I said nothing, and the next day, I left another card on his pillow. "What are you doing?" he asked. "I appreciate it, but you better not leave one each day up until our anniversary. I'd rather you put the money in our fund."

But I didn't. I left a different card every day, and though Ronald looked disgusted at first, he didn't complain any more, resigned rather than pleased. Trying to decide on a gift, I remembered the Christmas after my dad lost his job. He and Mom went to the Thrift Center to buy clothes for my brother and me.

Mom had a friend at church who worked for Hershey and got all the old chocolate, so we each received a stocking full of Halloween candy. I didn't bother any longer getting gifts for my dad, and I wrote a poem for my mom. It wasn't the "magical" Christmas in the midst of poverty that people claim is so wonderful and special, but it wasn't our worst.

Yet.

My family had taken a long walk in the cool air that evening to look at Christmas lights, and Mom told us stories about Christmas when she was a kid. When we got home, we found that someone had been in the house while we were out. The TV was gone, along with my dad's rifle and my mom's costume jewelry. Mom sat down and cried while Dad drove off somewhere. My brother and I just looked at each other, and then I handed Mom one of my candy bars.

She looked at me, cried some more, then took the candy bar and headed for the kitchen. We spent the next hour breaking up expired candy and making chocolate chip cookies.

I couldn't figure out what to get Ronald, so I finally gave up trying to make it meaningful. On our anniversary Monday evening, I suggested we stop briefly at a couple of bars, just to say hi to people.

"Okay," said Ronald, "but only for a few minutes. If we spend any money, I'll start looking for our next house to hit."

We stayed out for half an hour. As I looked around at everybody drinking and laughing, I noticed how different the scene looked from the way I remembered it. These people had smiles on their faces, but many of them didn't really seem happy, and being here in the bar didn't appear to be making them any happier.

Maybe we'd made the right choice after all. I'd taped an index card over my desk at home with the words, "Happiness isn't the goal. Lead a meaningful life." There were days the words felt as fake as any in the Book of Mormon.

Ronald and I certainly weren't the happiest people in the world, but we did at least have a sense of purpose. That had to count for something. For more than sitting at a bar drinking because you didn't want to be at home.

"Come on, let's go," I said after a while, and Ronald agreed immediately.

We walked past another bar on our way home, and there was a group of several guys laughing as they came out, a few still holding drinks. A single, grim man went in.

"God, that man's in pain," Ronald said as we walked on.

Maybe he was, I thought. Maybe he really did need companionship this evening. Perhaps he needed sex or simply to feel life in the people next to him, to remember that he was alive, too. Surely, there were other needs besides food and medicine. Didn't quality of life count for anything?

But then, wasn't being able to read, or having cataracts removed, exactly the kind of thing that brought quality of life to people, too?

"I bet these people could have just as much fun organizing a protest rally together or working at the Task Force," Ronald said. "They'd still be able to meet people, and they'd be doing something useful, too."

"Is it wrong to relax?" I asked. "Maybe that's a legitimate need, too."

"How can we sit back and have a good time when people are suffering and dying all around us?"

I thought for a moment before guessing at an answer. "Because maybe we'll die ourselves if we don't."

"What?" He stopped and stared at me.

"I want to help, and I'm going to help, but isn't the key word 'help'? It isn't 'solve.' Weren't we born to live, not to give up our lives? Is it so wrong just to want to live?"

"You're being selfish." Ronald didn't use a mean tone. "It's natural to be selfish, but we've got to rise above that."

"How many people have we helped?"

"I don't know. Not enough."

"How many people have we hurt?"

Ronald's face grew hard and he started walking again. "We haven't hurt anyone."

"How do you know? Maybe someone we robbed was trying to fight cancer. Maybe we crushed her spirits and instead of going into remission, her cancer kept progressing. Maybe someone was just on the edge between doing something good or something bad, and we pushed him over to the bad. Maybe—"

"Maybe, maybe, maybe. Maybe we just took some money from people who needed to be giving to charity instead of enjoying life all by themselves and ignoring other people's pain. 'There must needs be opposition in all things.' Maybe they needed to feel a little pain of their own."

"Maybe so," I said. "But why is it wrong for others to inflict pain but okay for us?"

"Because we're helping more people than we hurt."

"The end justifies the means?"

"Yes!"

"So in order to prevent the spread of AIDS, we should quarantine everyone who is HIV positive? That's a good end, isn't it? Think of the millions of lives we could save."

"That's different, and it isn't practical anyway."

"And our ability to cure every disease and feed every hungry person is?"

"If we want to live Celestial lives, we have to give more than Telestial donations."

"But aren't we just recreating Satan's plan? It was his idea to force people to be good, while Christ said they should have a choice." I paused. "And we left the Church because we don't believe its doctrine, right?" We believed Robin Hood fables.

We walked the next several blocks in silence, neither of us speaking, even at home. Ronald went off to the bedroom while I opened the hall closet to get his gift. I knew he wouldn't like it, that I'd made the wrong choice, and I wondered if this would be our last anniversary.

Perhaps that was best. I did love him, and I admired his conviction, but I couldn't live like this any longer. I wasn't strong enough or bold enough to do "something meaningful."

Even if what we were doing was a sin, though, and a crime, might destroy our marriage and suck all the joy out of life, allowing myself to be damned helping others might *still* be a worthwhile goal.

What was I supposed to do?

I sat at the kitchen table, staring at the wrapped box in front of me. Maybe I should put it back. Maybe—

The bedroom door opened and Ronald came out with a plain, unwrapped box in his hands. He set it on the table next to the other, but neither of us said a word. We must have sat there in silence ten minutes before he slowly pulled his gift over and halfheartedly ripped off the paper.

In the box were two crystal goblets. It had been a long time now since Ronald had asked for any luxuries. He looked at them carefully for a moment, slowly put them in the cabinet, and then went back to the bedroom.

I waited a few more minutes and then opened my package. Inside was a note signed and dated the day before which said, "I'll do anything you want me to do."

I looked toward the bedroom door. That note was still saying "the end justifies the means." He was just changing what "the end" was.

Perhaps therapy was what we needed to get over the past several months. I'd ask him tomorrow if he'd go with me.

Ronald was already in bed, facing away from me. I turned off the light and slipped in beside him, but we didn't touch. I lay awake, unable to sleep, and a few minutes later,

Ronald asked, "Should we pay them back? I still remember all the addresses, you know."

"Do you realize how much money that is?"

"Law school can wait another year or two."

"Do you think it'll be enough?"

There was a long moment of silence.

"No."

"Then…"

"I knew from the start it would come to this, Clyde. I've known you a long time."

"Are you mad at me?"

"I love you."

"Maybe if we get more involved with Lazarus House or the soup kitchen or with Amnesty International, we won't have time to worry about burglarizing."

"I already signed us up."

I smiled in the darkness. "Go to sleep, Mother Theresa."

I'd heard she was a bitch in real life.

Ronald turned toward me. "Not for another hour yet. This is our anniversary." I felt his toes brush against mine.

"Hey, mister," I said, "thanks for four good years."

He said nothing but reached for me in the dark.

The End of the World

I woke up at 2:00 a.m. to the sound of glass shattering on the kitchen floor. I jumped out of bed, threw on my slippers, and ran to the kitchen. Steve was standing at the sink with broken glass about his feet.

"I'm sorry," he said. "It slipped. I feel so weak."

Thinking he had an ulcer, Steve had taken four ibuprofen over the past day and a half for an allergy headache rather than aspirin. He'd started having bloody bowel movements, and last night, he'd thrown up some blood and had me pick him up from work because he didn't feel able to drive home.

"Well, go back to bed," I said. "I'll clean this up."

"Thanks, Bryan."

I swept up all the glass I could find and then went back to bed. "Sorry about that," said Steve. "I hate to cause you trouble."

"If you feel weak, just ask me for help," I said. I gave him a light kiss.

"Okay."

I felt a certain tenderness toward him now that I didn't always feel. This was my third relationship so far. The other two had ended in divorce, and I was never quite sure this one wouldn't as well. As a former Mormon, my dream had always been to find a soulmate I could spend the rest of my life with and then all of eternity, but the actual, real people I ended up "marrying" always seemed as flawed as I was.

Their biggest flaw, of course, was how often they were dissatisfied with *me*. There was no adequate way to put up with that fatal weakness.

But that little moment in the kitchen gave me hope again. Maybe we'd be okay. Maybe the Mormons would finally accept gays. Perhaps Steve would convert and we'd have a temple wedding. Maybe love really would triumph over oppression and weakness and imperfection. I sighed and walked back to bed.

I just hoped Steve hadn't aggravated his ulcer too much.

Despite my worries, I was soon back asleep. Then at 6:00 a.m. I awoke again to the sound of shattering glass in the kitchen. I threw on my slippers again and ran back, irritated. "Why didn't you wake me up to get you a glass of water?" I demanded as I entered the kitchen. Then I saw Steve lying on the floor with broken glass around him.

"Are you okay?"

"I hit my head." He reached to the back of his scalp and showed me blood on his fingers.

"Good grief. Let's get you back in bed. You're going to the emergency room today."

"Oh, I don't want to, Bryan." He sat up slowly.

"You've obviously lost a lot of blood internally. You need to go."

"Okay. In a little while. Just help me back to bed."

I was due for work at the University of New Orleans library at 8:00, so I would've had to get up within a few minutes anyway, but now I reset the alarm for 8:00, and when it went off, I called in sick. It was Tuesday, and Steve taught Portuguese at Tulane University on Monday, Wednesday, and Friday. He was off today and slept late, which he rarely did.

"Could you get me some apple juice?" Steve asked around 9:30, nudging me in bed. I got up and filled a plastic cup with juice. Steve drank and then dozed off again, and I soon followed his example. Unlike Steve, I slept late whenever I could. It was one of my weaknesses which Steve tolerated calmly. It was related to a serious bout of depression I'd had a couple of years before I met him. Ever since, even though I felt back to normal in most ways, I still slept more than I had before. Steve was practically a workaholic in comparison but had never once tried to make me feel I was wasting time in bed. I appreciated that.

My first serious episode of depression had come during my two years as a missionary twenty years earlier. I was having no success baptizing and decided it must be a result of my depravity. I was still a virgin, but God knew my soul was corrupt. I wanted to prevent my family from finding out the awful truth and one day almost stepped deliberately in front of a bus. My companion stopped me.

He'd asked what was wrong, and I broke down crying and told him. He'd hugged me and assured me God still loved me. He never told the mission president my secret. But a few years later when I wrote and told him I'd come out and been excommunicated, he wrote back calling me to repentance, and we'd never spoken again.

As well-adjusted as I felt I'd become in the years since, my latest round of depression had again been sparked by the Church. The First Presidency issued a public statement explaining in detail why gays should never be allowed to marry. Part of me had been angry, but part of me had also been worried. What if the Church was right after all, and I'd allowed myself to be deceived? After two decades of gay sex, I was probably irredeemable. One day while rimming a man, I suddenly felt very degenerate, and I tipped right over into the abyss.

With a little psychiatric treatment and a great deal of effort, I worked my way back to a semi-normal state. Part of me hated religion for making me feel worthless, another part was angry at myself for allowing them to do so, while yet another part always wondered if maybe it was true.

Steve and I finally got up around 10:30, and he headed to the living room to watch CNN. I read a little. We had a light lunch around 12:30, but still Steve didn't want to go to the hospital. "Let's wait a while," he said. "Maybe it'll pass."

Finally, around 1:30, he agreed to go but had to take a bath first. He took so long he wasn't ready until 3:00, and then we climbed into Steve's car. I'd been without one for five years now. Steve and I had been together almost four. He drove me to the bus stop every morning and picked me up from work in the evening, but he never let me drive his car.

It wasn't so much that he didn't trust me as he knew I hated to drive. He didn't much like it, either, but when I made an occasional offer to take over on a day I could tell he'd had enough, he always said, "I made the choice to keep a car. I'll take the responsibility."

"Be careful, Bryan. I can't handle an accident now, too."

We lived just off Manhattan Boulevard in Harvey on the Westbank of New Orleans, so I drove down to the Westbank Expressway. Then I turned left and rode up the high bridge over the Harvey Canal and got off at the Barataria exit. West Jefferson hospital was only a few blocks away. "Watch out for that car. You're driving too fast."

I drove up to the emergency room entrance, and Steve slowly climbed out. There were a few benches near the door. "I'll wait here till you park," he said.

I drove until I found the garage and parked on the third level. After I walked back to the emergency room, Steve and I walked through the doors together. Miraculously, there was no one in the waiting room, so the triage nurse took Steve right away. I sat and waited for them to finish. I could see the nurse take Steve's blood pressure and prick his finger to blood type him. Then Steve walked over to registration and a few minutes later came to sit beside me.

Around 3:50, Steve's name was called, and he went in back. Several more people entered the waiting room, and I watched as they were seen. A four-year-old boy who needed stitches on his forehead never cried at all. An obese woman in a wheelchair complained she wasn't being taken care of fast enough.

Around 5:30, I started getting antsy and walked over to a vending machine to buy some tiny chocolate chip cookies. Steve was always tolerant of my being fifteen pounds overweight, too, although he kept himself in perfect shape. I deluded myself into thinking he'd finally get to fully enjoy my body after the Resurrection. I threw the package away when I was finished and watched the news on TV.

Just before 6:00, the triage nurse came up to me. "Did you want to go back there with your father?"

I nodded. "Yes. May I?"

She ushered me through a door. Steve was sixty-one and I was forty-three, so other people occasionally mistook us for father and son. I didn't figure it was worth correcting the nurse given the circumstances. In another hallway now, I asked a nurse where Steve was, and he led me to an examination room. A Dr. Rubinstein was talking to Steve.

"We'll get some blood in you right away, and you'll start to feel better. Then we'll see if we can stop the bleeding."

Dr. Rubinstein instructed a nurse to give Steve two units by fast infusion and two at a normal rate. "He's lost maybe ¾ of his blood, so we need to get some into him right away."

Three-fourths of his blood. Good grief.

The thought came into my mind that spilling your own blood was the only way to atone for the most serious of sins, murder. I'd heard my Elders' quorum president say one day during Priesthood meeting that homosexuality was next to murder. I couldn't help but wonder if God was making Steve pay now by losing his blood.

Then I remembered that after the Resurrection, we'd have a perfect body of "flesh and bone," though not "flesh and blood." There'd be no blood in a perfected body. Maybe losing his blood just made Steve holier.

"Mr. Williams," the doctor addressed Steve, "you're in critical condition, and you'll be staying in intensive care tonight. We'll get a scope in here and see if we can find the source of the bleeding. Do you smoke?"

"No," Steve answered glumly.

"Drink?"

"A glass of wine with dinner."

"Drugs?"

"No drugs. Except four ibuprofen the other day."

Within a couple of minutes, the first two units of B negative blood was already infused and more was coming. Steve had two IV's, one in his left arm and one in his right hand, plus other plastic wires attached to his chest. "Everyone's been very good," he told me.

He held my hand, and I felt surprised. Steve would never even kiss me in the car when he dropped me off at the bus stop in the morning, afraid someone would see and beat me up after he left. I remembered when my first partner years ago had gone to the hospital for a kidney stone, and he told everyone there I was his cousin because he was afraid he'd be treated badly by the staff. But Steve didn't seem to care about that, and I was glad.

A few minutes later, a nurse came in with an endoscope, and Dr. Rubinstein turned to me. "I'm going to have to ask you to leave, but I'll come talk to you when I'm through."

I nodded and walked back to the waiting room. *American Idol* was on TV. I'd be suffering almost as much as Steve, it appeared. Then I felt guilty for joking like that, even to myself. I watched some of the other people in the waiting room. Steve had complained about an ulcer since we first met, saying he'd had symptoms for years. We knew we'd have to address the issue eventually, but we hadn't imagined it would be in such a dramatic way. It looked like we'd caught it in time, though, and that was good. Around 7:45, the doctor came out and motioned to me.

"I'm not finished," he said, "but I have to ask a very direct question."

My stomach turned. This wasn't HIV related, was it? I'd been positive for six years, but we'd always been very careful and didn't think we'd ever put Steve at risk. I'd die if I found out Steve's problem was related to my HIV status.

"How much does Mr. Williams drink?" the doctor asked.

"Half a glass, maybe a full glass of wine at dinner."

"That's it?"

I nodded.

"Well, it appears he has esophageal varices caused by severe liver damage, so I had to ask. We'll check his blood for hepatitis, too. I'll talk to you again." He turned and walked back through the door to the other hallway.

Liver damage. Hepatitis. We weren't nearly as careful about Steve not infecting me with something as we were about me not infecting him. I'd been immunized for hepatitis A and B, but maybe Steve had C. I felt guilty for worrying about myself at a time like this and quickly dismissed the concern. If it did turn out I'd been infected with C, there were probably treatments if it was caught this soon. I only hoped the same was true for Steve, that his liver wasn't irreparably damaged. I'd dated an alcoholic once who died of liver failure a couple of months after we broke up, found dead in his bed four days after he failed to show up for work. I knew this could be serious.

9:00 came and the doctor hadn't returned. How long did it take to do an endoscopy? I began worrying more. Ten minutes later, a nurse who'd been in the examination room earlier walked by. "You want to go see your friend?"

I walked back to the examination room. Steve had just one IV now, with saline solution. The other IV consisted of a few inches of tubing with nothing attached. "Como está?"

My two years as a Mormon missionary had been in Portugal, so I spoke Portuguese as well as Steve did. We usually spoke maybe half an hour a day in Portuguese. Steve preferred Brazilian Portuguese, so there were some differences, but we got by. We'd met in a bar four years ago, but as soon as Steve said what he did for a living, I was instantly intrigued. The language turned out to be only a small part of the overall attraction, but it had definitely been the initial one.

"Bem." Then he continued in English. "They gave me Demerol, so I was out when they put the tube down my throat. They saw some bleeding vessels and tied them off, so I should be okay now. Maybe they'll let me go home."

"He said intensive care tonight. I'm sure you're not coming home just yet."

Steve insisted I ask the nurse, so I did. "We're waiting on a bed in intensive care, but if we can't get one, you'll be here in the emergency room overnight."

Steve was tired and didn't talk much more. I stood nearby until I began to grow tired around 9:45. I felt bad for being less than 100% dedicated to making my partner feel comfortable. Maybe gays really weren't cut out for marriage, as the prophet claimed. I adjusted Steve's pillow. "I need to go home and take my pills and feed the cat, but I'll be back tomorrow morning."

"Okay."

I went home feeling exhausted even though I hadn't done anything. After I fed the cat and cleaned the litter box, I ate a sandwich and took my pills. I tried to stay on a 12-hour schedule, taking my pills around 6:30 in the morning and 6:30 in the evening. I'd been on the same cocktail for six years. My T cells were at 1200 and my viral load still undetectable. I had to take other pills for diarrhea and nausea, but overall I was healthy. I wondered what was in store for Steve if his liver was bad.

I went straight to bed after dinner and woke up at 8:00 and called in sick again. Then I drove Steve's car to the hospital, arriving around 9:00. He was in the Coronary Care

Unit, I assumed because they didn't have a bed in Intensive Care. He was lying in bed looking miserable.

The IV in his right hand was still unattached to anything, but Steve continued to receive saline solution in his left arm. He had a blood pressure cuff around his right arm and wires still attached to his chest. Monitors continually read his signs.

"How do you feel today?" I asked.

"Okay. But I need to go to the bathroom. Can you help me out of bed?"

I took the blood pressure cuff off, which gave him a little more mobility, but it was still hard to navigate with all the other lines. There was a potty chair a few feet away, and I helped Steve over to it. "I'll go guard the door," I said.

I stood outside the door for a few minutes. To my relief, Dr. Rubinstein soon came up. Maybe we'd get a few answers. "How's our friend?" he asked.

"Okay. He's on the potty right now."

"I'll come back in a few minutes."

But Steve seemed to be taking a long time. A few minutes later, I saw Dr. Rubinstein walk off. I could only hope he'd be right back.

Finally, Steve called and I went back in the room. There was a terrible smell, worse than that of a normal bowel movement, but I pretended not to notice. I closed the lid on the potty chair, but not before I noticed what looked like a cup's worth of tar inside. There was clearly blood still passing through his system. I could only hope it was old blood and there was no further bleeding.

I helped Steve back into bed and told him Dr. Rubinstein had passed by and should be back. A few minutes later, a student nurse from Charity came in and emptied the potty. "You know," she said, "there's a real toilet right under here." She showed us how to pull one out from underneath the sink. "If you can make it a few feet further, this one flushes."

A heads up might have been nice, but I knew they were busy.

The student nurse left and I stood beside Steve's bed. "Your color's better today."

Steve sighed. "I just hope we make it to San Francisco." Steve had lived there a year with his last partner, Frank, until his partner was killed in a car accident. Then Steve had moved back to New Orleans. But he'd made a couple of good friends in San Francisco and missed them both. We planned to move there together in another year, as soon as Steve could retire. He seemed to hate New Orleans more every day, and I was more than willing to move if it would help his mood.

He was becoming more of a Jekyll and Hyde every day, sweet at one moment and nasty the next. He grew angry if I suggested Prozac or therapy. "I have *real* reasons to be depressed," he insisted, "not some stupid chemical imbalance or self-indulgent pettiness. *I'm* not the one worried about God. I know there's no God." I'd always thought he was giving in to negativity and simply needed to focus more on the positive, but now I wondered if his physical health was causing the mood swings and was beyond his control. Having faced the same judgment when I was depressed, I should have known better.

"We'll make it."

Around 10:30, a woman announced that Visiting Hour was over, so I left and sat in the lobby until 2:00 when the next visiting hour was posted. I hadn't brought a book and tried to doze until then.

Steve was sitting up in bed when I walked into the room. "They did another endoscopy," he said, "but they didn't see any bleeding."

"That's good. Has the doctor come in to tell you if you have hepatitis or not?"

"No."

I turned on the TV and we chatted idly, watching judge shows for a while. After 3:00, Steve was allowed a clear liquid diet, and a nurse brought in some tea, broth, and Jello. "*You* must be hungry, too," Steve said. "You want my Jello?"

"I'm good, but thanks."

Steve had always been a Jewish mother when it came to food. No matter how nice our dinner had been, right before bed, he insisted we have dessert. Even when I was trying to diet, he'd hand me a saucer. "You don't need to lose weight," he'd say. "You're beautiful just the way you are. And you should enjoy life while you can, so have a piece of cake." He often complained *he* didn't enjoy life anymore since Frank died, but he wanted to make sure I did. I felt like a weak substitute for Frank, thinking that if Steve really loved me, he'd perk up more, and since he didn't, he must be merely tolerating my presence only because it was better than being alone. But on the weekends when he wanted to listen to music while he worked and I dozed, he'd always take a CD from my collection and make sure we were listening to something I liked.

After the meal in the coronary care room, I helped Steve once to the toilet that swiveled out from under the sink, and we waited for the doctor, who never returned. No one came to kick me out, so I sat there through three visiting periods. Finally, around 8:30, I glanced at my watch, and Steve said, "I know you can't wait to get out of here. You can go."

"I need to take my pills."

"You could have brought them with you if you'd wanted." I kissed Steve, who turned away, and then left.

The next day was Thursday, and I called in sick for the third day in a row. I was back at the hospital by 8:30, surprised to discover that Steve looked worse. "My back," he moaned. "I coughed last night and pulled a muscle. It hurts every time I move. This place is a torture chamber." He'd had a cough for several days. It was because he thought he had a cold or bad allergies that he'd taken the ibuprofen in the first place. It seemed unfair that something unrelated to the bleeding should be causing such discomfort now.

I helped Steve to the toilet again and stood guard at the door a few minutes. When he called, I went back in and helped him to bed. "I've got to check out," he moaned. "If I stay here another day, I'll die."

"Okay, you can check out."

"They won't let me."

"You can do anything you want. You want me to tell the nurse you're checking out?"

"Yes."

I went to the desk and told a nurse, who said, "Well, it's up to him, but you know, the insurance won't pay if he checks out against medical advice."

Good grief. I went back to Steve's room and asked for his insurance card. I called the number on the card and eventually talked to a girl named Libby. She said if the stay had been approved, and it had, they would pay. So the nurse was just trying to scare us. I told Steve and he had me go back to the nurse to get the paperwork started.

Another nurse came in to take out his IV's. She had just removed one when a man came in with an ultrasound machine. He was scheduled to do an ultrasound of Steve's abdomen. "Should I do it?" Steve asked me.

"Well, it'll have to be done eventually. If they do it now, your doctor should have the results available when you see him next week." Steve had made an appointment for next Thursday before all this started.

He agreed and lay back in bed for the test, which basically involved some cold jelly on his stomach and a wand pressed against it for a few minutes while the man took pictures. Then the nurse took out Steve's remaining IV line, and he finished dressing. A man came with a wheelchair and took him downstairs to a little office, where a woman told Steve the hospital bill for two days came to $19,000, and because West Jefferson was out-of-network for Steve's insurance, his part of the bill came to $5,000.

"Great," Steve grumbled, "and we just had one extra uncovered test added to the bill." He sent a glare my way. "So much for moving to San Francisco. We'll never be able to afford it now."

As nice as Steve could be when he tried, and as well as we usually got along, his depression had become increasingly difficult to take. I'd resisted marrying him because I didn't want to get sucked into a black hole, but he'd brought me flowers every week, took me to movies, and told me in Portuguese how much I meant to him after he thought he'd never find another man to love.

He seemed a genuinely decent man who deserved happiness. I wasn't sure I could give that to him, but I wanted to try. If gays were damned to Hell, the only happiness we had any chance of enjoying was during this life. I didn't want Steve to be damned after he died *and* damned now. He should have at least some minimal, temporary happiness. But the smallest things still sent him over the edge, and a $5000 bill wasn't a small thing.

I drove us home, and Steve took a bath as soon as we got in. I could hear him moaning, and as he dressed, he said, "My back's killing me. It feels like a knife. What am I going to do? I can't stand it."

"You can't take aspirin or ibuprofen, and acetaminophen is processed by the liver, so if you have liver problems, you can't take much of that. Maybe just one pill."

"Can you go get me some?"

"You need anything else?"

"How about a heating pad, too?"

"I'll be back in a few minutes." I was off to Walgreens, bought what we needed, and came back.

I'd only just handed Steve a pill with a glass of water when we heard a gagging noise. The cat was throwing up. Rocky did that about once a week, and it always drove Steve crazy. Now, he was livid. "Get rid of him! Bring him to the SPCA! I can't take any more! I can't take any more!"

"I'll clean it up. It's not the end of the world."

"No! Take him to the SPCA! I mean it! Take him now!"

Steve had been on edge for several months, so anxious to leave New Orleans he found fault with everything, including the cat he'd had for twelve years. It was Frank's cat and Steve's last tie to the man. Steve and I had separate bathrooms, and Steve insisted on keeping the litter box in his own bathroom and cleaning it himself. I knew he hated cleaning the box and had offered several times to do it, sometimes simply doing it without a word. But Steve always told me he was afraid I'd catch something because of my HIV. It was his responsibility, he said, and I wasn't his slave.

He'd talked before about getting rid of Rocky, so I knew he meant it this time. I looked up the address of the SPCA on Japonica Street and got directions on Mapquest. Then I took Rocky and left. The cat hissed and hissed when I brought him into the building, and I felt bad to leave him, but what could I do? We had no friends to take Rocky, and even if we could find someone through the paper who might accept a twelve-year-old cat, we had too much on our plate now to be fielding calls. Feeling like a murderer, I left the cat carrier with the SPCA and came home. We were both horrible people.

Would Steve throw me away just as casually one day?

I was really here for his sake, not mine. He let me live with him rent-free. I only had to help with utilities and food, but the absence of rent let me catch up on the $40,000 I still owed in student loans. Despite that, I'd been happy as a single man, and the financial situation wasn't what led me to move in.

After I turned down Steve's first two proposals, he threatened to kill himself. "Life has no meaning without a partner. If Frank's dead and you don't love me, I have no reason to live."

"But I do love you."

"Then move in with me and make me happy."

I suggested Wellbutrin again and group therapy, and he almost walked out of the apartment. "You always say you believe in doing the right thing, even if the Mormons think you're a sinner. If you'd just move in with me, I'd be happy again."

Then he played Scott Joplin's "The Entertainer" for me on his piano.

My mind told me it wouldn't work, but he was so sweet when he wasn't in the depths of despair that I wanted to make him feel better. So when Steve proposed a third time, I gave in. He cried for fifteen minutes after I said yes.

Steve was a little calmer when I came back today from the SPCA, sitting on the sofa with the heating pad. "My back is still killing me, and I have all this fluid in my abdomen. What is *that* from?"

"It's probably from all the saline solution they kept pumping into you. It'll go away eventually."

"Well, I can't stand it. I feel bloated and obese. Look it up in your medical book."

I did and found that he probably had ascites, which could be caused by liver problems. He'd never had it before, so it seemed odd he developed liver ascites the same day he went to the hospital. It was *probably* from the IV. But still, it was worrisome. Maybe his liver was going downhill fast.

"Could you boil some water for my tea?" Steve asked.

I did and brought the tea back to him.

"Could you fix me some grits?"

I did, and he made his way to the kitchen to eat. "Could you go to the store and get me some back rub? Make sure it doesn't have aspirin in it."

I went back to Walgreens and bought some Capzasin. Steve tried to eat soft foods during the next couple of days. I called in sick Friday as well and made a few trips to the store for Jello and soup and sherbet. I made tea and grits a couple more times. Steve wanted some yogurt but was afraid to eat any dairy products because he still had residual phlegm from his coughing.

On Sunday, he asked me to buy him a box of Kleenex. When I got in the car, the motor wouldn't turn over. I went back in the kitchen. "What's wrong?" Steve asked.

"The battery's dead."

"Oh my god. Oh my god! The battery's dead! What are we going to do? What are we going to do!"

"I don't know how to put a battery in, so I guess I'll have the car towed to Sears."

"Oh my god! Oh my god!"

"It's not the end of the world, Steve."

"It *is* the end of the world. It *is* the end of the world. What if I need to go back to the hospital, Bryan? What are we going to *do*?"

"There are taxis and ambulances. I'll just go get a new battery. It's really not the end of the world."

"It *is* the end of the world."

It reminded me of Steve's attitude at the bowling alley each Wednesday evening. We played purely for my benefit because Steve hated any and all sports. But he knew I liked bowling, and he wanted to please me. Yet he didn't bowl all that well, and if after three frames he had fewer than twenty-five points, he'd give up and not even aim his next few balls. If he somehow miraculously bowled a strike or a spare after that, he'd perk up and try again, but just the slightest lack of success sent him into apathy, a fraction more, into despair.

I knew it was easy to get depressed when you were feeling sick, and with his predisposition toward it, I'd have to work hard to keep him focused.

I called a tow truck, which cost $65, and Sears put in a new battery for $100. It was expensive and inconvenient but not a catastrophe. I wished Steve wouldn't overreact to everything. Things were hard enough without that. I had to keep up my own spirits, too. On the way home, I bought some tissues for Steve.

I went back to work Monday, and we made it through the next few days. I photocopied some sheet music at the library I knew Steve would like. He cheered up briefly when he saw the music and went straight to the piano, but his back hurt too much to sit on the bench for long, and he started crying instead.

Steve's back slowly improved over the next couple of days, but the fluid remained around his waist. On Wednesday night, the day before his appointment with his doctor, Steve started pounding his stomach. "I can't take it! I can't take it! I'd rather die than have this bloating! What will I do if the doctor doesn't want to give me something for it tomorrow? I can't keep suffering like this! What will I do?"

"Insist he give you a diuretic."

"What if he won't?"

"Then we'll go to the emergency room at Touro." We'd found out that Touro downtown was covered by his insurance. "We'll leave right from the doctor's office and go straight to Touro. But he'll give you a diuretic. You'll see."

Steve was in a foul mood the rest of the evening. I tried to take it in stride, knowing he was both uncomfortable and scared, but it was wearing me down. We watched a DVD, and I went to bed at 10:00 while Steve stayed up to worry some more. He'd always stayed up later than I did to prepare for class.

Our normal routine was to come home from work, then I'd prepare a salad, feed the cat, and cut us each a slice of cheese while Steve prepared the main meal as we watched *Family Feud*. We usually ate while watching the *McNeil-Lehrer News Report*. Then we retired to the den, where we watched a movie we'd checked out of the library. We saw several at home each week, and on Fridays we went to the movie theater to see another.

But after Steve tucked me in bed, he'd grade papers or read his class notes until around 1:00 before coming to bed himself. We'd then cuddle the rest of the night. Since he came home from the hospital, though, Steve was cuddling his pillow and not me. Was he realizing he didn't love me after all? Would he just keep me around till he got better and then tell me things weren't working out?

I felt guilty for worrying about myself but also wondered if breaking up might not be for the best. If we broke up, though, Steve might slip even further into depression. It didn't seem fair to make Steve's happiness my job, but I did love him and wanted him not to suffer.

I suppose it was natural in times of stress to revert to Mormon ways of coping, a kind of unconscious bias that felt instinctive but was really learned. My mind told me these things were a test from God, and my heart believed though I simultaneously knew it was a lie. Why would God need to test a man He'd already condemned?

If God was involved at all, perhaps this illness was a gift. If Steve and I both passed the test, the experience might bring us closer together. Maybe God was deciding if gays finally deserved marriage, and we were one of His test cases.

The scriptures showed numerous times that God could be reasoned with and convinced. The very episode of Sodom and Gomorrah which so often condemned us demonstrated God's willingness to negotiate. Was God looking especially hard at Mormon relationships to see if He would change His mind on homosexuality, the way He'd already changed His mind about blacks?

Believing there was nothing out "in the universe" felt delusional, and believing anything religious at all did, too.

The lyrics from Mary MacGregor's "Torn Between Two Lovers" flashed through my mind.

Thursday, I left work at noon to take Steve to his 2:00 appointment with Dr. Strother. Steve had me wait in the car because he didn't want the doctor to know he was gay. I didn't know why that mattered now when it hadn't before. Was this another sign he was pulling away? He came back an hour and a half later.

"What's the verdict?" I asked when he slowly climbed into the car.

"He didn't say."

"What about hepatitis? Didn't he have the results from the tests? He's affiliated with the hospital."

"He didn't have any results. He told me he thinks it's a duodenal ulcer. He wants me to go in for blood work and a CAT scan next week."

"No results from the ultrasound?"

"No results at all. I didn't want to tell him how to do his job."

"Did he give you a diuretic?"

"Yes, he gave me a prescription for a diuretic and one for stomach acid." He read the prescriptions. "Spironolactone and omeprazole."

"Well, at least you got the diuretic."

"I have a return appointment in two weeks."

"Two more weeks before we hear any results. Sheesh."

"I know it's hard on you, Bryan. I'm sorry."

"I just don't want *you* to have to worry two more weeks without knowing anything."

"If I have the diuretic, I'll be okay." He leaned over and gave me a kiss. "I couldn't do this without you. Thank you for being there."

"I'll always be here for you."

Steve looked down for a moment then, and I didn't know if he believed me or not. Finally, he just said, "Let's go."

We headed to Walmart, where Steve had his prescriptions filled. Then we went home, and he took his pills right away. He smiled for the first time in days and pulled out the Scrabble board. "You need to have some fun," he said. "You can't just take care of me all the time."

He was hopeful at first that the diuretic would work, but after two days when he still hadn't lost any of the fluid, he began to despair again.

"It's not working. I'm not peeing any more than normal. I'm never going to lose this fluid. My life is over. I can't go to work like this Monday."

"It'll be okay. It just takes time. And if this diuretic doesn't work, we'll get you another."

"But I don't see the doctor for two weeks! I can't wait two weeks!"

"We'll call him up Monday if you haven't started losing the fluid. He can call in a prescription for you."

"Well, my life is over. We're going to have to break up. You'll need to move to San Francisco by yourself."

"Your life isn't over. The fluid will go down. You're going to be fine. You may have hepatitis, but we'll deal with it. Naomi Judd has had hepatitis for fifteen years and she's doing fine."

Steve seemed only mildly placated but instantly got in a better mood later when his friend Andrew from San Francisco called. He'd called a few days ago as well and wanted to check today on Steve's progress. In the last several days, Steve had called his sister, Alice, and his mother, both in Chicago, for moral support, and even his first partner who he hadn't been with in thirty years, a man named William living in Baltimore.

Steve seemed to thrive after talking to other friends and family but didn't care much what I said. He still complained and moaned whenever I tried to say something positive, though he'd perk up if another friend or relative said the same thing. It made me feel stupid, but I at least took comfort knowing he was getting support from somewhere, even if not from me.

By Monday, Steve had finally started losing some of the fluid around his waist, so he didn't call the doctor. He seemed to lose it more quickly when he walked, so I tried to get him to take a walk after dinner each evening. "But if we walk," he said, "you won't have time to see your movies. I know you like to watch your movies."

"They can wait. Let's try to get this bloating down."

On Tuesday, he went in for blood tests, and on Thursday, he went in for a CT scan.

"I had to drink two shakes of barium sulfate. It was awful. Then they injected me with an iodine dye. It made me need the bathroom bad. I barely made it to the bathroom after the scan and had bad diarrhea. I was afraid I'd poop in the car on the drive home. But I'm okay now."

I was still taking it all one day at a time. I didn't know Steve's condition yet, so I couldn't accept or deal with the possibilities. Everything was still on hold. I missed the calm, quiet times we had listening to music, playing Scrabble and backgammon, or watching *I Love Lucy* when we weren't watching movies.

Despite his one attempt to play, there was a steady, morose atmosphere. Steve used to lie against me on the sofa, but now he sat apart. He pulled away when I tried to hold him in bed. Although we weren't officially married, I knew I was committed to him "in sickness and in health." He'd stood by me with my HIV, and I would stand by him with his hepatitis.

"Sorry I've been neglecting you these past couple of weeks," Steve said Thursday night. "It's always me, me, me. I'll pay attention to you soon. We'll have sex this weekend."

"It's the least of my worries," I said. That was true enough. Steve had made it clear early on that sex was an essential part of a relationship, but he was so terrified of my HIV that we didn't have much of a sex life. He was a bottom, so he wouldn't fuck me, with or without a condom, and he was afraid the condom would break if I fucked him, so we didn't do that, either. He was afraid he'd get HIV from even a drop of precum if he sucked my dick, so that was off the table as well.

We ended up doing the same exact thing every single time. He'd jack me off and then I'd suck his dick. I liked performing oral sex, of course, but not as my only sexual activity, and having a handjob as my only form of release was far from satisfying. But he was willing to accept me despite his constant fear, and he wouldn't do that unless he truly liked me. Right?

Still, I felt like a leper most of the time and wasn't sure how such a limited sexual relationship could work on a permanent basis for either of us, but I also thought that perhaps we could just help each other out for a few years. I'd make sure he got to San Francisco since he might otherwise talk about it without ever doing it. Perhaps we'd break up shortly after arriving, but I hoped he'd find more happiness there. If so, our mutual sacrifice in staying together these few years would have served both of us reasonably well.

Of course, I didn't want a third divorce on my record. Whatever that might say to other prospective partners, it had to say a lot more to God.

Steve hadn't kissed me the past several days, but Thursday night he kissed me good night. Everything seemed possible when he was in a good mood. He was so sweet and considerate it was easy to remember why I loved him. He straddled me in bed and gave me a back rub. "I don't want all the tension to knot up your back. After my back has been so sore lately, I don't want you to suffer like that, too."

On Friday on the way home from work, however, Steve was in a bad mood yet again. He complained about the traffic and how awful it was to live in New Orleans. Wouldn't it be great, he moaned, when we finally moved to San Francisco. Talking of San Francisco *almost* put him in a good mood by the time we reached home. He could go up and down so quickly it was tiring. After putting his briefcase on the desk in his study, he listened to the messages on the answering machine. One was from the doctor's office. "Your test results are in."

"Why didn't they tell me the results in the message?" Steve demanded. "Does that mean the results are bad?"

"No. They just like to talk to you before they give results. They never leave them in a message."

"And now I have to wait till Monday before I hear the results? Why did they call on a Friday afternoon? Don't they realize people work?"

"Well, you didn't think you'd be getting the results before your next appointment Thursday. So how is it worse that you only have to wait till Monday?"

"Because now I'm worrying. You just don't understand."

"You knew you took tests. You knew there'd be results. Now you find out there'll be results. I don't see what's changed in the last five minutes except that you'll be getting the results *sooner* than you expected." I wasn't trying to be contrary. I was trying to find a rational way of calming him down.

That was clearly the wrong tack.

Steve didn't answer but left for the bathroom. I went in the kitchen, set the table, and took leftovers out of the refrigerator to warm up. Steve didn't say anything when he came in the kitchen. We prepared dinner quickly, in silence.

After we sat down to eat, though, Steve said, "I know it'll be bad. And I'm not going to die here in New Orleans. I'm going to live with Alice in Chicago. Well, I'm going to *die* with her. I don't know what you're going to do."

"You don't know the results are bad. It might be okay. Why don't you wait until you hear the results before you drop into despair?"

"I know it's bad, Bryan."

"How do you know?"

"I just know."

"Well, it *might* be bad. But we'll deal with that when it happens. It *might* be okay."

"You think it's going to be bad, too. I can tell. You're detached. You've already given up on me."

"I'm not detached. I care very much what happens."

"No, you're detached. I'm very perceptive."

Well, maybe I *was* a little detached, I thought. His mood went up and down so often I *had* to detach myself a little to avoid the roller coaster ride. But it didn't mean I didn't care.

"I probably have cirrhosis. You think I have cirrhosis?"

"Well, you *might* have cirrhosis. But since you're not drinking any more, even that can be dealt with. It's not necessarily the end of the world."

"You can't even give me some false hope, can you? I need someone who can give me unconditional support, someone who can say, 'You're going to be fine,' even if it's a lie. You're so negative. I need someone positive around me."

I was dumbfounded. *I* was negative? Everything that came out of Steve's mouth was negative. "I'm trying to be positive, but you won't hear it."

"I really need to be with someone else right now, someone who can give me unconditional support. You haven't even hugged me since we got home. If I have to ask for it, it's not worth very much."

"We've been arguing ever since we got home, and you expect me to have hugged you?" An argument *he* started. As usual.

"I'm not arguing. It's just like you to see it as an argument." He paused and actually pouted. "And I *still* don't get a hug?"

I was irritated but went over and gave him a hug. Why was this man so unreasonable all the time? I was a person, too, with my own feelings to deal with. His behavior might be worse now, but it was only a difference in degree, not in kind. Still, I knew I had to forget what I was feeling and concentrate on Steve. He was the one suffering most right now. I felt bad my own feelings had even come into the picture. We finished our meal in silence except for the TV in the background.

Then Steve said, "You still want to go to the concert?" We had tickets to see Josh Groban, tickets bought over two months ago. But we hadn't been out even to a movie since all this started. We certainly hadn't discussed a crowded music venue.

"You up to it?" I asked. "If you're just going to be miserable, there's no point going."

"No, I want to go."

I drove down to the arena by the Superdome and found a parking space on the street. "If the car is stolen tonight, I'll just kill myself now," Steve said. We walked over to the arena and climbed to our seats in section 310. We were on row 5, so there was an aisle in front of us, with rows 1-4 several feet beneath us, and we had an unobstructed view.

"My legs feel better," Steve told me. "Walking always seems to help."

"That's good." I squeezed his arm.

We watched as the entirely white audience filed in, well over half of them in their sixties and seventies. We made small talk, commenting in Portuguese about the many heavy people walking by, some 300-pound girls in their twenties with bare midriffs and low cut blouses showing lots of cleavage. Steve encouraged me to take up bike riding, maybe join a gym. "I don't want you to suffer like that," he said. I was afraid he'd make another comment about his ascites and crater again.

The concert started at 8:00 with Chris Botti, a trumpet player, warming up the audience with some smooth jazz. Steve liked it and seemed to perk up. "I'm feeling better," he said. "I can't be that sick if I'm feeling better, can I?"

"No," I said. "It's going to take a little while, but you're going to be fine."

After an intermission, Josh Groban came out. He sang one song in Spanish and a few in English, but by far the most he sang were in Italian. Even though we couldn't understand him, the sound was glorious, beautiful and exhilarating. Steve was smiling and joking by the time the concert was over. I still felt subdued, remembering how just a couple of hours ago Steve had wanted to break up. Hoping to avoid triggering him, though, I pretended to be cheerful.

I wondered if I might not really be happier alone. It hadn't been loneliness in this life I was worried about. I'd always taken into consideration that only those who qualified for the highest degree of the Celestial Kingdom would be married throughout eternity. But maybe it wasn't so much because gays were "bad" that they wouldn't be allowed to marry. It might simply be that we'd be happier as ministering angels in the hereafter, single forever and unfettered with all the drama of a relationship.

Mormons taught that being single was a curse, but maybe it was a blessing.

We walked back to the car after the concert. The vehicle hadn't been stolen. I drove home, and we shared some cookies and milk before bed. "I'm sorry I was so depressed earlier," Steve said. "You know I love you."

"I love you, too." But I also knew he could ask me to move out again tomorrow. I knew it wasn't his fault for behaving irrationally, but of course it still put me on edge. What could I do, I wondered, to ease his suffering?

Saturday went okay. I read most of the day and vacuumed, while Steve prepared his lessons and graded papers. That night, we went to see a movie. It was awful, and the audience was awful, putting Steve in a rotten mood again. The next morning, he was feeling better, and we had sex for the first time since all this started. Steve suggested it, but he didn't want to come himself, and I basically just hugged him and masturbated myself. I wondered if he was afraid to come in my mouth now, afraid he'd make me sick.

If there was any danger of that, it would already have happened, of course. If I'd contracted hepatitis C from him, I'd simply have to live with it. I didn't regret what little pleasure we'd been able to get from our sex life. I wasn't with him for the sex anyway. I was with him because when he was in a good mood, he was a pleasant guy. I just had to remember that while he was frequently in a bad mood now, this wasn't the way it always was.

And that maybe when we got to San Francisco, things truly would get better and we could be happier. People went through four or six or eight tough years of school to get a good career. Weren't a few tough years of a relationship worth the trouble, too, if you finally got something you wanted? Even twenty or thirty years of a tough, mortal relationship would be worth it if we earned the right to an eternal, happy one.

If heaven was as wonderful as we'd been told all our lives, at the very least, it should have decent mental health counseling. No one made it through life without baggage that had to be dealt with before we could finally enjoy the hereafter.

I knew that the brief moments now when Steve wasn't depressed, he could be delightful, and I held on to the hope that if I put my time in with him here, we'd have more of that later.

I read again on Sunday while Steve prepared for class. At one point, he came in and sat beside me on the bed. "What are you reading?"

"*The Secret Garden* in Portuguese."

"Will you read some to me?"

He lay down in bed with his head in my lap, and I read about Mary following the robin and finding the key to the garden. After a while, I could hear Steve sniffling. I put down the book and held him for several minutes. Finally, he got up, kissed my forehead, and went back to his study.

We went grocery shopping at Walmart later, and after dinner we watched a video of *Far from Heaven*. "Julianne Moore was robbed," Steve said. "She deserved the Oscar."

Monday, Steve picked me up from work as usual. "I've got good news and bad news," he said as I got in the car.

"Yes?"

"The good news is I feel stronger. I took the stairs again today at work instead of the elevator. I can't be all that sick if I'm feeling stronger, can I?"

"No."

"The bad news is the doctor's office called again this morning. I talked to the assistant. She said my test results were in and I had to come in and see the doctor right away. I said I had to work today and that I had an appointment Thursday, and she said that would be okay. But after I hung up, I got really irritated that she'd made it sound so urgent and then just kind of blew me off, so I called back and asked if I could make an appointment for tomorrow. I'm going at 8:45 tomorrow morning."

"Well, that's good. It's terrible to have it hanging over your head. They were wrong not to give you the results while you were in the hospital. And it was wrong of your doctor not to get the results for your last visit. I'm sure it's not awful, but you still need to hear it."

"You don't think I have cancer?"

"No."

"You don't think I'll need a liver transplant?"

"No."

"Well, I feel stronger."

Steve was in the mood for something light this evening, and after dinner, we watched two episodes of *I Love Lucy* and three of *The Golden Girls*. We cuddled when we went to bed.

But the next day was agonizing. I knew Steve had seen the doctor early, but I also knew he wouldn't call to tell me how it had gone. What if this turned out to be HIV-related after all? Steve had told me he and his last partner had sex with other men the last few years of their relationship. I was sure he'd been reasonably careful, but if he could get hepatitis, he could get HIV. Even though you could easily live twenty or twenty-five years with HIV before showing symptoms, it would be devastating news. He hadn't been tested in years, so even if he tested positive now, there was no reason to think I was the one who'd infected him. But Steve would feel certain it was me and the relationship would probably be over.

So when 6:00 came and Steve picked me up from work, I was worried. "How'd it go?"

Steve shrugged and waved his hand in a "so-so" gesture. We walked to the car in silence, and after we kissed, Steve gave me the news. "The doctor said I had cirrhosis, and hepatitis B, but he doesn't know yet if I still have an active case or not."

"Okay."

"And he said there's a growth on my liver. It may just be a mass of blood vessels that isn't supposed to be there or it might be cancer. He said it was probably cancer, and I should take a leave of absence from work."

"But…but you've been having these symptoms for twelve years." I almost felt dizzy. "It seems unlikely it's cancer."

"Why does the doctor want me to quit work when he isn't even sure yet I have cancer?"

"It seems premature." I took a breath. "And mean, to scare you when he doesn't even know."

"He asked me where I got the hepatitis from. How should I know?"

"And what difference does it make? That was just prurient on his part." Homophobia reared its head again.

We talked all the way home and throughout dinner. Steve wasn't sure he wanted any more tests, including the biopsy, and wasn't sure he wanted chemotherapy even if he did have a biopsy and they confirmed cancer. "It's a slippery slope. They want control of your life, and soon you have no quality of life left. And I really wanted to get to San Francisco next year."

"Why don't we go at the end of this semester? I'll get a job that has health benefits for domestic partners, and so you'll have health insurance even if you don't get a job right away." I didn't add "or can't work."

"What if you can't find a job?"

"We felt sure I was going to find one next year. I'll just start looking a year earlier. We won't go till I find something, but I could start looking now. Almost everything is San Francisco has benefits for domestic partners. Whatever I find will be enough for us to get started."

Steve wasn't convinced, but I wanted to show him there were options. He didn't know what to do. Steve had trouble making decisions under the best of circumstances. He'd stand in the grocery for five minutes, deciding which of two types of bread to buy. It took him fifteen minutes to decide which of three movies to see. Now he felt overwhelmed.

I'd support whatever decisions he made about treatment or moving, but I couldn't make the decisions for him. My last partner had full blown AIDS, so I was used to bad news, but with my last partner, I'd known from the beginning it was coming. This was sudden and unexpected.

Finances would be a problem, too. We lived in Steve's house, but the mortgage was more than I could pay by myself. We'd have to move to an apartment. There'd be so many hassles in addition to the illness itself. I could live with a lower quality of life, but it would be hard for Steve, who was used to suburban comfort.

I wondered if this was a test to qualify us for a higher reward in heaven. Maybe gays had so many points deducted for our promiscuity and sex outside of marriage that we needed additional trials to regain points. Maybe that was the whole reason God had inflicted AIDS on so many of us in the first place.

I could hear the homophobia in my own head.

But was it true?

We waited a week before we could go in for the biopsy. Steve had to go in to Meadowcrest one day to preregister, which took two and a half hours, then go in another day for a blood test to see if his blood coagulated quickly enough. If it didn't, they couldn't do the biopsy. Steve still had a cough that came and went. He thought now maybe he'd gotten tuberculosis from the blood transfusion, but I assured him that wasn't the case. He'd drank no alcohol since he found out he had liver problems, and he didn't seem to miss it.

The day of the biopsy finally came, and I took off from work to be with him. "If they do another CAT scan to line up the needle, I might have an accident on the table. Maybe I ought to bring an extra pair of underwear."

"I can carry them in a bag," I offered.

"No, I wouldn't have easy access to them."

"Then you should carry them."

"But there's no room in my jacket pocket. And I don't want to bring a bag."

"Well, those are your only options. Either I bring them or you bring them."

"I'll bring them."

We arrived at Meadowcrest at 6:15 a.m. for Steve's 6:30 appointment. I sat in the lobby with a book and waited as Steve went inside. I read for a while and dozed for a while, but a man outside was using a pressure hose to wash the building, so there was too much noise to either concentrate or sleep. The front door kept opening by itself even with no one near it, so the noise was deafening. Some nursing students sat nearby for a while and then moved on. By 9:30 I was beginning to worry but convinced myself I was being impatient. By 10:30 I was still more worried but told myself to calm down. By 11:30, I knew I had to do something.

I went to the information desk and asked where Steve was. He was in Endoscopy and I could go see him. I walked down the halls, following the signs, and finally rang at a desk. A nurse ushered me in, and I went to a bed where Steve was lying down. He had what looked like a bar code on his forehead, a plastic card continually taking his temperature.

"Tudo bem? They did another endoscopy on you?"

"No, this is just where they brought me after. An Indian doctor did the biopsy."

"It went okay?"

"Fortunately, I wasn't coughing. He wouldn't have done it if I was coughing. He said the coughing is probably from the fluid in my abdomen pressing against my diaphragm. He said the fluid might never go away. He also said I have hepatitis C, not B."

That was bad, obviously, for a couple of reasons. First, C was worse on the liver than B, and second, I'd never had C and couldn't be vaccinated for it. Also, C had a higher correlation with liver cancer.

"He said the mass on my liver was close to my heart, so he could only do the biopsy if I could hold my breath. We practiced a dozen times, him pushing me in and out of the

CAT scan and me holding my breath. They didn't give me any iodine this time. But he finally deadened my abdomen and stuck a needle in me. I didn't watch. But I have to stay here till 1:30 to make sure I'm not bleeding internally."

"You feel okay?"

"I feel fine. Except for this IV. I told them not to put too much saline in me. They're ordering my lunch. I'm hungry. I haven't eaten since last night."

The nurse soon asked me to leave, and I went to the cafeteria. At 1:30, I went back, and Steve was in the bathroom dressing. We went straight home, and things went fine until 2:00 in the morning when Steve woke up with a pain in his mid-chest where the needle had gone in. He moaned and moaned for about thirty minutes and then seemed to be fine. He was fine the next day, too. We were never sure if it was a pain from the procedure or just gas, but at this point, everything seemed ominous.

And Steve continued to be irritable. We'd be watching a video and some scene would set him off and we'd have to stop watching the movie. Or a commercial for some new drug would appear on TV and Steve would change the channel. The teenagers playing in the street outside irritated him. The other drivers on our way home irritated him. The other shoppers at the grocery store irritated him.

Everything I did irritated him.

On Friday morning, the day we expected to hear results from the biopsy, Steve said, "So should I call this morning and go right to work after hearing I have cancer? Or should I wait till I get home and hear a message on my machine to call back and then wait all weekend to hear?"

"Can you call them from work?"

"And then go teach class?"

"Can you call just before you leave work?"

"And then have to face that drive home?"

"Well, it'll be the same thing Monday. You'll have to wait till your day off on Tuesday if you don't want to work the same day you hear results. You can wait till Tuesday?"

"I guess I'll have to. Those bastards."

But there was no call on the machine Friday evening. "It doesn't matter. I know what they're going to say."

If he had hepatitis C, I was afraid his suspicions might be right but didn't want to say so. "Whatever it is, we'll get through it."

We went out to eat as we often did on Fridays but hadn't done much since all this started. But spicy foods and undercooked vegetables gave Steve digestive problems, so he complained all day Saturday about the meal Friday night.

"I don't even care about the cancer," he said Saturday evening. "I just want something done about the bloating and the gas and the coughing and not being able to sleep at night. I want something done about the hepatitis and the cirrhosis. Why can't they start treating those problems? Regardless of the cancer, they know I have all that."

"I think they're wrong not to be treating those things."

"My next appointment with Rubinstein isn't for another month. They're just going to tell me over the phone I have cancer and then make me wait a *month* to see him? They said I could see a Physician's Assistant sooner but not the doctor. What kind of a system is that? Should I try to find a new doctor?"

"First appointments are usually a few weeks away, too. You'd think in the richest country in the world, we'd have a better healthcare system."

"I can't take this anymore! I need to start getting treated now! I don't know what to do!"

"Call Monday and see if something earlier has opened up with Rubinstein."

"And if it hasn't?"

"Make an appointment with the Physician's Assistant."

"I don't want to see a Physician's Assistant!"

"Then call a new doctor."

"That'll still take three weeks!"

"Then your only other choice is to do nothing. You have four options. And that's them." He wanted me to make everything all right, and I couldn't. All I could do was help him make the best decision from the choices available.

But Steve was so angry he turned and left the room without speaking. It was twenty minutes before he spoke again. "I guess we ought to break up," he said. "You obviously don't understand."

I understood that he was scared and mad at the world. I understood he wished he had more options. That didn't make his being irritable much easier to put up with, but I said, "I'm not going anywhere. I'm staying with you."

It was Wednesday before we heard the results from the biopsy, eight days after it had been done. It came the day Steve got a flat tire driving me to the bus stop in the morning. He turned the car around, moaning, and went back to change the tire while I walked half an hour to the bus stop. When Steve picked me up from work that afternoon, he told me he'd gotten a call from Rubinstein. "The flat tire was the good news of the day," he said. "It was just as I expected, Bryan. I have cancer."

It was surreal to hear. I'd half expected it, too, but it was different to have it confirmed. Instantly, I thought of the chemotherapy and the many days of sickness before the inevitable end. But what should I say?

"I'm not upset," Steve said. "I expected it. There's no sense wondering if I should have gone to the doctor sooner. No sense screaming and crying. It's not like it's the end of the world. I have options. I can get treatment."

"That's right. More people are surviving cancer than ever before. And you've been having symptoms for years, so it's obviously a slow-growing cancer."

"He's going to see me next week and we'll make plans. Until then, I'll just go on as usual."

But the usual wasn't so good. Steve still coughed every day. And he still had fluid in his abdomen despite the diuretic. And he had his down moods when he was sure he was going to die. Two days before Steve's next appointment with Rubinstein, he pulled a muscle in his back again from coughing and was in terrible pain. He moaned and yelled all through the night. I felt bad for him, but at the same time I was exhausted and just wanted to sleep. When I suggested he take some cough syrup and he muttered, "That'll just make it worse," I wanted to hit him.

Steve finally went to see Rubinstein again and told me about it over dinner. "He gave me Mytussin for the cough," he said. "It has codeine, so that should help. And he gave me furosemide for a second diuretic. I think it's called Lasix."

"It's to replace the other diuretic, or in addition to it?"

"In addition. He said the cancer is a primary cancer, that it hasn't spread to the liver from somewhere else. He said he would call two oncologists, one to do surgery and one to do chemotherapy. The surgeon wasn't in, and the other said there was no chemotherapy for liver cancer. That can't be true, can it?"

"I don't think so."

"He also said he'd see about getting me on a list for a liver transplant. Was that his way of saying it's hopeless?"

"Of course not. They wouldn't waste a liver on a hopeless case. That's a good sign. You have cirrhosis in addition to the cancer, so they can take care of both problems if they just remove the liver. They'll probably cut out as much of the cancer as they can, and then they'll do chemotherapy while they wait for the transplant. Transplants are very successful these days. You'll be sick until you get one, but then you'll live a perfectly normal life again."

The next day at the library I looked up liver cancer. The book said that indeed chemotherapy was not effective, that the only hope for a cure was surgery, and it was possible in only 30 to 40% of cases. Without that, death came in four to seven months, from liver failure or blood loss from gastrointestinal bleeding. The cancer also spread easily to the diaphragm and the lungs and had to be caught before that. It wasn't great news, but it wasn't hopeless, either. Over dinner that night, I mentioned that surgery was successful in 40% of the cases. "That's not an insignificant number," I said, hoping to cheer him up.

"It's nice that you can be so detached," Steve said. "But it's my life. I can't be so detached."

He wouldn't speak to me during the rest of dinner, and I was bewildered at his reaction. I figured he just needed to feel like a martyr, feel misunderstood and alone. It was irritating, but I tried to assure him I loved him and was not detached.

That night at bedtime, Steve sat on the edge of the bed. "There's something else," he said. "I didn't tell the doctor. It's too embarrassing. I'm not sure I even want to tell you."

"What's wrong?"

"My balls are swollen. I thought it was because we've only had sex a couple of times in the last two months, but I looked on the Internet. I think it's more ascites, fluid seeping into my scrotum. It's grotesque. It's as big as a grapefruit. I'm a freak. I just want to die."

"You've got to tell the doctor. They can drain it."

"I can't go in and spend all day at the hospital. Besides, it's too embarrassing."

"Doctors have seen everything. They can deal with it. It's nothing to be ashamed of."

"Can I borrow your sewing needle? I'm going to drain it myself. I can't take it anymore."

I got out of bed and found my sewing kit and handed Steve my needle. He got some antibiotic ointment and boiled some water to sterilize the needle, and he spent the next hour in the bathroom piercing himself. I couldn't sleep till I knew how he was. He finally came out and said, "I drained half of it. It may come back again, so I'm going to keep the needle for a few days."

This was a downward spiral, with things getting worse from day to day. I hoped the surgery would come soon, that it would be successful. It had already been two months since all this started, and the book said he might only have four months to live, which would give him only two more months. Why didn't they hurry?

The next couple of days continued with the coughing and swelling, but there was a new symptom. Steve became forgetful. It was probably a reaction to the stress, but he'd lose his glasses three times a day, and we'd have to search the house. They were always easy to find, but that didn't prevent him from having a nervous breakdown every time.

He couldn't find an exam for school. He searched through his two briefcases, his boxes of class material, and everywhere else, moaning and moaning about having lost the exam. Finally, he found it in a folder, right where it was supposed to be. Another morning, we were getting ready to leave, and Steve couldn't find his keys. We searched the whole house. He finally found them—in the pocket of the pants he was wearing.

The swelling in his scrotum finally became too much and Steve went one Thursday to the emergency room. They told him it was too dangerous to drain it, that he should elevate his legs more and wear a jockstrap. He bought three pairs on the way home but then said they were too uncomfortable.

The ER doctor said he didn't think the coughing was due to the ascites pressing on his diaphragm but didn't offer any other answer, so we still didn't know what was causing that. All we knew was that Steve was coughing so hard in the mornings he was running to the bathroom gagging. One morning he vomited. Fortunately, just dry heaves.

Steve still managed to get to work and pick me up in the evenings. One day when we got home and he looked through the mail, he said, "I wonder who sent me a card. You didn't tell anyone I was sick, did you? You know I don't want any of your family to know."

He opened the card and read it. I didn't say anything, but I knew it was a get-well card I'd mailed the day before. There'd be a "thinking of you" card from me arriving tomorrow. I'd bought five cards altogether and was going to send one every couple of days.

But Steve didn't say anything tonight about the card and just threw it away. Had I done something wrong? I felt every day that my worth as a human being rested on the success of my relationship with another man. My worth as a spiritual being rested on it, too. It was agonizing every day to wonder if the answer was finally that I was indeed worthless. I had no intention of abandoning Steve, but even at this stage of the disease, he could divorce me.

My last partner, down to a hundred pounds, had kicked me out after reading my journal and discovering I had fantasized about sex with another man. Jerry and I had sex maybe three times a year because he was always so sick, but I'd remained monogamous throughout the relationship. Still, just the thought that I was fantasizing about someone else led him to dismiss me overnight, regardless of his own condition. I could never quite tell if all these failures were my own fault, just a natural result of gay life, or if I was putting up with crap no normal person would put up with.

The next weekend, we flew up to Chicago to celebrate Steve's mother's eighty-fifth birthday. Alice, her husband, their two kids, and their families were there, as well as a few cousins and neighbors. Steve felt miserable and didn't want to go, but he was afraid this would be the last time he saw his family. He joked and laughed with everyone, but as soon as we were alone, he was depressed again.

The following Thursday, Steve had an appointment with Dr. Kellogg downtown at Tulane to evaluate him for a liver transplant. The appointment was late, so Steve couldn't pick me up from work, and I had to catch the bus home that evening, arriving around 8:00. "How'd it go?" I asked.

"You don't want to know."

"Of course I do. What happened?"

"He looked at the films of my CAT scan and said, 'Oh, this is terrible! This is awful! Oh, this is bad!'"

"No." What an asshole.

"He said the tumor was right in the center of the liver and it couldn't be cut out. It's also near some large blood vessels. I wasn't sure exactly why that was bad. I gathered he was afraid some tumor cells would break off and spread."

"Did he put you on the transplant list?"

"He said he'd have his assistant contact me next week."

"They just keep dragging this out."

"He prescribed folic acid for my circulation and epivir for my hepatitis. Oh, and he says I have hepatitis B, not C."

"Good grief. How hard can it be to get that right? Can't they make up their minds?"

"He said all he can offer me is palliative care. He says I have about six months left."

"Unless the transplant comes through."

"If they even put me on the list."

I hugged him while he sobbed. "Don't let me die, Bryan. I don't want to die." I held onto him tightly. I'd watched my mother, grandmother, and grandfather all die of cancer.

"You're not going to die. The transplant'll come through. More people are becoming donors every day."

"It's hopeless."

"It's not hopeless. It'll be hard for a while. But you'll get better." He didn't believe it, and I didn't believe it, but it seemed the thing to say.

"You know I don't believe in God. Frank's dead and I'll never see him again. I'll never see San Francisco again. I'll never see my family again. At least I get to see you for a little while longer. Please don't ever leave me."

A few days later, the whites of his eyes turned yellow. His skin, too. His abdomen and legs were still swollen, and even with the increased diuretics, he wasn't peeing as much. I was worried his kidneys were shutting down. He was supposed to get blood work to check his kidney function, but he wouldn't go because the last phlebotomist had given him a bruise the size of an orange.

One day he got in the mood for canned grapefruit sections, so I went to four groceries looking for them. Another day, he wanted canned kiwi. Fortunately, I remembered the one store that carried it and went back. He had me go to the next room to get his tissues, go to the kitchen to put his juice back in the fridge, put his dishes in the dishwasher for him, go get his socks.

He was becoming incapable of doing even the tiniest things for himself. I wanted him to be stronger so he could make it till a liver became available. Was his depression making him give up, or was the disease just progressing that quickly? I waited on him as efficiently as I could, hoping he'd feel at least a little peace with fewer worries.

But he became increasingly critical. He complained one evening I hadn't emptied the dishwasher yet, and when I started, he complained I was in his way while he was trying to get juice. He complained I didn't fix the blankets on the sofa right, that I didn't clean the bathroom right, that I didn't talk enough, that I didn't clean the table well.

He complained that I drove too fast, I was too slow checking out movies from the library, that I rubbed his feet too hard, that I didn't rub his feet enough. I understood why he was bitchy, but it was still irritating. I felt guilty for being irritated and tried not to show my annoyance, but misery was everywhere in the house.

If this illness was a test from God, it was going to give Steve bad marks right at the end. He might have had an A average going into the final, or at least a high B. Now he'd end up with a C for the course. What kind of omniscient God would put someone in that position? Certainly not a benevolent one. For the first time in my life, the suspicion that perhaps there really wasn't anything else out there at all started feeling more like a fact.

Final exams at the university were finally over, and Steve was almost finished grading them. One of his students, a smart, pretty girl, killed herself just before finals week. Steve was deeply distraught.

One of Steve's doctors had prescribed Xanax for him a few weeks earlier, but Steve had resisted filling the prescription because he felt the pills were only for weaklings. Then Andrew in San Francisco suggested they'd help him sleep better, and as it had been weeks since he'd gotten a good night's sleep, one Sunday he asked me to fill the prescription. I went to three Walgreens before I found one with a pharmacist on duty, and Steve happily took a Xanax that night. Then he had me read more of *The Secret Garden* to him in bed.

Coincidentally, or as a side effect of the medication, that night Steve started hiccoughing. He lay next to me in bed for an hour hiccoughing while I tried in vain to sleep. He hiccoughed with his mouth open, so he sounded like he was being stabbed, and after each hiccough, he would moan loudly. "Try a spoonful of sugar," I suggested several times. "It works with regular hiccoughs. Give it a try."

He finally did and came back to bed without hiccoughs. I sighed in relief and tried to get some sleep. About an hour later, though, the hiccoughs and moaning started again. "I have to get some sleep," I said. "I'm going in the living room."

"Don't leave me, Bryan."

"I've got to get some sleep." I felt like a bastard, but even in the best of circumstances, I was no good without sleep. If I had two or three more months of this, I couldn't face them with a lack of sleep. I still had a job I needed to keep.

I brought my pillow to the sofa and went to the kitchen for a glass of water. There was sugar all over the floor. I spent several minutes cleaning it up and then lay on the sofa. I didn't need a blanket because Steve was so cold all the time he kept the house quite hot. Of course, Steve's discomfort was much more severe than mine. Now, worried I was offending him, it took me forever to fall back asleep.

Sometime later, I heard Steve calling my name. "Come back to bed." Reluctantly, I went to the bedroom. Steve was no longer hiccoughing and after a while I was able to get to sleep. But before long, he was hiccoughing and moaning yet again. "Try some sugar," I said.

"It doesn't work."

"It worked last time."

He went to the kitchen, returning a few minutes later without the hiccoughs. Even if it only lasted an hour, it was something. I tried to get back to sleep. Sure enough, an hour later, he was hiccoughing and moaning once more.

"I've got to get some sleep," I said again. I brought my pillow to the sofa another time. I'd closed the bedroom door, but Steve was making so much noise I could still hear him.

The alarm rang at 5:30 and I staggered to the kitchen for breakfast, fixing Steve a cup of tea. "Well, the Xanax worked," he said cheerfully. "I slept better than usual."

I looked at him in astonishment. He seemed serious. "You've got to be kidding," I said. "I only got two and a half hours of sleep last night. I'm dying."

"Maybe you should try some. I'm sure I can get extra if I need it. Everything that's mine is yours."

Steve had two doctor's appointments today, so I called in sick and took him to his first appointment at 7:00 downtown at Tulane Medical Center. He had to get an MRI with injected dye before he could be further evaluated for a liver transplant. We were out by 9:30 and went home. I had to hold Steve's arm both while walking to the hospital and then back to the car. He was too weak to walk on his own.

I had to help him again for his 1:30 appointment with Dr. Maynard, a surgical oncologist at West Jefferson. He disagreed with the other doctor who'd said the tumor was inoperable. He felt they could go in and first cut the blood supply to the tumor and then go in and zap it. They'd schedule something for next week.

"So maybe I'm not going to die," Steve said as we climbed back in the car.

"You're not going to die. Even if they can only get 90% of the tumor, that'll give you a few more months to be on the transplant waiting list. And maybe they'll be able to get all of the tumor. But in any event, they'll get enough to give you time to get a transplant, and after that you'll be fine."

"I don't want to die. I want to live my life with you. You've been so good to me lately."

But things quickly deteriorated. Steve grew weaker by the day. Perhaps because of the fluid pressing on his stomach, he was never hungry. He drank half a glass of Carnation instant breakfast in the morning, a little juice in the afternoon, and half a can of Ensure in the evening. If he ate anything at all, it was three spoonfuls of soup, a few mouthfuls of Ramen noodles, or three bites of tuna salad. He wasn't getting anywhere near the nutrition he needed, but he couldn't force himself to eat any more. His arms were bone thin and his back and shoulders just knobs. Because of the fluid, I had to buy him size 38 boxer shorts instead of his usual 32's to wear around the house. His legs and feet were swollen. Above the abdomen, though, he was a skeleton.

One day on my lunch break at the library, I went to the university bookstore and bought a CD of the opera *Tosca,* featuring a singer Steve particularly liked. He already had two other versions of the opera, but because he knew I'd never acquired a taste for this kind of music, he only listened when he was home alone. The smile on Steve's face was so genuine when he saw the CD that I told him he needed to play it right then.

"You should listen to your favorite operas every day," I told him. "It'll help you heal." He put in the new CD immediately.

He became so weak I had to help him to the bathroom or the kitchen or to bed. He was still hiccoughing and moaning at night, so I no longer even attempted to sleep in the same room. But I got no sleep anyway because he was up six times a night, calling out for help every time.

He also began taking more and more baths, saying it was the only time he felt good, but he couldn't get out of the tub without assistance. After his sixth bath in twenty-four hours, I forbid him from taking any more. My back was hurting from lifting him out of the tub. I wanted him to feel good, but I simply wasn't strong enough. What if he slipped and broke a leg?

My prayers to God started becoming angrier. If this life was the only time gays had to experience love, how could He be so mean as to take so many of our partners away so callously?

For the past couple of weeks, Steve had gone through dozens of facial tissues a day to get phlegm out of his mouth.

I picked up used tissues by the handful near the sofa, on the kitchen table, by the bed, and on the floor. But now I saw that Steve had lots of white, chunky goo in his mouth all the time. He must have thrush, I realized. What next?

The next day was Sunday. It had been exactly three months since all this started with the bleeding from his esophagus. It seemed strange one's life could change so completely in such a short time, and worse, that one could get used to it. "I'm sorry I'm so much trouble," Steve whispered as I brought him some tea in bed.

He looked so miserable that I tried to comfort him. "You're the best thing that ever happened to me," I said. I didn't just mean the trip to Lisbon last year or the proposed move to San Francisco. He sent donations to the Sierra Club and the Nature Conservancy because he knew the environment was something I cared about. He even subscribed to *Dialogue: A Journal of Mormon Thought*, although he hated religion, because he wanted to support "progressive" Mormons. Every few months, he'd boil peanuts for me, even though he hated the smell, because he knew I loved them.

Why did I doubt so often that this man loved me? I wanted him to get better and be his old self again. Maybe a close call with death would help him get over his depression. Maybe he'd finally be willing to take some Prozac. If the surgery was successful and we got the transplant, this still might be my one relationship that succeeded. I'd recently read an article about co-dependency, though, and wondered if my own condition was just as pathological as Steve's.

If only we had universal healthcare here. And if that included mental healthcare, too. Sick people couldn't cure themselves by snapping their fingers.

Perhaps after all the dust settled, I'd learn how to take more emotional space for myself. But that was all in the future. For now, I could only hope today would be a good day. Steve smiled weakly and asked me to read to him again.

Then in the morning around 9:00, I heard Steve call from the bathroom. I went in and found him sitting in the tub.

"Another bath?" I said, exasperated. I hated being short with him, but I was wiped out.

He mumbled something about "deserving this," though I wasn't sure what he meant. I stepped in the tub and put my hands under his arms.

"I don't want to be mean," I said, "but I'm telling you. This is the last bath. If you get in here again and can't get out, I'm calling an ambulance to take you to the hospital. Do you understand?" I'd thought he had a couple of months left, but now it looked like it might only be a few weeks. There would be no time for a transplant, I realized.

I hoped I could hold out. It wasn't that Steve's being ill was "inconvenient." I was simply afraid I might fall back into my old depression as well, and two depressed people wouldn't be good for each other. I had to be strong for him.

Steve nodded weakly, and after a few minutes we had him standing in the bathroom with his new boxers on. "I'm okay," he said and closed the door on me. But not two minutes later I heard a loud "whump."

I opened the door and found Steve sitting next to the box he used as a table. He'd knocked the box over and was sitting by the toilet. "Let's get you back up," I said.

We tried for several minutes, but he couldn't stand.

"I'm going to have to call an ambulance," I said.

"No," Steve moaned.

"But Steve, you can't walk. I can't carry you. What are we going to do?"

"Crawl," he mumbled. He couldn't speak in complete sentences anymore.

"Crawl where?"

"Sofa. Help."

I tugged on his arms while he scooted forward on his butt with his legs in front. After twenty minutes, we'd made it to the bathroom door. "Steve, this is hopeless. You need to be in a hospital."

"No," he said. He lifted his arms again. "Help."

After an hour—an *hour*—we'd made it eight feet to the den. We tried for several more minutes to lift him so he could sit on the sofa, but we finally gave up. "Sit here," he said. I could hardly hear him.

"What'll we do when you need to go to the bathroom? It'll take another hour to get back. And how can we lift you to the toilet? You need to go to the hospital."

"No."

I was so frustrated I left him watching TV alone, telling him to call if he needed me. But he never called. I was afraid he was too weak to call, so I went back and checked on him every half hour. I should have stayed to talk to him, but I was irritated and couldn't hear him anyway. I could have rambled about anything, read to him, listened to music with him. I wanted to focus on Steve but kept thinking of myself, too.

I kept hearing the voices of the prophets and apostles saying gays were selfish and hedonistic and shallow. Every second of the day when a negative thought flashed through my mind, I judged myself worthy of Hell.

How was I going to get through three more weeks of this? How was I going to get through today? Somehow, I had to get enough sleep and be ready for another day of work in the morning. I only had two more days of sick leave left. I'd have to save them for when things got bad. But if Steve was like this now, how could I leave him home alone for a whole day? He needed to go to the hospital.

I'd had Steve write out a few checks for bills the previous couple of days. I said we needed to get my name on the checking account so I could write bills if he couldn't, but I realized that the time had come and gone for that. He'd also talked about leaving me the house and his $42,000 in CD's and his $20,000 in life insurance and his $160,000 pension, but he'd never gotten around to writing a will or making me his beneficiary and obviously never would.

He was so depressed after Frank died that he never could bother worrying about what would happen if he died, too. Now his sister would get everything. I hadn't married him for his money, so it didn't really matter. I knew the house note wasn't due for another week, but I wrote out the check and had Steve sign it today. I could tell in a few days he'd be too weak. He misspelled his name the first time, so I wrote the check out again and had him sign it another time. We had to be able to stay here at least until Steve died. I could find an apartment on my own after that.

Steve had been farting uncontrollably for days and was embarrassed, but today when he farted, he didn't apologize. I put a T-shirt on him in the bathroom, and already there were several pink stains on the front from his drooling.

"New T-shirt," he said.

"You've been wearing that one two hours. You'll just get a new one dirty, too. I can't put five T-shirts on you today." Why was I being so disagreeable?

"New T-shirt," he repeated.

After we got the new shirt on him, which took almost ten minutes, he asked for an ice pop. It was past noon and this was his first food of the day. I brought him a cherry popsicle and he ate most of it, his shoulders slumped and his head drooping. I brought him a little juice later, but he moved so little he looked stoned.

"Please let me take you to the hospital. I promise I won't abandon you. You have an appointment tomorrow with the surgeon. How are we going to get you there? We'll need an ambulance tomorrow. Why not just go today? I'll stay with you the whole time. You've got to see the surgeon or they can't cut the tumor out Tuesday."

"No hospital. Got to promise me."

That was the closest thing to a sentence he'd said all day. "I can't promise that." I *wanted* to respect his wishes. I'd certainly want mine respected. But…

"Please."

"You want me to buy some Depends? If you're just going to sit there on the floor for days, we'll need to get you some diapers."

"Don't worry 'bout it."

"I am worried about it. It's been four hours since you've been to the bathroom. Usually, you go every two hours. You need to crawl back?"

"No."

I knew he needed to go to the hospital, but what could I do? If he told the paramedics he didn't want to go, they'd be forced to leave him. On the other hand, I was afraid of being charged with abuse for letting him suffer here when he clearly needed hospitalization.

I called Alice in Chicago for some moral support. She told me to take him to the hospital. After I hung up, I went back to the den. Steve was lying on his back now, unable to sit upright any longer. I waited fifteen more minutes until he was too weak to protest, and then I went back in. "I'm so sorry," I said, beginning to sob, "but I'm going to call an ambulance." I felt miserable, but how could I care for him for two more weeks in this condition?

An ambulance arrived ten minutes later. When the paramedics came into the room, the first thing Steve said was "No."

"You don't want to go to the hospital?" one of the paramedics asked. I held my breath.

"No."

"Can you tell me what day this is?"

Steve couldn't.

The paramedic turned to me. "He isn't rational enough to make a decision. We'll take him in."

I sighed in relief, though I knew the question wasn't fair. Steve hadn't had to go to work in days. There was no reason for him to know what day it was.

Because I'd told them he'd fallen earlier, the paramedics strapped Steve to a backboard. It seemed to take forever, but finally he was in the ambulance. I followed them to West Jefferson, arriving a few minutes after they did. As I stepped out of the car, a female paramedic from the ambulance hurried up to me.

"Does he have a living will? An advance directive?"

"No."

"Because the doctor says he's not looking too good."

The emergency room doctor greeted me inside. I could see a nurse inserting an IV into Steve's neck. "Does he want extraordinary measures?" the doctor asked. "Because we're at that point."

I couldn't believe it. I'd known it was bad, but not this bad. "No," I said, "no extraordinary measures." Would they listen to me, someone who wasn't family?

"You can come hold his hand while we work on him."

"Blood pressure is 40 over 20," someone said.

"Heart rate is 30," someone else called out.

"Blood glucose is 8," said another voice.

That couldn't be right.

Steve wore an oxygen mask and was gasping for breath. What the hell? He'd been breathing fine at home. "It's agonal breathing," the doctor said. "He probably doesn't have much longer."

They checked his potassium, which was 8.6, about twice normal, the cause of the heart problem. It was the result of renal failure, they said. I realized Steve probably knew he couldn't urinate anymore and that was why he wasn't worried about getting back to the bathroom. He probably realized he was dying and wanted to die at home.

Why hadn't I listened to him? If only I'd realized he was this close, I'd have let him die in peace. Why couldn't he have told me he knew he was about to die? After all this time trying to help him, had I betrayed him at the last minute?

"We've got to get some medicine into his stomach right away and get the potassium down," one of the nurses said. "We'll have to use a nasogastric tube." He and another nurse slid a tube down Steve's nose, but he couldn't swallow to help guide it, and after two attempts, they gave up. "We'll do an enema instead." All this invasiveness. It was exactly what Steve didn't want. Were my last memories of him going to be the extra suffering I made him go through at the end? Why were they even bothering?

As they gave Steve an enema, I watched the monitor show his heart rate ranging from 33 to 50 and back.

"Glucose is 17 now," someone said.

No one was frantic, and they didn't mind my being there. Steve's eyes were half open, but when the nurses talked to him, he didn't answer.

The nurse on duty asked me about his symptoms and medications and I answered as best I could. They seemed surprised Steve hadn't been in any pain, just discomfort because of the bloating. He looked seven or eight months pregnant.

They did a blood gas, complaining about the low blood pressure, and they injected two huge syringes of something into the IV line in his neck before hanging a bag of solution in a drip.

I sat there holding Steve's hand, but he was oblivious. His head was turned away from me. Was it coincidence, or was he mad at me for bringing him here? He had a right to be angry, but I didn't want him to hate me right at the end. What if this really was the conclusion of everything? Perhaps Steve was right and there was no God, no heaven, no eternity for lovers to share together.

Oh, *why* was his head turned away from me? Maybe he was completely out of it and couldn't focus on anything anymore. Perhaps that meant at least he wasn't suffering right now.

"Steve," I said, hoping he could hear me. "You're going to be with Frank again." I squeezed his hand, but it was limp.

We'd arrived at the hospital about 4:30, and by 6:00, the doctor said it would be "hours, not days." I watched as Steve's blood pressure went down to 28 over 17. His gasps were coming at longer intervals.

A few minutes before 7:00, he spurted some blood into his oxygen mask, and the nurse suctioned his mouth. I wondered if they'd injured him earlier with the nasogastric tube or if this was new esophageal varices. I suppose it hardly mattered at this point.

I continued holding his hand and watching him slowly gasp. At 7:05, the nurse came over to me. I hadn't seen Steve gasp in a couple of minutes.

"I'm so sorry for your loss."

"Is he dead?" I said, surprised despite everything. It couldn't be true.

"I'm afraid so."

We discussed the need for me to make arrangements with a funeral home. And then I walked out of the hospital, my throat thick and sore. I wanted to cry but knew I couldn't. Gay men didn't feel true love. I'd heard it from my friends and teachers for years. I'd watched my missionary companions so disgusted at the sight of gay guys they tried to beat them up.

I'd never see my sweet husband again, because his sweetness had died before he did. I'd even have been happy to take his bitchy self back. How could he really be gone? Even with three months of warning, it seemed too sudden.

Now we'd never have San Francisco. We'd never have heaven. We'd never have anything. We were supposed to have years left together. Why hadn't I done more to help? Why hadn't I been more patient? Why hadn't I found some way to make him even a little bit happier?

I wanted him back to try again. "I'll make you happy this time," I said. "I will." I prayed to Steve, to God, to the Universe. To nobody at all.

When I stepped outside, I was surprised to see it was still daytime. How could it still be light, I wondered, when I'd just lost the man I loved?

I sobbed uncontrollably as I walked back to the car. It was the end of the world.

The Lithium Prophecies

I was twenty the first time I heard a voice that wasn't there. Of course, at the time, working as a Mormon missionary in Rome, I thought the voice was real. It told me to make an appointment with the Pope, that I'd be able to convert him, and as a result, millions of Catholics would end up being baptized into the LDS Church.

That didn't go so well, and within a few months, I'd been diagnosed as schizophrenic and sent home from my mission six months early. The early release was as big a blow to my family as the diagnosis. After all, I could get treatment for the illness. There was no way to make up for the disgrace of a premature return home, even if it was medically required.

I lived with my parents in Seattle while I earned a degree in Communications, missing only one semester due to a particularly bad episode, and upon graduating six months ago, I started working full-time as a teller at City Credit Union. I was twenty-five and finally earning my own way. I'd saved up several thousand dollars, as my parents hadn't insisted I pay them back for college, and I didn't need to pay rent. I wanted to move into my own place soon.

At home, I was treated like a sickly child. I took my meds every day and hadn't heard voices in a couple of years. I was a man now, and I needed my independence.

"Eric, how are you?" It was Randi, one of our regular members at the credit union. She worked in the TV studio in the basement of City Hall. My branch of the credit union was located one floor above her, still in the basement, down a long, deserted hallway. We could hear each member as they made the long walk from the elevator at the far end of the hall, clickety clackety click on the tiled floor. "No sneaking up on you here," they'd say, laughing.

"Hey, Randi. What can I do for you today?"

"I need *money*." Randi was a tall, black woman with red-tinted hair, always laughing.

"I can do something about that. How much would you like?"

"$40."

"And whose account did you want that out of?" I looked at her innocently.

"Can I take it from the mayor's?" She laughed.

I went straight to Randi's account with a smile. I remembered numbers easily, and Randi came in often enough for me to be familiar with her member number.

"$40 from savings. No, let's make that $60. It's the weekend."

"Two twenties and two tens?"

"Sounds perfect."

I printed out the receipt, had Randi sign it, and handed her the cash.

"Thanks, Eric."

"You have a good day. And by the way, that scarf looks really good on you."

The rest of the day went well until my lunch hour at 2:00. I cashed some checks, deposited others, took in $25 in rolled coin, and opened a Money Market for one of the women on the city council. I joked around with James, a Eurasian security guard about my age who liked to chat on his rounds of the building. He was short, with close-cropped dark hair and black glasses.

But while I sat in our little kitchen behind my coworker Sandy's desk, I started to get a headache. I'd never had a migraine before and wasn't sure if that's what this was, but my head hurt far more than it had from any previous headache.

I couldn't eat the can of soup I'd brought, or even drink my chocolate milk. I sat at the kitchen table next to our large fig tree. It had been given to us by Marketing to spark dialogue about our "green" loans. I peeked through the Venetian blinds at Sandy, working alone during my lunch break. She was fifty, heavy, and always wore checkered shirts, boasting she hadn't needed to buy new clothes in years. I wondered if I should ask her for some aspirin.

My head was bursting. After twenty minutes, with each pounding pulse through my brain, I started hearing the word, "explosion," "explosion," "explosion."

I sat up straight. It *did* sound like a word. It sounded like a *voice*.

I tried to think back to this morning. Had I forgotten my pills?

By the time lunch was over and I logged back onto my computer, my headache was gone. But the word "explosion" kept resounding in my head. I chatted and joked with our members the way I always did, yet in the back of my mind, I couldn't keep my fear at bay. They were going to lock me away this time.

"You have a good day at work, Eric?" my mother asked when I walked in the door just past 6:00, after the 106 dropped me off half a block from home. My mom was nearing sixty, still trim, with short, bobbed gray hair. She always dressed as if expecting company.

"A woman named Lavitra came in today," I said, smiling.

My mom's face was blank at first, but then she frowned when she recognized the drug's name. "Don't say such things, Eric."

"I'm just telling you who stopped by."

"Anything *good* happen today?"

"A Korean guy named Man Sup came in."

My mother's eyes narrowed. "I'm going to ask the bishop to have a talk with you. In the meantime, supper's ready. And then you better shower so you can go to the Single Adult dance down at the stake center. You need to find yourself a nice young girl."

"Isn't pedophilia against the law, Mom?"

"A nice young *woman*."

I didn't feel like joking anymore and asked what I'd asked many times. "Do you really think any decent girl's going to marry someone like me?" I certainly wasn't interested, and I couldn't imagine they'd be, either.

"It's a commandment to marry. And the Lord giveth no commandments to the children of men save he shall prepare a way for them to fulfill them."

"Do you know where that comes from?" I teased, trying to be playful again though not really feeling it.

"I Nephi 3:7."

"You'll make a good missionary one day, Mom."

"You know my patriarchal blessing says I'm supposed to serve with your father. But we can't go till you're married."

"I'll do my best tonight."

I ate, read a little, did some push-ups, and then showered and caught the bus to church. The entire time, there was that tiny voice in the back of my head. I smiled, tried to be charming, and asked five girls to dance, but I kept growing more and more worried. What if the meds had stopped working? What if the voice told me to do something terrible? What if I listened to it?

Suddenly, just after 11:00, the voice stopped altogether. I sighed in relief and spent the rest of the evening talking to Jeremy, the Single Adult chair who looked like he wanted to leave the dance as badly as I did. Jeremy was a few months older than I was, almost six feet tall, with mousy brown hair the same color as mine. He towered over me at 5' 9" and probably weighed twenty pounds more than I did, maybe 180 pounds, perhaps 185.

I wondered what his weight would feel like on top of me.

Jeremy usually left as soon as the dances were over, but tonight he stayed to help clean up and then drove me home so I wouldn't need to take the bus. Once alone in my room, I fell asleep quickly, enjoying the silence in my head.

The next morning was bright and sunny, always something to celebrate in Seattle. I hummed brightly as I ate my cereal.

Then all at once, in mid-bite, I heard it. "The city will be destroyed by a nuclear explosion."

I stopped chewing. The voice was no longer an isolated word. It was a complete sentence. I looked at the TV but already knew it wasn't on. Neither was the radio. I looked at my dad in the living room, reading the paper in silence.

No one heard the voice but me. I always took my pills just before breakfast and wondered if I should take an extra dose. Maybe I should email my doctor.

I was too afraid to do either.

"I'm taking a walk, Mom. See you later."

I headed down Renton Avenue till I came to Kubota Garden and continued in. I loved the winding and convoluted pathways, the waterfall and koi pond. Today as I wandered back and forth through the park, the voice kept growing louder and clearer. "We can see through time. There will be a nuclear explosion in the city of Seattle in four days. You must save as many people as you can."

The message kept repeating over and over. The voice felt different than I remembered previous voices. But it was still the same type of preposterous message, asking me to "save the world." I knew it was simply a product of my illness.

I had seen *A Beautiful Mind*, and I could do what John Nash did, experience the hallucinations and accept them for what they were. The meds were probably working, after all, if I still understood that.

By 1:00, I'd wandered through the garden for five hours, my anxiety creeping back up. Even though I knew the voice wasn't real, it was impossible to hear the message 1200 times and not begin to wonder just a little.

Hearing even a *real* message 1200 times would drive someone crazy, like Chinese water torture inside my brain.

I finally sat on a bench, too tired to walk any further. Two young women walked by, heavy in conversation. "My brother-in-law saw it," one of the women said. "Everyone in Marysville saw it. The newspaper tried to make it sound like mass hysteria. But my brother-in-law works for Microsoft. He's not an idiot. If he says he saw a UFO, I believe him."

The women walked on, and I decided to interact with my imaginary voice for the first time. "Are you an alien?" I joked.

I felt a sharp pain in my head. Then I heard an answer. "We are trying to help you. Can you hear me?"

Uh oh. Now I was really scared. I'd encouraged my illness. I'd let these women influence my paranoia through the power of suggestion. I had to stop this before it grew any worse.

"No, I can't hear you. Go away."

"Your military forced us down. There are three of us left. They are interrogating us. But we cannot communicate with them though we try. We are attempting to reach anyone who can hear. You must evacuate the city. Call your leaders and tell them what we have told you."

I was sitting with my hands over my ears, but I kept hearing the voice. What was I going to do? I was only months away, maybe just weeks, from being able to live on my own. I didn't want to spend the rest of my life in an institution. The doctors would say I was dangerous if I told anyone about this.

I walked home quickly and went straight to the bathroom, where I took four sleeping pills, swallowing them in one gulp with a handful of water. I didn't want to overdose but did want to sleep soundly and break the cycle that had started this.

I passed my father on the way to my room. "See any flying saucers out there?" he said, chuckling. He was sixty-three, in as good shape as my mom.

"Huh?"

"The paper said there was a sighting the other day. You were gone a long time. Not out there talking to E.T., were you?" He smiled, but I could tell he suspected something.

"Just took a long walk. All I do at work is sit. Got to stay in shape. Going to the gym twice a week isn't enough."

He nodded, and I continued on to my room. I was too nervous to fall asleep quickly despite the dosage, but I did eventually doze off. That didn't entirely help, however. I still dreamed of a spacecraft being shot down, of survivors actively rounded up by the military, of beings which looked remarkably human being medically examined and then harshly interrogated.

Even in my sleep, I questioned the absurdity of it all. Why would the military behave aggressively toward aliens before even knowing their intent? Wouldn't forcing them down be likely to spark some kind of aggression in return? If these other beings were advanced enough to travel to another planet, wouldn't we suspect they'd have more advanced weapons as well? Perhaps it would be safer to get on their good side rather than antagonize them.

And yet, the predicted "explosion" didn't sound like a threat of retaliation.

None of it made sense. I tossed and turned for hours, on the edge between sleep and consciousness, hearing the voice the entire time. "Your city will be destroyed by a nuclear explosion four days from now. It is up to you to save your people."

Finally, at some point, either the alien stopped communicating, or the pills started working, and eventually I fell into a deep, deep sleep. When I awoke, it was 4:00 in the morning, and there was no more voice.

I stepped out of bed and got down on my knees. "Heavenly Father, you said in Corinthians we would never be tempted above that which we were able to bear, that you would provide an escape. I need you to keep your promise."

After I finished, I stayed beside my bed reflecting on my paper-thin relationship with God. As a teenager, I was told if I prayed after reading the Book of Mormon, I would hear a "still, small voice" telling me it was true. I did pray, and I did hear some type of voice, but I had to wonder now, was that the beginning of my illness? What about Joseph Smith, who both saw and heard God the Father and Jesus Christ? If anyone else today said such a thing, they'd be labeled schizophrenic in an instant. Why was *he* called a prophet instead?

Was Joan of Arc crazy as well? Were all prophets and seers by definition crazy? Maybe there was no god to begin with, for *anyone* to hear.

But what if these aliens had been around for centuries, visiting occasionally, arriving with messages each time for those who *could* hear? Perhaps "God" was simply an alien race trying to help.

Or maybe we were all just really fucked up.

I was completely awake now. I didn't want to go back to sleep, so I went to my computer and emailed some friends in Italy, the few who still liked me. Part of me wished the Church would've let me try to make an appointment with the Pope, after all, just to see what would have happened. At the very least, he might have had some counsel that would have benefited me. But it would have been a PR nightmare for the

Church, and they were, if anything, conscious of their public image. I knew they wished defective Mormons like me didn't exist. We were "awkward."

I could feel it every time I went to church. People were friendly and shook my hand and asked how I was doing. But I could see them whispering to each other about me, nudging, pointing. It wasn't just prurient interest. I could see the disapproving looks, noticed how they steered away young women who were visiting or who'd just moved into the ward. I hadn't found any of those girls attractive, but I still felt irritated I was judged too poor a man to be with. I could tell they all wished I simply wasn't there.

"Why doesn't the Lord take people like that home?" I heard one woman saying. "What good is he to anyone?"

When I talked to the bishop about it, he said it was all in my head.

Mom and Dad were up by 7:30, and I had sausage and eggs ready for them by the time they came out to the kitchen. Sunday mornings were the only time I cooked, but I figured Mom needed at least one break a week.

"That walk must have really tired you out," Dad said, glancing through the newspaper.

"I'm fine now."

"I was afraid you'd try to get out of church today," Mom said carefully. "The Church is about the only thing you really have going for you, you know."

"Thanks a lot."

"You know what I mean. As long as you're faithful, the Church will always be there for you when you need it."

"It's like being in the Marines," my dad said, as if that was supposed to sound appealing.

I wasn't in the mood for services, but the voice hadn't returned, and I was grateful for that, so I figured I ought to go. Sacrament meeting was first. I sat with Jeremy, who reminded me of the Single Adult fireside that evening on the topic of righteous dating. Since I couldn't date the people I wanted to date, the idea sounded tedious. But Jeremy offered to give me a ride.

I sat back and sang along with the rest of the congregation. "We thank thee, O God, for a prophet to guide us in these latter days." A couple of announcements followed, then a song about the atonement, and next the deacons passed the bread and water. I wondered again if being crazy was a sin, that perhaps I should refrain from partaking of the sacrament. If I was strong enough, faithful enough, wouldn't I be cured? Wasn't still being sick a sign I lacked sufficient faith?

In any event, I should probably refrain from the sacrament just on account of the masturbation. If I never married at all, though, would I need to abstain from even self-release my entire life? It felt harsh. Why couldn't the prophet receive a revelation condoning the practice for those cursed with celibacy? Why was it always so necessary to suppress our sexual nature anyway?

I wanted to know the answers.

I wanted a revelation of my own, to help me understand a great many things.

Listening to Sister Barrows talk about some pronouncement from President Hinckley, one of our recent prophets, I felt Jeremy's leg accidentally brush up against mine. The contact felt good, so I didn't move away. But I suddenly felt very, very alone.

"Are you out there, Voice?" I thought wearily.

"You do not believe me." The voice was back instantly. "Let me convince you we tell the truth."

Oh God.

"We foresee that one of your airplanes will crash just outside the city tonight. Once you see we speak the truth, you must warn your leaders about the explosion in three days."

"Okay, okay, then go away until tonight."

The voice ceased, and I smiled. Jeremy saw me smiling and smiled as well. I was happy to be able to negotiate with the voice. That meant it didn't have absolute control.

And now I'd have proof. If a plane crashed, then the voice was real. And if it didn't, I'd know I simply needed to add a new med to the mix, and I'd be fine again.

I wondered, though, if this truly was an alien trying to help, why he didn't give me more details about the plane, so I could save those lives, too. This alien beneficence seemed fuzzy at best.

Sunday School came next, about the prophecies of Isaiah, and then came Priesthood, about sacrificing to serve others, and then I was free for the rest of the day.

I considered talking to the bishop, but what advice could he give me? Mormon theology proclaimed the existence of life on billions of other planets throughout the universe, so there was nothing blasphemous about entertaining the possibility of aliens. There was even some talk that perhaps the lost ten tribes might have migrated to another planet and would come back in a spectacular way in the last days.

The fact I was obsessing about this, however, wasn't a good sign.

Yet if it were true…

Back home in my room, I pulled out my Patriarchal Blessing, which the stake patriarch had given me when I was fourteen. We'd talked for twenty minutes before he laid his hands on my head and pronounced God's plan for my life. He mentioned missionary work, without specifying it would be cut short. He encouraged me to pursue college and said the right career choice would fall into my lap.

Then he'd gone on to say I "would help others through perilous times," which had always led me to believe maybe I'd be ordained a bishop one day. The last part of the blessing told me not to despair in finding a mate, that God would provide when the time was ripe. There was no mention of children, though. I didn't know what to make of that.

In the past, patriarchal blessings were treated like personal scripture. These days, we were encouraged to accept them as mere guidelines. Still, my older sister's blessing had mentioned her "sons and daughters," and after bearing two sons and one daughter, she was sincerely hoping her fourth child would be a girl so she could retire from her womb. When the fourth turned out to be a boy, she cursed and accepted she had to keep trying till she got "all the spirits" God had "in store" for her to bring to this planet.

I read part of an LDS novel in the afternoon, took a walk, and browsed Yahoo News every hour to check for any report of a plane crash in the area. There was nothing.

I wasn't thrilled about going back to church for the evening, yet I had to admit, things got a bit lonely with no real friends. I had a habit of disclosing my diagnosis too early in a relationship with classmates at school, and the other person *always* pulled away afterward. I couldn't truly blame them, I supposed. I did have "friends" at church, though no one who ever wanted to get together outside of religious activities. I wasn't sure that counted.

Jeremy picked me up at 6:40 and asked me to say the opening prayer when we started at 7:00. "Help us to be in tune with thy spirit tonight," I asked.

I sat in the front pew to listen to the speaker, Brother Clemmons, our stake high councilor. Jeremy sat next to me.

The fireside went well. I didn't zone out or become too irritated with what Brother Clemmons said, always a danger. Then, just as I glanced at my watch at 7:53, it happened. "The plane is crashing right now!" The voice blared inside my head. Its return was so sudden and powerful I jumped up and shouted, "The plane! The plane!" I sounded like the dwarf on *Fantasy Island.*

Brother Clemmons stopped speaking, his mouth frozen open. Everyone stared at me. I felt my face burning and ran outside, mortified. I ran and ran, down the block, down a second block, all the way to the bus stop. I wanted to keep running forever. But I also wanted to jump on the very next bus and ride far, far away.

"Eric!" I heard a voice shouting. "Eric!"

I turned. It was Jeremy, running to catch up. I thought about running away again. Why was there no bus? Why couldn't there be a cab?

"Eric!" Jeremy caught up and leaned over, holding his side. "What happened? Are you okay?"

I didn't want to talk about it. Why did he have to follow me? Did he feel obligated because he'd given me a ride? Because he was the Single Adult chair? Because he felt sorry for me?

"I had a vision of a plane crashing near the city right at that moment," I said bluntly. I figured if I made myself sound crazy enough, he'd leave me alone. Perhaps *choosing* loneliness was better than being abandoned into it.

"Really? Does—does that kind of thing happen often?"

"Only when I skip my meds."

He looked at me uncertainly. "Did you skip them?"

I looked back at him. "No."

He nodded and put his hand on my arm. "Come on, I'll take you home."

He turned and started walking, and I followed reluctantly. We were both quiet on the drive back, the radio playing soft pop music. I listened to Chris Isaak and tried to relax.

When the song ended, an announcer came on. "American Airlines flight 66 has crashed just outside of Renton, killing all 131 people on board and two people on the ground. The plane disappeared from radar just before 8:00 p.m. and reports soon began pouring in from the ground. Investigators have released no information yet on the cause of the crash, but weather is not believed to be a factor."

The reporter went on for another few moments before the air was again filled with mellow music. The car pulled off to the side of the road and stopped. Jeremy turned off the engine. The music ceased.

"Eric, what do you suppose it means?"

"I—I don't know. I'm scared, Jeremy."

He put his hand on my arm again. "Do…you know what went wrong onboard? Can you steer the investigators in the right direction? Maybe prevent this from happening again?"

"I heard a voice in my head," I said slowly. "It's told me other things, too."

"Like what?"

"You do realize I'm crazy, right?"

"Who isn't a little crazy?" He shrugged. "What else did the voice tell you?"

"Let me figure out what I'm going to do first."

"Will you tell me tomorrow night at Single Adult Family Home Evening?"

I thought for a moment. "Yes," I said. "I should know what I'm going to do by then."

"Okay." Jeremy started the car again.

"You understand that just because this one thing turned out to be true, anything else I might hear from the voices in my head could still be pure rubbish. Lithium can only do so much."

Jeremy laughed. "Prozac can only do so much, too."

I realized then I'd been thinking an awful lot about my own problems lately and forgetting there were other people out there with their own issues. The apostles always said gays were self-centered. Of course, to be fair, wondering if it was solely up to me to save a million lives *was* a bit distracting.

"You okay, Jeremy?"

"Sure."

"You need to talk?"

He sighed. "Oh, you know how it is. Just wondering if I'll be in the Single Adult group the rest of my life. I'm twenty-six already. But that's a boring topic. Yours is more interesting."

"There's a lot to be said for boring sometimes."

"We'll talk more about your voices tomorrow."

"Sounds like you hear voices, too. Even if it's only your nagging inner voice. Or the Church pressuring you every day to get married."

"Yes, I do hear a voice every day." He looked at me. "Someday, I'll tell you what it says. But tomorrow we focus on you. Be prepared to talk."

I walked into the house and went to the kitchen for a glass of milk. "Good speaker?" Mom offered me a cookie.

"I learned we're not supposed to kiss our girlfriend until we're kneeling across the altar." I forced a smile. "Lavitra isn't going to be happy when I tell her."

"Now, Eric. You're at church four times a week. And your mind is still a garbage heap." She put her hand to her lips as if she just realized she'd said something improper. I continued smiling.

"No sweat, Mom. I happen to agree."

It wasn't even 8:30, but I went to my bedroom and climbed under the covers. "What now?" I asked the voice.

"Now you understand the gravity of the situation. Tomorrow you must contact your leaders. You must insist they evacuate the city."

"Can't you just tell me how to stop whoever is going to set off the bomb? I'd get more results sending in a good tip to Homeland Security."

"We do not have those kinds of details. We only see the larger scene."

"Can't you read my mind and learn how to write our language? You could tell the military yourself. Can't you get a pen and draw a picture?"

"Humans are strange creatures. We offer you assistance, and you do not seem to care about saving your own lives."

"You don't understand. My brain is defective. No one will believe me."

"You must make them believe."

"Okay, okay. I work at City Hall. That's the seat of city government. I'll see if I can talk to the mayor tomorrow."

"That is exactly what you must do."

"All right already. Now let me get some sleep."

I lay in bed and stared at the light filtering in through the window. I felt like an alien myself. I could just imagine the expression on the mayor's face if I did manage to get in to see him. He'd see that I was fired for sure.

Wait a minute. My credit union was based solely in Seattle. If the bomb went off, I'd lose my job in any case. My parents would lose their home. Dad worked for Boeing. They might be put out of business if the bomb was big enough to send radiation their way.

Even a moderately-sized bomb would likely put them out of business. Since it was impossible I'd be able to get everyone to evacuate, even in a best-case scenario, hundreds of thousands of people might die. What would happen to Microsoft? To Costco? I smiled wryly. Starbucks might go out of business, too. If I could convince the mayor of *that* threat, he might see the seriousness of the danger.

My life was in the toilet no matter how I handled the situation.

I felt sorry for my parents. They tried so hard to be good to me. It would really hurt them if I was sent away for treatment. The plane could have been a coincidence, after all. It didn't really prove anything.

I smiled. That was exactly what they told us in church about asking for miracles. If we had faith, we didn't need miracles, and if we didn't have faith, even miracles wouldn't give us proof. We'd still rationalize them away.

Wait a second. Even if the plane crash did prove something, it only proved it to *me*. Maybe *I* believed the other warning now, but why would the mayor believe me? A schizophrenic nobody, convinced of his own preposterous claims, wasn't enough to make the mayor issue a mandatory evacuation. And what if I only created the warning about the plane retroactively in my own memory? I hadn't written it down with a time and date. Maybe I hadn't even really been warned at all.

"Hey, Spock," I said, "I need another prediction for the mayor."

"We have thought of that." The voice returned instantly, loitering outside my consciousness. "Tell your leaders there will be another plane crash tomorrow night."

"Another one? What's going on?"

"We only see through time. We do not know why these things occur."

"And that crash will be near Seattle again?"

"That is correct."

"Okay, I'll tell him."

"After you save the city, we will ask you to save us."

"If I convince any leaders that aliens saved a million lives, they'll never let you go. They'll want to keep you forever."

"You must not tell them we are responsible. You must say you saw this in your own brain."

I sighed. "Whatever. My brain is tired now. Go away till tomorrow."

The voice was silent immediately. I wondered if I ignored it or never called it back, if it would stay away. Still, if this was all real, sticking my head in the sand wouldn't help anyone, including me. I'd have to talk to the mayor, for whatever good it might do. Then I'd have to convince my parents to leave, no matter what the mayor decided.

Then I realized something else. My parents loved me, but they wouldn't *believe* me. They might not lock me up, but they certainly weren't going to leave town. My parents would be dying on Wednesday.

Perhaps I should keep the warning to myself and die along with everyone else. Life was too hard. I'd be doing us all a favor. Of course, what was so hard about life was always trying to do the right thing. If I'd made it this far *mostly* doing right things and then did one really bad thing at the end, it would make my whole life worthless.

I sighed wearily and tried to empty my mind of my own voice. I thought about taking some more sleeping pills but didn't want to get addicted. I had enough problems already.

I eventually fell asleep but tossed and turned all night, my sleep filled with odd, bizarre dreams. And then, far too soon, it was morning. I hit the snooze button twice but realized I couldn't put off the inevitable forever.

I staggered to the kitchen for a bowl of cereal. Dad had already left, but Mom was having toast. "You look terrible, dear. You all right?"

"I had a bad dream."

"What was it?"

"Another plane's going to crash in Seattle tonight."

Mom shook her head. "Well, think about something happy." She smiled brightly. "Two planes wouldn't crash in the same area in two days. Not unless someone was shooting them down."

I stopped with a spoonful of Cheerios halfway to my lips. Were *terrorists* responsible for the two plane crashes? Was it a trial run before setting off the bomb?

I put the spoon back in the bowl. Oh my god. Maybe the *aliens* were responsible for the crashes. Were they sacrificing those lives to convince others to leave before the bomb leveled the city?

Wait a second. What if the aliens weren't trying to help us at all but hurt us instead?

I frowned. How could evacuating possibly hurt us? Make us miss a day of work? The warning had to be legitimate.

"You okay, Eric?"

"I'm not very hungry. I think I'll just head on."

"Did you take your pills?"

I realized I'd almost forgotten. "I'm taking them right now."

"You might take a vitamin C, too. You don't look so good. You think you should stay home?"

"I'll be fine. You have a good day, Mom."

On the way downtown, I looked more closely at my fellow passengers. Every one of these people might die if I wasn't successful today. The teenage black girl with the wet afro she kept shaking every few seconds, spraying everyone within a yard of her with water. The middle-aged Asian man who kept staring at the young Asian high school girl. The Hispanic man contributing far too much to the methane pollution our planet was already suffering from.

These lives were in my hands. I suppose I should have felt powerful but instead I felt very, very weak.

Someone was standing on the escalator leading out of the bus tunnel from Pioneer Square, so it took extra long to get up to 3rd Avenue. Then there was the steep block uphill to 4th

Avenue and City Hall. As I approached the building, I could see some kind of activity in the street. There were police at the entrance, blocking perhaps two hundred people gathering near the doors. And this wasn't even the main entrance, which was up on 5th Avenue. Most of the people gathered looked homeless or at least down and out, but not all. They were shouting and gesturing and trying to bully their way into the building. The Noah's Bagels on the ground floor, which opened onto the street, was locked.

"What's going on?" I asked a businessman on the corner.

"I don't know. Looks like some kind of anti-war demonstration. I heard someone shout something about nuclear bombs. These bleeding-heart liberals make me sick."

Oh my god. I wasn't the only one who heard the voice. Maybe every schizophrenic in town heard the warning. Maybe other people, too.

I breathed a sigh of relief. The message would get through without me. I pushed my way into the crowd, making my way to the door, where I was met by several police officers. I showed my badge to get into the building, and they let me inside.

I rode up the elevator to L2R and walked down the long hall. James, the security guard, hurried toward me. "Jesus, it's crazy out there! You okay?"

"Are they letting any of those people in? Surely, some got through before the police barred the doors."

"I don't think so. Those people were out there before the building opened, so when the first employees got to work this morning, they called 9-1-1. The police were already stationed out front when I got here at 7:00."

"Is someone going down to hear what they have to say?"

James shrugged. "They look like kooks to me. But the mayor may send someone down just to placate them."

"Well, come back and let me know what you find out."

"Concerned about the democratic process?" He laughed.

I smiled weakly. "Something like that."

James slapped me on the shoulder. "If you get any people causing trouble in the credit union today, you give me a call, and I'll be right down."

"Thanks."

"You be good and don't spend all your free time looking at internet porn at work today." James nodded goodbye and headed off down the hall. He often made sexual jokes, asking how many times I came over the weekend or saying his friends thought he was a big dick, but that apparently some people liked big dicks. I did like James and wondered if I should ask him out for a drink after work sometime. I'd only have a Coke, of course, but if I wanted to have a real friend someday, I had to start making more of an effort.

But that was hardly a priority right now.

I used my badge to open the door to the credit union and then hurried to turn off the alarm. I switched on the light and copier, logged onto my computer, and pulled the money bag out of the locked drawer so the courier could take it to the main branch and process the previous day's checks. Then I flipped on the radio to The Mountain.

Sandy came in then, looking bewildered. "We usually get a warning about scheduled demonstrations. Did I forget something?"

"I hear they're predicting a nuclear explosion on Wednesday."

"You think they're terrorists?"

"I don't know, but you might consider calling in sick Wednesday and visiting your mother in Maple Valley."

Sandy laughed. "And that's better than being blown up?"

We checked our emails, sent one down to our manager at the main branch letting him know the situation, and opened the folding metal gate at 9:00. We had a light crowd at this branch in the best of times, but it was almost dead today. Members from the Municipal Tower across the street apparently weren't willing to run the gauntlet to get in.

Randi, from the TV station downstairs, came in just before 11:00. "The crowd's bigger now," she said. "The mayor's talking about closing the building and sending us home."

"Is there a spokesperson for the group? Have they given their message to the mayor?"

"God only knows. I need $40. Then I'm cutting out regardless of what the mayor says. They're looking unruly out there."

After she left, I went on the internet, which we weren't supposed to do on our work computers, and clicked on KIRO 7 News. I clicked on "Demonstrators Mob City Hall" and the video loaded.

"Hundreds of protestors gathered at City Hall and our own KIRO 7 headquarters today, demanding to be heard. They claim the city will be destroyed by a nuclear bomb on Wednesday. Officials say the demonstrators do not appear to be organized. Some insist angels have given them the warning. Others say God himself. Some mention aliens. Others mention Native American or Hindu gods. Experts say this is some kind of unusual mass hysteria, perhaps sparked by the UFO sightings a few days ago or related to the chemical spill near the city's major water supply last week. Officials at Seattle Public Utilities insist there is no contamination of the city's water."

The report ended. I was disturbed the protestors were being labeled crazy, but of course, that's exactly what I'd expected. It looked like no prediction of the plane crash tonight had been reported, though, and that made everything else useless.

Suddenly, an alarm went off in the building. "We'd better lock up," Sandy said nervously.

I told her to call our manager while I quickly relocked the front gate. Just as I was sliding down the second bolt, James came running by. "They've rushed the police and are inside the building. You better get out." Then he was gone.

Sandy started crying. I didn't know if I should be happy or not. Then I started hearing shots and knew the answer.

"It's dangerous to leave. Let's turn out the lights and hide in the kitchen."

We did so, and Sandy called her husband on her cell. I called my mom. "We're watching it on the news right now," she told me breathlessly. "The National Guard's been called to make mass arrests. It says City Hall employees are locked in their offices. They're using tear gas in the street. Are you okay?"

"No tear gas in here yet."

"There are protestors outside the Army base at Ft. Lewis. And there's a group at the power company. There's even a group at the airport for some reason. Oh, wait." She paused a moment. "The mayor's declared martial law! It's just like the WTO riots. Everyone's being ordered back to their homes. No one's allowed on the streets after 1:00."

"I may be spending the night here."

"Not with all those crazy people?" Mom said worriedly. Then she huffed in frustration. "You know what I mean."

"Mom, you might want to leave the city."

"Without you? I don't think so."

I heard yelling down the hall then and hung up. Sandy and I remained motionless. Someone rattled the gate out front, shouting, and then ran off again. Most of the protestors who'd gotten into the building must have headed to higher floors rather than the basement. We could hear muffled bangs and shouts and screams and more bangs. Sandy and I just sat quietly, waiting for the storm to pass.

"Voice," I said silently, "what now?"

"We still foresee disaster. Your leaders do not know about the plane tonight. Without that, the larger apocalypse will still occur. You must do something."

I shook my head. With all those other people involved, how could it still be up to me? "The building's under siege. I haven't got a chance."

"You must do something."

"Okay, okay. Let me think."

But this time, the voice didn't leave me alone. Every couple of minutes, the message repeated. "You must do something. You must do something."

After about an hour, it was silent in the building. Another fifteen minutes later, I heard footsteps again in the hallway. The gate rattled. "Eric? Sandy? You in there?"

It was James. Both Sandy and I ran to the gate. "Is it safe?" Sandy asked. "Can we leave?"

"It looks like everyone's been carted off. They're convoying the employees out from the upper floors."

"Thank God, thank God." Sandy started crying again.

"You guys follow me."

"James, I need to see the mayor."

Both Sandy and James stared at me in astonishment. Finally, James spluttered, "Are you crazy?"

"I know what's behind all this. I need to speak with him."

James's eyes narrowed. "What do you know?"

"I need to speak to the mayor. Can you get me upstairs?"

"There must be ten police officers outside his door. I can't get you past them."

I considered. James probably knew the mayor's phone number, but the chance of getting through that way was probably nil. He certainly wouldn't be checking email, with his official work email crammed on the best of days.

"Get me upstairs and let me talk to whoever's guarding the door."

"I want to go home!" Sandy pleaded, still crying.

"James, escort Sandy out and then come back to get me. I need to see the mayor before he leaves."

"I don't want to get fired."

"I can solve this whole problem. You'll be a hero."

James's eyes narrowed again. "I'll come back, but you'll still have to convince me."

They walked off, and I went to the faucet in the kitchen for a glass of water. After a few sips, I decided I needed something stronger, opened our mini-fridge, and took out my chocolate milk. I started to contact the voice but decided to pray instead.

"Heavenly Father, what should I do? I'm scared. Is talking to the mayor the right thing? How can I convince him? What should I do?"

There was no response.

I sighed. "Voice," I said, "I'm on my way upstairs in a minute."

"Your military interrogations are growing harsher. We may not be able to communicate much longer. Make sure you save your city. If you succeed, my people will try to make official contact next time, public contact. If we see we can communicate with your people, we will come back sooner."

I felt a flash of irritation. There wasn't *enough* weight on my shoulders? Now the responsibility for interstellar peace was in my hands?

"Yeah, yeah, yeah," I said. "You better put some good words in my mouth."

There was no answer to this. Instead, I felt a sharp pain in my head again, as I had that first day. Were they torturing the aliens? I heard silence for several minutes and then began hearing isolated words that meant nothing.

I noticed footsteps in the hall again and hid. A moment later, James was at the gate. "Eric?"

"Thanks for coming back."

"Can I escort you out of the building now?"

"We need to go upstairs."

"How can you possibly know what's going on? Besides, the National Guard has arrested everyone. It's all under control."

"There's more to the story."

"What?"

I struggled to come up with a reasonable answer. "I volunteer at the homeless shelter." That wasn't true, of course. I was so involved with the Church I never had time to do anything for the community.

"So?"

"One of the men there is Saudi Arabian. He was a doctor but then became an alcoholic and lost everything."

"What has any of this—"

"He overheard something." I hoped using Islamophobia to manipulate the security guard didn't make me too much of a monster. Expediency was a pretty shitty excuse.

James looked at me.

"There's a terrorist cell that's going to set off a nuclear bomb here Wednesday. The homeless guys, and I guess some of their relatives, are just doing their patriotic duty and trying to warn the mayor. But they're too poor and disturbed or whatever to go about it in a civilized way. No one's going to believe them. *I* didn't believe them at first. But some of the men told me the details. I can help stop this."

James looked skeptical, frowning so hard he looked like a caricature. There was really no plausible explanation. If what I'd said was true, why wouldn't I have reported it sooner? I took a deep breath and joined James in the hallway.

"I need something more."

I suddenly remembered Nephi killing Laban in the Book of Mormon to get the plates of brass. Killing was a sin, but sometimes you had to do terrible things to achieve a higher goal. I put my hand on James's arm.

"Come over here a minute," I said. I couldn't take him into the credit union. The security cameras were still recording in there. I led James instead to the public bathroom just twenty feet away.

"What's up?"

I motioned for James to keep following. He was curious if guarded but stayed with me. I pushed open the door to the bathroom and then the door to the handicapped stall at the far end of the room. James looked thoroughly puzzled but kept following. Once we were both inside, I shut the stall door and latched it.

"Eric—"

Without another word, I reached forward and put my hand on his crotch. His eyes widened but he didn't protest. I'd wanted James for a long time but resisted. If I had to sin to save a million people, though, *or* be damned for letting them die, I had to make some kind of compromise.

There was no time for sophisticated moral debate. I unzipped James's pants and continued. I'd never done oral sex to anyone before, yet there didn't seem to be much mystery over how it was done. I couldn't help but consider the possibility I was going to be killed ten minutes from now or locked up and die in Wednesday's explosion. Part of me wanted to remain pure up until the very end, so I might at least have a chance at a decent afterlife. Another part was determined to enjoy as much life right now as I could.

I did my best, and soon we were finished.

"All right," James said, zipping up. "I'll take you upstairs."

I was disappointed the truth hadn't been an option in convincing him, or even an elaborate story or any other kind of reasoning. It was basic animal lust that did the trick. What did that say about the human race? Were we really worth saving?

I had to admit, however, I felt strangely positive about what had just happened there next to the toilet filled with discolored, recycled water. I didn't feel guilty. Whether that was the result of a dispensation like Nephi had been granted, I didn't know. I felt uncommonly alive, instead of the general hazy half-life I usually sensed. For now, though, I had to focus on the immediate task ahead.

I followed James to the elevator, where he put in a special key to get the elevator to move. We went up a few floors and the doors opened. There were three armed soldiers leading five employees into the elevator next to us. Two armed soldiers met us as we stepped out into the hall.

"He's an employee from the credit union on L2," James explained, offering nothing further. We walked down the hallway to the mayor's office, blocked by several armed guardsmen. I'd never been to this floor before. In fact, I'd never been above the lobby.

James stopped in front of the soldier blocking the mayor's door. "He's an employee here." James motioned to me as I showed my ID badge. "He heard something about what's going on. He has information for the mayor."

The guard looked at us scornfully, and I realized how pathetic my "authority" sounded, but miraculously he nodded, and two other men patted me down. Then the lead guard opened the door and ushered me in. James didn't follow. There were several guardsmen in here, too, a few employees, and the mayor, who was on the phone. This wasn't going to be a private audience. If I said anything unbelievable, I'd be arrested on the spot.

When the mayor finally put down the phone, he looked at me in frustration. "Yes?" he demanded.

"I think these people are kooks," I said carefully. "But one of them made it into the credit union and insisted I tell you there will be a plane crash tonight. And once you see that part is true, you'll believe the part about the bomb on Wednesday. He wanted to make sure you knew about the plane crash." I could still hear isolated words in my head, making it hard to concentrate. I hoped I wasn't stuttering.

"The plane crashed yesterday, you idiot."

"No, it's a second one. Tonight."

"Are you fucking kidding me? Who let this jerk in here?"

The mayor waved his hand and picked up the phone again. The guard looked at me sternly, and when he opened the door, I hurried out. Three soldiers were just leading another small group onto an elevator and let me join them. James was nowhere to be seen. I was relieved not to face him.

Then I wondered if I'd ever see him again. I heard you always remembered your first time. Mine had been far from romantic, but I did feel a special connection with the man now. I hoped he'd be okay. What if he didn't evacuate?

I looked at the broken glass in the lobby. "Voice," I said silently as the guards led us to the door, "I did it. I told the mayor."

I couldn't hear a clear response, still sensing a jumble of words. I didn't know what to think and just wanted to get home. I wanted to tune out the voice from here on out. I'd fulfilled my obligation. My job was done. All I needed now was to evacuate with my parents and worry about myself. No more risking myself for others. I'd done enough.

Walking toward the bus tunnel, I decided to make one last effort. I'd thank the aliens for helping us and tell them I was sorry for their suffering, but I wasn't going to be able to help them any further. The cascade of thoughts made it difficult, so I concentrated even harder.

"It's a trap!"

"I'm in Ft. Lewis!"

"They're giving me drugs!"

"There are no aliens!"

"Where's Elvis?"

"They're sticking wires in my head!"

I stopped. A man rushing behind me ran into my back. I stepped out of the way. What the hell was going on? "Hey!" I called out in my mind. "What's happening?"

My knees buckled under the intense wave of pain I felt throbbing inside my skull. I no longer heard isolated words. I heard dozens of voices. Had more aliens been captured? I tried to focus on just one voice, pick one from the crowd.

"We're all being interrogated."

"I know. You told me that days ago."

"We were just arrested *today*."

"What do you mean arrested?"

"At the airport, I tried to warn them about the plane."

I was confused. "Who am I talking to?"

"Jeff Hunter. I'm a custodian at Seatac. I heard a voice telling me about the plane crash tonight."

Other voices still seemed to be fighting inside my brain, but I tried to stay focused. "An alien told you?"

"What alien? Brook Shields told me. We've had a psychic connection for years."

"What's happening right now?"

"I'm in some medical facility. An Army hospital. There are lots of military guys around. I heard someone say, 'Everyone who responded was schizophrenic.' I sure wish people would stop calling me schizo. I'm not schizo. Hey, they're coming back. They said they want to put me in an

MRI while Brooke is talking to me. They're—" The voice cut out. It was like a phone being disconnected.

I kept walking slowly downhill and soon reached the tunnel entrance. I was afraid to continue down, though, afraid I wouldn't get any "reception" underground. The street was packed with people trying to get home before the curfew. Probably everything would return to normal tomorrow, now that all the "protestors" had been arrested. I offered up a silent prayer of thanksgiving to God for helping me avoid capture.

"That's what you think." I heard the voice loud and clear.

"Huh?"

"If you heard the voice, they're onto you. They know it's *all* people with schizophrenia now. I heard someone say they're going to read every psychiatrist's patient list."

"Who are you?"

"They said they're going to keep on medicating the water supply and see if anyone else reacts."

"Who's they?"

"The military, of course. They're going to lock us up forever. I know because they talk freely in front of us. Unless they don't think anyone would believe a crazy person. But I think we're all goners. I should've known it wasn't my dead husband contacting me. I've been taking my meds regularly for years."

The voice stopped, and I suddenly noticed people passing by me on the sidewalk giving me odd stares as I stood there motionless gazing into space. One woman put a scarf over her mouth and nose as if she thought some airborne disease was making everyone act crazy.

What if the aliens had accidentally triggered my auditory hallucinations and the rest of this really was delusional?

I wanted to hurry home before the buses stopped running. But if this *was* all some plot by the military and they had access to my patient information, they'd soon know where I lived. I didn't understand why the military might be experimenting with telepathy. What could they hope to gain? Certainly, none of today's events seemed to be working out. The city was in chaos.

Wait a minute. If this was the military, how were they able to predict last night's plane crash? And what about tonight's? The military wouldn't deliberately kill people just to pursue some experiment. Something wasn't right. I *must* be getting crazy information from crazy people, if I wasn't generating this myself.

If the military wanted to get residents to believe the warning about the nuclear bomb and evacuate, why not simply tell everyone they'd uncovered a plot? People would be a lot more likely to believe that than a bunch of unbalanced rioters.

I tried to latch onto another voice, but I couldn't sort through the competing minds. I heard sirens nearby and remembered the urgency of my situation. If the military did need my help for some reason and wanted to interrogate me, I should probably cooperate. But something told me that wasn't a good idea.

I couldn't go home, so what could I do? The homeless shelters might be raided to look for any last mentally unstable people. Should I try to walk up to Volunteer Park and hide in the bushes? It was still cold at night. And it wasn't a very big park. Maybe the Arboretum would offer more protection. I wished I had a friend or two I could rely on.

Wait a second. What about Jeremy? He seemed to be making an effort on my behalf, but we'd still never so much as gone out together to see a movie or a Seahawks game. How much could I really rely on him?

There was no way to know without asking. I turned on my cell phone and looked up his number. Since he was the Single Adult chair, I had him in my contacts.

"Jeremy, it's Eric."

"Are you okay? The world's going crazy. I'm on my way home. I'm not supposed to be on the phone while I'm driving."

"Could you pick me up? I'm sorry to ask, but the buses aren't running."

There was a pause. "Are you in trouble? Is this connected to last night? All these people are making prophecies. And the news says most of the people are…are…"

"Are like me. I know. We'll talk when you get here." I told him which corner I'd be on, and at 12:40, he pulled up to the curb. We'd be hard pressed to get anywhere by 1:00, but I hoped the military would give us a little leeway. Downtown was getting deserted, but there were still people out.

"Thanks, Jeremy." I climbed into the car.

"No problem."

"It may be. I have another favor to ask."

He looked at me quizzically.

"Can we stop at one of those cheap motels along Aurora? I got some cash from the ATM. I'll pay. But I don't want to use my credit card there. I'm afraid I'm being tracked."

"You *are* connected to this? What's going on? You said you'd tell me tonight anyway."

As Jeremy began driving north, I told him what I knew. It wasn't much. I concluded with, "So we can't tell anyone where we are for a couple of days, till this all settles down. Just call your parents and tell them you got caught out after curfew and had to stop somewhere, but don't say where. Then turn off your phone."

"Okay, Eric. Okay." Jeremy frowned.

"Just think of me as a service project for church."

He looked over and shook his head. "You're not a service project."

We pulled up to a motel along a dirty stretch of Aurora at 1:05. I stayed in the car and told Jeremy to only sign himself in, not to mention me. I could be paranoid in the best of times, so I was sweating now. Jeremy paid with his credit card, and I handed him cash when we got in the room.

"You keep it for now. You can pay me later."

I thanked him and looked about the room. There was a small table with a single chair, a double bed, a heating unit near the window, and a TV bolted into the inner wall. A tiny bathroom that looked almost clean was in the corner.

"Sorry about the bed, but when I said it was just me, I couldn't very well ask for two."

"It's okay." I smiled. After what I'd done earlier, sleeping next to a man who would probably sleep in his clothes all night wasn't a problem. I wondered if guilt was postponed because of everything else happening. I wasn't even sure I felt the need to talk to anyone about it. Certainly not with Jeremy, who was probably freaked out enough as it was.

He was good looking, I supposed, with oddly attractive eyebrows, and I wouldn't have minded propositioning him sometime if I ever did decide to come out, but not now while he was doing me a favor. And while he did seem to like me, his father was our bishop. Jeremy wouldn't return any interest I might show, despite his offer of friendship, even if he was gay. But I was still glad to be here with him.

He smiled, too, and sat on the bed. "Well, shall we watch the news?"

We did. The reports were consistent throughout the day. Martial law at least through tomorrow, but it looked like most of the rioters had been caught, and they were being questioned to determine if there was any real threat. There was video of people being sprayed with water or shot with rubber bullets or clubbed with riot sticks for being out past curfew. Perfectly innocent people just trying to get home.

There was lots of footage of the broken glass at City Hall, making it look like half the city was destroyed.

By 7:00, programming was pretty much back to normal, and Jeremy and I lay on the bed watching *The Amazing Race*. "I love seeing these people run around like crazy for nothing." He looked over at me. "Sorry."

"You can use the word 'see' around blind people, too, you know."

"Okay, Eric."

We started talking about disabled people we'd known over the years, including a deaf missionary in Jeremy's mission to Cincinnati. I'd known a boy who always walked on tip toe when we were six, though I never knew what that was about. Autism? And there was a woman in our ward who'd had a stroke and used a walker. Plus a guy who'd served in Iraq and lost the bottom half of his left leg.

"That war was such a waste," Jeremy said.

"We do need to fight terrorists."

"That's not what that war was all about. Not really. We created more problems than we solved."

"I guess that was the President's fault. The military was just trying to do a good job."

Jeremy shrugged. "I suppose. I mean, I know most of the guys fighting were doing it for their country. But you have to wonder about military *leaders* sometimes, don't you?"

"What do you mean?"

"My family's from St. George. Three of my cousins got leukemia because of the military."

"Really? How do you reckon?" Was *he* crazy? I made a conscious effort not to back away even a millimeter.

"Don't you know about all the above ground nuclear testing in the Nevada desert back in the late '50's? Bomb after bomb after bomb. And all that radiation just drifted right over St. George. Leukemia rates shot up 300%."

"That was an accident. They didn't do it on purpose."

"This was years after Hiroshima. You don't think they had any idea of radiation by then?"

"Well…"

"And you know about the military doing LSD experiments on troops in the '60's, right? And the U.S. Public Health Service did that terrible syphilis experiment on almost four hundred men in Tuskegee. You can never really trust the government."

Who was paranoid now? "That's not a very Mormon sentiment," I said. "This is supposed to be the promised land. America was founded by God."

"Maybe. But that doesn't mean it hasn't become a little corrupt. It's not the Church, is it? Government can apostatize."

We were quiet then, and I couldn't help but wonder about the current crisis. Surely, the military wouldn't bomb an American city. This still had to be about preventing disaster, not causing it. I wanted to try contacting someone again, but I didn't want to look glazed or spaced out in front of Jeremy. Still, I needed to know more, to—

"Oh my god!"

"What?"

"Aren't you paying attention? A plane just crashed near Lynnwood. Alaska Airlines Flight 6. A hundred and forty people were killed." He looked at me. "I've got to call my family and tell them to leave the city. My dad needs to call every member in the ward."

"Not tonight. No one can leave now anyway."

"But you told the mayor. He'll want to start evacuations tomorrow, won't he?"

I thought for a second. "Okay, call your dad. That way everyone can be ready to leave at first light. They'll have at least one full day to empty the city. And maybe part of Wednesday." A little voice was nagging at the back of my mind. Something wasn't quite right, but I didn't know what. It was the kind of feeling I'd always been taught to associate with the promptings of the Holy Ghost, but now I suspected it was just the methodical workings of my own brain.

I remembered a Shakespeare quote about methods and madness.

"Wait a second," I said as Jeremy reached for his cell. "Do you mind if I try to contact someone first...you know...in my head?"

Jeremy swallowed. "I don't know if I want to watch."

"I have to find out something." I stared at the wall and concentrated. "Are we in any real danger?" I asked silently. "What is this really all about?"

Like before, once I tried to tune in, I could hear a multitude of competing voices. "They gave me electric shock therapy," someone said.

"They doubled my meds," said another.

"They gave me some new drug by injection. I feel funny."

"They're about to put me out so they can cut into my brain."

I had no idea how much of this was true or simply the rantings of other mentally ill people. I tried to focus on just one voice, someone strong, hopefully someone not completely crazy.

"They said they're going to keep us locked up forever," someone said. "Now that they know who they can contact, they want to do all kinds of experiments."

"How did they manage to contact all of us?" I asked. "Schizophrenics have never been able to use telepathy before."

"I don't know. They gave some soldiers all kinds of drugs, from what I can gather, and hooked them up to all kinds of machines."

"But why?"

"They're trying to find ways to infiltrate enemy countries and cause havoc and disruption. I got this from some other voice, I think from one of the soldiers. I don't know who. They're experimenting on an American city first because they feel they'll have more control. What a bunch of sick fucks."

"So is there really a bomb on Wednesday?"

"There's no bomb. They're just trying to scare everyone and cause panic. They say at the last minute they're going to announce that there *was* a plot to bomb the city, but they caught the people responsible in time. Probably us."

"So what now?"

"The drugs'll wear off soon. I don't think the military is sending out any more messages. None of us have heard any lately. But they may try to round up every schizophrenic in the country as a security risk. I know they're never letting us go."

I asked a few more questions, but there was no answer. I realized I was going to miss hearing voices when life went back to normal, if a schizophrenic could be said to have a normal life to begin with.

If the military tracked me down, though, it might never be normal again.

I wondered if there was any way to get the media to report what I knew. I'd have to try thinking of something in the morning. It might be the only way to save myself, and to save the other people like me out there. I wouldn't be saving a million fellow Seattleites, but maybe I'd be saving thousands of people with schizophrenia across the country. We were worth saving, too.

I felt a hand on my arm. "You okay?"

I looked at Jeremy. "There's no bomb," I said simply. "It's all a trick." I repeated what I'd just heard. It was quite possibly incorrect information, given by some still delusional person, but something inside told me it was true.

"People will do anything to hold power over others," Jeremy said. "Boss them around. Torment them. Cause them grief any way they can." He looked disconsolate. "Even my dad does it sometimes." He paused. "Even the Church."

"Jeremy!"

He shrugged. "Don't you ever feel you're being told to live a life that just doesn't apply to you? We're not all cut out to be an apostle or there would be a lot more of them. Some of us are good at missionary work. Some of us aren't. I'm a terrible leader, but I keep getting called to all these leadership positions. I hate it. Some of us are blind or deaf or schizophrenic or infertile or whatever. We can't all live the same lives, but the Church only has one path open for us. Just like the government here and everywhere else only has one goal—to be in power, whatever the cost. There's a cost to bullying, no matter who's doing it, however 'lofty' the goal."

I nodded slowly. Unrighteous dominion. We turned off the TV and tried to talk about innocuous subjects. Jeremy mentioned his stamp collection and some French art deco books he bought on eBay. I told him I loved playing on the Church basketball team and staring for hours at Snoqualmie

Falls. He talked about listening to his campus counselor by majoring in business though what he really liked was music.

Jeremy revealed that his grandparents had disowned his aunt for getting pregnant before marrying and choosing to raise the child by herself, how he'd never even learned of the woman's existence until last year. He admitted that although he'd been a zone leader on his mission and eventually assistant to the mission president, he'd never received a witness the Church was true. He had, naturally, dutifully borne his testimony regularly that he had.

"Still, you hear every week, sometimes every day, that other people have heard the Holy Ghost, so you can't help but wonder why you don't hear it, too. You think something is wrong with you. And you just live your life based on what *they've* heard. But it's never quite the same as having heard it yourself."

"I thought we were going to talk about simple things." I smiled.

"You don't know how lucky you are to be crazy. You're not responsible for anything. You're absolved."

I laughed. "I don't think it works that way."

"I wish...I wish..." Jeremy lay back on the bed and closed his eyes. He looked terribly unhappy. It seemed inconceivable that someone without a mental handicap could still seem so, well, handicapped. Without thinking, I reached over and ran my fingers gently across Jeremy's hair. I stroked his head a few more times, and he slowly opened his eyes. He turned to look at me.

"I told you I heard an unspoken voice once," he said softly. "It was the first time I saw you when you moved into the ward. I knew right then that one day we'd be together." He sighed. "But I still thought I needed to live off my father's beliefs. So I avoided you most of the time. Lately, though, I've felt I simply had to listen to my own mind. Do you…do you think you'd ever want to be with me?"

Despite what I'd done with James this morning, I'd never kissed anyone before. Now I leaned over and slowly lowered my face to Jeremy's. A feeling flowed through me I'd never experienced before. It was like hearing the word of God. Jeremy reached up and put his arms around me, and we made love slowly and passionately for a very long while, falling asleep in each other's arms a couple of hours later.

The next morning, I awoke to see Jeremy sitting up in bed, smiling down at me. I smiled back and sat up, too.

"Well, as much as I'd like to spend the day here with you," I said, "I think I need to contact a news crew or something."

"We're back to the credibility issue," Jeremy replied. "Can you get anyone to believe you?"

"I'll make them listen." I wondered if I could email Randi, and if the Seattle Channel would be enough.

"Let's check the news first." Jeremy turned on the TV to the middle of a report.

"—because the two flights that went down were Flight 66 and Flight 6. The Southern Baptists have issued a statement that the numbers 666 prove the Antichrist is speaking through the mentally ill, perhaps possessing them. 'All this has been predicted in Revelations.'"

It was a clip now of a preacher speaking in Atlanta. We must be national news.

"'The Apocalypse is upon us.' Seattle remains under curfew. The mayor intends to make an announcement at 9:00 a.m."

"Well, we can't leave just yet," I said. "But I'm going to try calling the news station." I turned on my phone and looked up the number for KIRO 7 News. It took me a while to get a live person, but eventually someone was on the line.

"I'm have schizophrenia," I told the woman bluntly, "and I've been hearing voices." I told the reporter my name and then explained everything that had happened over the last few days. Whether it would help or not, I didn't know. After I hung up, I called *The New York Times*, too, and told my story again.

When I hung up this time, Jeremy looked at me happily. "You did it," he said. "I know it. I can feel—"

The door to the motel room suddenly burst open and six armed soldiers surged into the room. There was a lot of shouting and cursing and pushing and grabbing, and I was whisked out of the room, my last vision of Jeremy being him lying face down and handcuffed on the bed.

I was kept handcuffed as well, in the back of a truck. We drove for at least an hour. I was blindfolded and pushed out of the vehicle when we stopped, stumbling along until I was shoved into a chair in some room. When the blindfold was ripped from my face, I squinted and saw three men in military uniforms. I didn't know their rank.

"Eric Matthews," one of the men said carefully. "You're quite the man."

I frowned but didn't say a word.

"As far as we can tell, we reached 463 men and women. We've arrested all but four of them." He stopped and looked at me shrewdly. "But out of everyone, you're the only person who got through to the mayor personally *and* told the full story to the media." He waved his hand dismissively. "Not that the story will ever be reported, of course, but you're an extraordinary man. And one of the last five to be caught. I have to say, I'm impressed."

Was I going to be executed then, I wondered? Maybe I'd disappear mysteriously and never be found. Or just lobotomized and left to languish in a hospital somewhere. Perhaps I'd simply be kept prisoner the rest of my life.

What would happen to Jeremy?

"We have a proposition for you," said one of the other men.

I looked up curiously.

"We'd like to recruit you to lead our infiltration program. We see you're good with languages. Spanish and French in high school, and Italian and Russian in college. Even a little Mandarin. We could use a man like you."

I was thoroughly appalled, and yet almost immediately intrigued as well. Was I going to be like Mia Farrow in

Rosemary's Baby and go over to the dark side? The men sat down and took the next two hours to explain the program and all its benefits to the country. They also emphasized the benefits to me, to Jeremy, and our freedom.

It was still the same story. Other people were trying to force me to live the life they wanted. And enlist me to make others do the same. Yet I had to admit I'd felt more alive the past few days than I'd felt in years, maybe ever. If I was in charge, perhaps I could somehow tailor the program to be more humane. And there was always the possibility I could eventually get enough evidence to go public in a way I'd be heard.

No useful change had ever been made from within a corrupt system. I didn't need *any* voice to tell me that.

I sat there wondering what to do, calling out to any minds that might still be talking, but there was no response. Then I sent up a quick prayer. There was no answer to that, either. If there was a God at all, maybe he wanted me to rely on my own voice rather than keep asking for his all the time.

I thought about Mormons dying of leukemia and black men suffering with syphilis and J. Edgar Hoover's files on gay men.

I could hear voices, but these military leaders couldn't hear *my* thoughts.

"Okay," I said. "I'll do it." But I wouldn't play the long game. I was in charge already. They just didn't know it.

The men smiled, handed me two dozen papers to sign, and then left the room one by one. Two guards came a few minutes later and led me to a small private room with a bed and a toilet. It wasn't a prison cell, though, and one of the guards assured me, "This is just temporary. The mess hall is down the corridor to the right." So I wasn't being locked in.

I lay on the bed making plans, my thoughts clearer than they'd ever been.

An hour later, I heard a knock, and a guard opened the door. "Eric!" Jeremy said, rushing into the room. We hugged and kissed and hugged again, and the guard closed the door and left us alone.

"Our lives are going to be different from now on," I said carefully, "but we're going to be all right."

"Oh, I know," Jeremy said firmly. "I know."

I was surprised at the confidence in his tone. "*How* do you know?" I looked at him intently.

He smiled happily and gave me a quick kiss. "A little voice told me!" he said impishly.

I smiled at that, too, and then pulled Jeremy down gently onto the bed beside me. The truth was that no one could predict the future. There was always danger ahead. But for now, at least, we had our sanity, and we had each other. I rolled on top of Jeremy and began kissing him.

We didn't lock the door, but no one came in.

Books by Johnny Townsend

Thanks for reading! If you enjoyed this book, could you please take a few minutes to write a review online? Reviews are helpful both to me as an author and to other readers, so we'd all sincerely appreciate your writing one! And if you did enjoy the book, here are some of my others you might want to look up:

Mormon Underwear

A Gay Mormon Missionary in Pompeii

The Golem of Rabbi Loew

Marginal Mormons

Gayrabian Nights

Invasion of the Spirit Snatchers

Mormon Misfits

Gay Gaslighting

Sexual Solidarity

Out of the Missionary's Closet

Sins of the Saints

The Mysterious Madness of Mormons

A Mormon Motive for Murder

Going-Out-of-Religion Sale

Escape from Zion

Breaking the Promise of the Promised Land

I Will, Through the Veil

Am I My Planet's Keeper?

Have Your Cum and Eat It, Too

Strangers with Benefits

Constructing Equity

Wake Up and Smell the Missionaries

Kinky Quilts

Racism by Proxy

Orgy at the STD Clinic

Please Evacuate

Please Evacuate Again

Recommended Daily Humanity

The Camper Killings

10 Things to Do Before the Apocalypse

Repent! The End of Capitalism is Nigh!

An Eternity of Mirrors: Best Short Stories of Johnny Townsend

Inferno in the French Quarter: The UpStairs Lounge Fire

Latter-Gay Saints: An Anthology of Gay Mormon Fiction (co-editor)

Available from your favorite online or neighborhood bookstore.

Wondering what some of those other books are about? Read on!

Invasion of the Spirit Snatchers

During the Apocalypse, a group of Mormon survivors in Hurricane, Utah gather in the home of the

Relief Society president, telling stories to pass the time as they ration their food storage and await the Second Coming.

But this is no ordinary group of Mormons—or perhaps it is. They are the faithful, feminist, gay, apostate, and repentant, all working together to help each other through the darkest days any of them have yet seen.

Gayrabian Nights

Gayrabian Nights is a twist on the well-known classic, *1001 Arabian Nights*, in which Scheherazade, under the threat of death if she ceases to captivate King Shahryar's attention, enchants him through a series of mysterious, adventurous, and romantic tales.

In this variation, a male escort, invited to the hotel room of a closeted, homophobic Mormon senator, learns that the man is poised to vote on a piece of anti-gay legislation the following morning.

To prevent him from sleeping, so that the exhausted senator will miss casting his vote on the Senate floor, the escort entertains him with stories of homophobia, celibacy, mixed orientation marriages, reparative therapy, coming out, first love, gay marriage, and long-term successful gay relationships.

The escort crafts the stories to give the senator a crash course in gay culture and sensibilities, hoping to bring the man closer to accepting his own sexual orientation. And to give them both a better future.

Inferno in the French Quarter: The UpStairs Lounge Fire

On Gay Pride Day in 1973, someone set the entrance to a French Quarter gay bar on fire. In the terrible inferno that followed, thirty-two people lost their lives, including a third of the local congregation of the Metropolitan Community Church, their pastor burning to death halfway out a second-story window as he tried to claw his way to freedom.

A mother who'd gone to the bar with her two gay sons died alongside them. A man who'd helped his friend escape first was found dead near the fire escape. Two children waited outside a movie theater across town for a father and "uncle" who would never pick them up.

During this era of rampant homophobia, several families refused to claim the bodies, and many churches refused to bury the dead. Author Johnny Townsend pored through old records and tracked down survivors of the fire as well as relatives and friends of those killed to compile the first full account of a forgotten moment in gay history.

This second edition on the 50th anniversary of the fire includes additional research and information not available previously.

A Gay Mormon Missionary in Pompeii

What's a gay Mormon missionary doing in Italy?

He's trying to save his own soul as well as the souls of others, terrorized by homophobic doctrine into committing acts of cultural imperialism to prove his worthiness.

In these tales chronicling the two-year mission of Robert Anderson, we see a young man tormented by his inability to be the man the Church says he should be. After enduring a major earthquake, encounters with organized crime, a serious bus accident, and conflicts with horrendous mission leaders, he dreams of nothing more than escaping his suffocating existence any way he can.

But one day, he meets another missionary who loves him, and his world changes forever.

Am I My Planet's Keeper?

Global Warming. Climate Change. Climate Crisis. Climate Emergency. Whatever label we use, we are facing one of the greatest challenges to the survival of life as we know it.

But while addressing greenhouse gases is perhaps our most urgent need, it's not our only task. We must also address toxic waste, pollution, habitat destruction, and our other contributions to the world's sixth mass extinction event.

In order to do that, we must simultaneously address the unmet human needs that keep us distracted from deeper engagement in stabilizing our climate: moderating economic inequality, guaranteeing healthcare to all, and ensuring education for everyone.

And to accomplish *that*, we must unite to combat the monied forces that use fear, prejudice, and misinformation to manipulate us.

It's a daunting task. But success is our only option.

Orgy at the STD Clinic

Todd Tillotson is struggling to move on after his husband is killed in a hit and run attack a year earlier during a Black Lives Matter protest in Seattle.

In this novel set entirely on public transportation, we watch as Todd, isolated throughout the pandemic, battles desperation in his attempt to safely reconnect with the world.

Will he find love again, even casual friendship, or will he simply end up another crazy old man on the bus?

Things don't look good until a man whose face he can't even see sits down beside him despite the raging variants.

And asks him a question that will change his life.

Please Evacuate

A gay, partygoing New Yorker unconcerned about the future or the unsustainability of capitalism is hit by a truck and thrust into a straight man's body half a continent away. As Hunter tries to figure out what's happening, he's caught up in another disaster, a wildfire sweeping through a Colorado community, the flames overtaking him and several schoolchildren as they flee.

When he awakens, Hunter finds himself in the body of yet another man, this time in northern Italy, a former missionary about to marry a young Mormon woman. Still piecing together this new reality, and beginning to embrace his latest identity, Hunter fights for his life in a devastating flash flood along with his wife *and* his new husband.

He's an aging worker in drought-stricken Texas, a nurse at an assisted living facility in the direct path of a hurricane, an advocate for the unhoused during a freak Seattle blizzard.

We watch as Hunter is plunged into life after life, finally recognizing the futility of only looking out for #1 and understanding the part he must play in addressing the global climate crisis…if he ever gets another chance.

The Camper Killings

When a homeless man is found murdered a few blocks from Morgan Beylerian's house in south Seattle, everyone seems to consider the body just so much additional trash to be cleared from the neighborhood. But Morgan liked the guy. They used to chat when Morgan brought Nick groceries once a week.

And the brutal way the man was killed reminds Morgan of their shared Mormon heritage, back when the faithful agreed to have their throats slit if they ever revealed temple secrets.

Did Nick's former wife take action when her ex-husband refused to grant a temple divorce? Did his murder have something to do with the public accusations that brought an end to his promising career?

Morgan does his best to investigate when no one else seems to care, but it isn't easy as a man living paycheck to paycheck himself, only able to pursue his investigation via public transit.

As he continues his search for the killer, Morgan's friends withdraw and his husband threatens to leave. When another homeless man is killed and Morgan is accused of the crime, things look even bleaker.

But his troubles aren't over yet.

Will Morgan find the killer before the killer finds him?

What Readers Have Said

Townsend's stories are "a gay *Portnoy's Complaint* of Mormonism. Salacious, sweet, sad, insightful, insulting, religiously ethnic, quirky-faithful, and funny."

D. Michael Quinn, author of *The Mormon Hierarchy: Origins of Power*

"Told from a believably conversational first-person perspective, [*A Gay Mormon Missionary in Pompeii*'s] novelistic focus on Anderson's journey to thoughtful self-acceptance allows for greater character development than often seen in short stories, which makes this well-paced work rich and satisfying, and one of Townsend's strongest. An extremely important contribution to the field of Mormon fiction." Named to Kirkus Reviews' Best of 2011.

Kirkus Reviews

"Townsend's lively writing style and engaging characters [in *Zombies for Jesus*] make for stories which force us to wake up, smell the (prohibited) coffee, and review our attitudes with regard to reading dogma so doggedly. These are tales which revel in the individual tics and quirks which make us human, Mormon or not, gay or not..."

A.J. Kirby, *The Short Review*

In *Dead Mankind Walking*, "Townsend writes in an energetic prose that balances crankiness and humor....A rambunctious volume of short, well-crafted essays..."

Kirkus Reviews

"The Rift," from *A Gay Mormon Missionary in Pompeii*, is a "fascinating tale of an untenable situation...a *tour de force*."

David Lenson, editor, *The Massachusetts Review*

"Pronouncing the Apostrophe," from *The Golem of Rabbi Loew*, is "quiet and revealing, an intriguing tale..."

Sima Rabinowitz, Literary Magazine Review, *NewPages.com*

The Circumcision of God is "a collection of short stories that consider the imperfect, silenced majority of Mormons, who may in fact be [the Church's] best hope....[The book leaves] readers regretting the church's willingness to marginalize those who best exemplify its ideals: those who love fiercely despite all obstacles, who brave challenges at great personal risk and who always choose the hard, higher road."

Kirkus Reviews

Zombies for Jesus is "eerie, erotic, and magical."

Publishers Weekly

In *Mormon Fairy Tales*, Johnny Townsend displays "both a wicked sense of irony and a deep well of compassion."

Kel Munger, *Sacramento News and Review*

"While [Townsend's] many touching vignettes draw deeply from Mormon mythology, history, spirituality and culture, [*Mormon Fairy Tales*] is neither a gaudy act of proselytism nor angry protest literature from an ex-believer. Like all good fiction, his stories are simply about the joys, the hopes and the sorrows of people."

Kirkus Reviews

In *Inferno in the French Quarter* "author Johnny Townsend restores this tragic event [the UpStairs Lounge fire] to its proper place in LGBT history and reminds us that the victims of the blaze were not just 'statistics,' but real people with real lives, families, and friends."

Jesse Monteagudo, *The Bilerico Project*

In *Inferno in the French Quarter*, "Townsend's heart-rending descriptions of the victims…seem to [make them] come alive once more."

Kit Van Cleave, *OutSmart Magazine*

Marginal Mormons is "an irreverent, honest look at life outside the mainstream Mormon Church….Throughout his musings on sin and forgiveness, Townsend beautifully demonstrates his characters' internal, perhaps irreconcilable struggles….Rather than anger and disdain, he offers an honest portrayal of people searching for meaning and community in their lives, regardless of their life choices or secrets." Named to Kirkus Reviews' Best of 2012.

Kirkus Reviews

Dragons of the Book of Mormon is an "entertaining collection….Townsend's prose is sharp, clear, and easy to read, and his characters are well rendered…"

Publishers Weekly

In *Gayrabian Nights*, "Townsend's prose is always limpid and evocative, and…he finds real drama and emotional depth in the most ordinary of lives."

Kirkus Reviews

Gayrabian Nights is a "complex revelation of how seriously soul damaging the denial of the true self can be."

Ryan Rhodes, author of *Free Electricity*

Gayrabian Nights "was easily the most original book I've read all year. Funny, touching, topical, and thoroughly enjoyable."

Rainbow Awards

Lying for the Lord is "one of the most gripping books that I've picked up for quite a while. I love the author's writing style, alternately cynical, humorous, biting, scathing, poignant, and touching…. This is the third book of his that I've read, and all are equally engaging. These are stories that need to be told, and the author does it in just the right way."

Heidi Alsop, *Ex-Mormon Foundation Board Member*

"While the author is generally at his best when working as a satirist, there are some fine, understated touches in these tales [*The Last Days Linger*] that will likely affect readers in subtle ways….readers should come away impressed by the deep empathy he shows for all his characters—even the homophobic ones."

Kirkus Reviews

In *Lying for the Lord*, Townsend "gets under the skin of his characters to reveal their complexity and conflicts….shrewd, evocative [and] wryly humorous."

Kirkus Reviews

In *Invasion of the Spirit Snatchers*, "Townsend, a confident and practiced storyteller, skewers the hypocrisies and eccentricities of his characters with precision and affection. The outlandish framing narrative is the most consistent source of shock and humor, but the stories do much to ground the reader in the world—or former world—of the characters....A funny, charming tale about a group of Mormons facing the end of the world."

Kirkus Reviews

"Townsend's collection [*The Washing of Brains*] once again displays his limpid, naturalistic prose, skillful narrative chops, and his subtle insights into psychology...Well-crafted dispatches on the clash between religion and self-fulfillment..."

Kirkus Reviews

"Written in a conversational style that often uses stories and personal anecdotes to reveal larger truths, this immensely approachable book [*Racism by Proxy*] skillfully serves its intended audience of White readers grappling with complex questions regarding race, history, and identity. The author's frequent references to the Church of Jesus Christ of Latter-day Saints may be too niche for readers unfamiliar with its idiosyncrasies, but Townsend generally strikes a perfect balance of humor, introspection, and reasoned arguments that will engage even skeptical readers."

Kirkus Reviews

Orgy at the STD Clinic portrays "an all-too real scenario that Townsend skewers to wincingly accurate proportions…[with] instant classic moments courtesy of his punchy, sassy, sexy lead character…"

Jim Piechota, Bay Area Reporter

Orgy at the STD Clinic is "…a triumph of humane sensibility. A richly textured saga that brilliantly captures the fraying social fabric of contemporary life." Named to Kirkus Reviews' Best Indie Books of 2022.

Kirkus Reviews

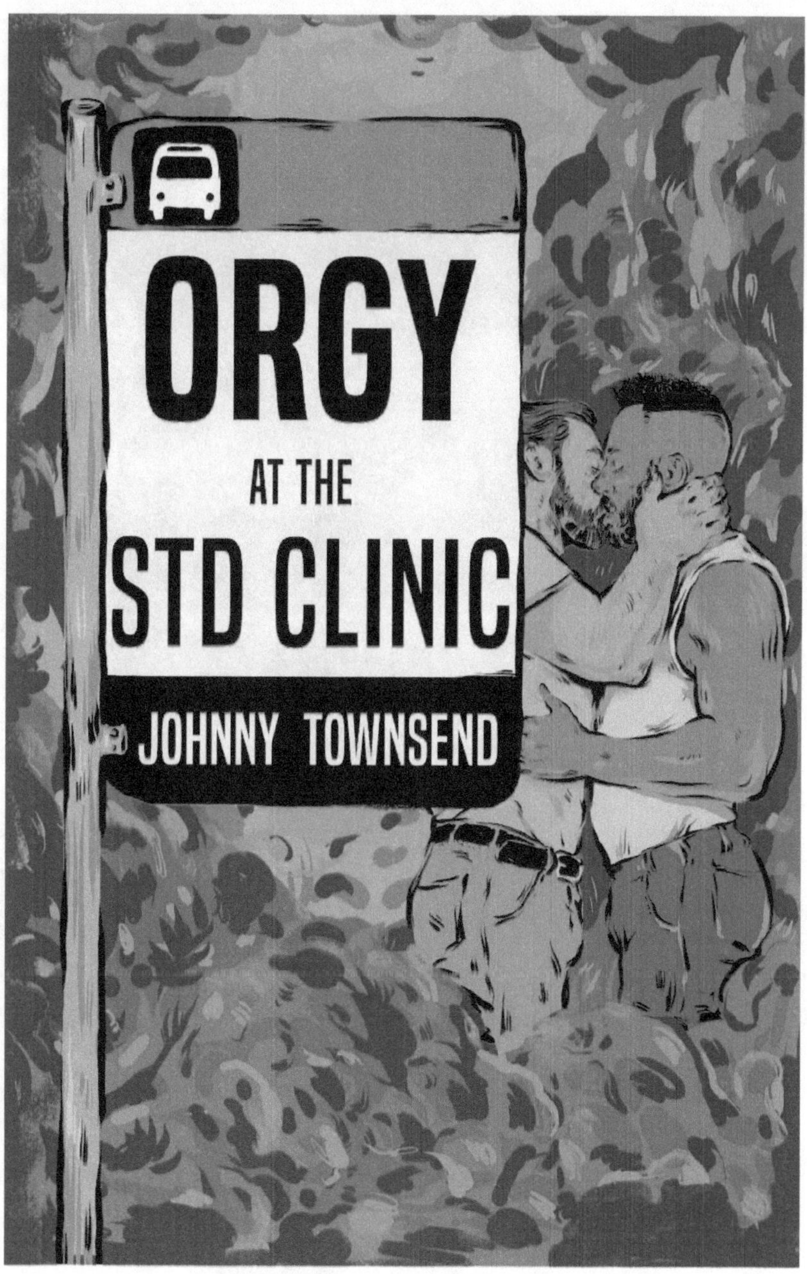
ORGY
AT THE
STD CLINIC
JOHNNY TOWNSEND

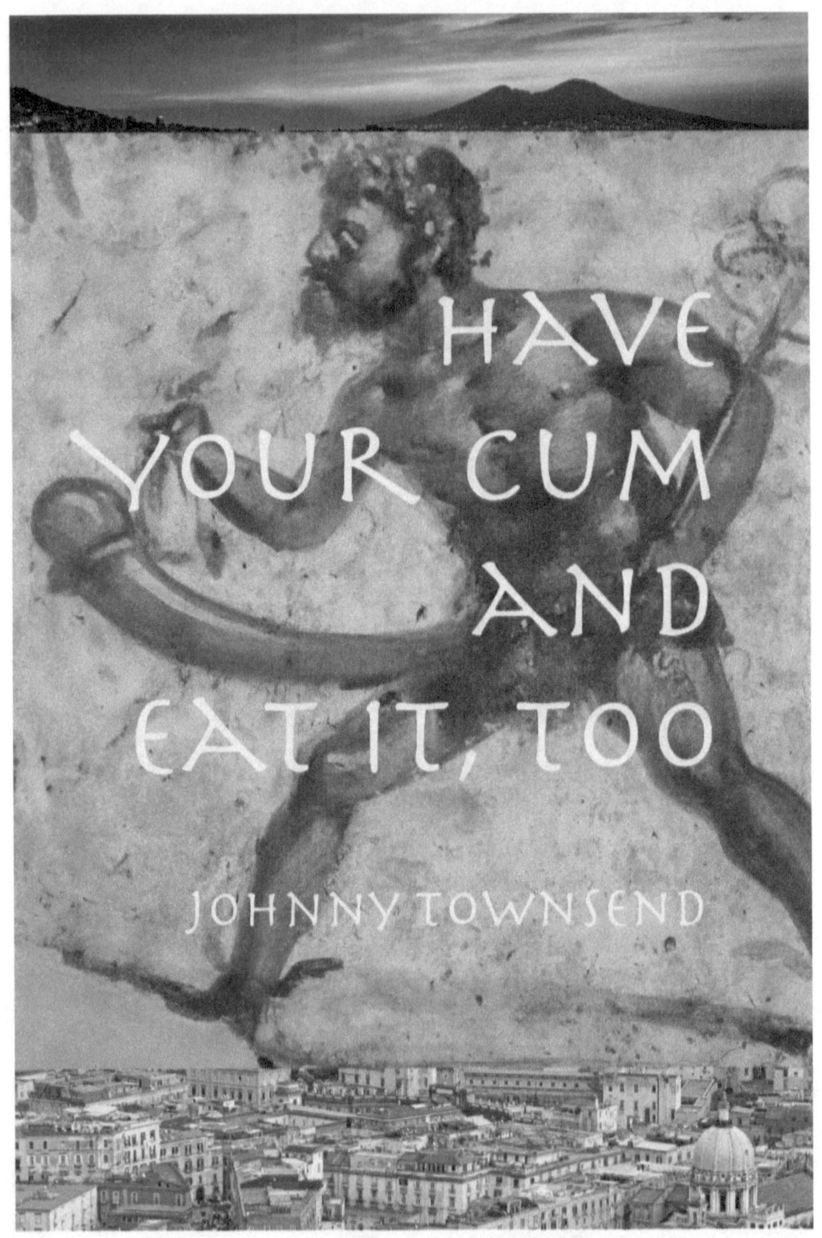
HAVE
YOUR CUM
AND
EAT IT, TOO

JOHNNY TOWNSEND

AN
ETERNITY
OF
MIRRORS
JOHNNY TOWNSEND